All I Cannot Save

*To Deirdre,
With best wishes
from a fellow writer!

Veronica Polloy

Dec. 2024*

All I Cannot Save

Veronica Molloy

Copyright © Veronica Molloy 2024

First published in Ireland by

The Limerick Writers' Centre
c/o The Umbrella Project
78 O'Connell Street, Limerick, Ireland

www.limerickwriterscentre.com

www.facebook.com/limerickwriterscentre

All rights reserved

No part of this publication may be reproduced or transmitted in any form or by any means, electronic or mechanical without permission in writing from the publisher, except by a reviewer who may quote brief passages in a review.

1 3 5 7 9 10 8 6 4 2

Book Design: Catherine Shiels
Cover Design: Catherine Shiels
Managing Editor LWC: Dominic Taylor

ISBN 978-1-7384997-5-5

This is a work of fiction. Names, characters, businesses, places, events, locales, and incidents are either the products of the author's imagination or used in a fictitious manner. Any resemblance to actual persons, living or dead, or actual events is purely coincidental

ACIP catalogue number for this publication is available from
The British Library

For Liam – determined protector

*'My heart is moved by all I cannot save:
so much has been destroyed…
I cast my lot with those who
age after age, perversely,
with no extraordinary power,
reconstitute the world.'*

Adrienne Rich

Contents

Prologue   11

I

Chapter 1 My Day Had Come   15
Chapter 2 Recollections of Martha   23
Chapter 3 Back to Ballymac   33
Chapter 4 Rossnagh   41
Chapter 5 The Road to Dublin   47
Chapter 6 Martha's Wake & Funeral   53
Chapter 7 The Crushed Reed   61

II

Chapter 8 Ballygraigue   73
Chapter 9 Prima Donna   81
Chapter 10 Retreat   87
Chapter 11 The Bliss of Solitude   95

III

Chapter 12 Principalship & Friendship   107
Chapter 13 The Good, The Bad   117
Chapter 14 The Ugly   127
Chapter 15 The Tree of Knowledge   141
Chapter 16 The Little Ones   151

IV

Chapter 17 There's a Change a Coming   161
Chapter 18 These Past Few Days   167
Chapter 19 What the Old Men Say   175
Chapter 20 The Poisoned Tree   181

V

Chapter 21 The Crushed Reed Revisited   189
Chapter 22 The Long Goodbye   197
Chapter 23 What is Truth?   205
Chapter 24 Giving to the Mystery   219

Epilogue   227

Prologue

I lay in the bed where she was found. I wrapped the soft quilt around me. This bed, this room, had become her nest. A place of peace at the back of the house where her life began again. I leaned into the pillow where she took her last breath. I searched for her scent. I heard her say 'I had two daughters.' I saw her raise her hand. I saw her smile. I would never have guessed the darknesses she knew, the horizons she had straddled and overcome, the realities she had kept from me. I wept.

James and Tom knew. They had known all along. James did not just know. He understood. He had built this room for her down a small, softly carpeted hallway away from the bedroom she had once shared with my father. Away from the room where her daughters had slept and laughed and where one died.

I

1

My Day Had Come

That day should have sounded a note of caution. Even from a distance, I noted the change in my mother's demeanour. Her broad shoulders sunken, her long arms and legs visibly thin beneath the pale blue chiffon suit, a cream scarf wrapped around her neck tapering across her shoulders. She was beautiful, elegant and changed. I glimpsed her in a sideways glance as she smiled. I took note but refused to allow any pain to enter my heart, any acknowledgement of questions arising. I smiled back. I had spent seven long years coming to this moment. It was glorious, and very simple. The year was 1953.

Four years before, I had completed my training first as a postulant, the second year as a novice and finally my third canonical year, referred to as *a closed year*. I had no contact from anyone outside of the community. The isolation was real. It helped me focus on the stark reality of the choices I was making. The singular purpose of our chosen community life was sealed. This was the year you stayed or left. Few, if any, left. This year culminated in my first profession. I walked up the aisle in bridal white, my hands folded in piety, my spirit lit by rapture. In the presence of my community, I was received by Rev Mother Columba. Kneeling close to the sanctuary, I received my veil and signed my commitments, co-signed by Rev Mother. My robe was blessed that I would seek a life in holiness, justice and truth. I committed to die to the world and live only for Christ. I meant it.

Now, I was celebrating my final profession. The rehearsals had all finished the evening before. Sister Peter, with the assistance of Maisie and Molly, prepared the dining room setting long tables with freshly pressed white linen cloths and bone china accoutrements. Sister Gregory conducted operations in the kitchen for the reception. Dozens of eggs were boiled. Three large hams cooked. Local hands were brought in to help. Paddy and his son, John, had the garden dressed in all the beauty of late summer. The roses, however, drenched with rain, were already dropping their petals. The weather was still changeable, and Paddy lamented that the professions would not be celebrated at the end of May rather than August sixth, the Feast of the Transfiguration.

Sisters Mary and Ciaran prepared the chapel. The red carpet which lined the nave was swept to infinity. The white marble steps gleamed. The brass candlesticks were polished to perfection. An abundance of white and blue hydrangeas, dahlias and chrysanthemum, all freshly picked from the garden, dressed the altar and the sanctuary. Veni Creator Spiritus, the incantations from prelates and choir rose to the arches of our community chapel. The spiritual struggle, the desire for Christ, remains undimmed but the path that lay before me was beyond all I could possibly have imagined. We may say this of any life but not all of us are born and live through times of unprecedented change. Many were caught in the tsunami that eventually hit the shores of certainty. But my perpetual profession was solemn and beautiful and all that I had worked and hoped for.

***

I could not wait to meet my family, privately at first and later in the dining room for high tea. As I turned the brass knob on the heavy oak door and swept in, I was met with some restraint. James stood at the back admiring Paddy's handiwork through the long sash window. His young wife, Angela, sat nearby on a heavy ornate chair, her small hands resting on the highly polished mahogany. Their two boys, Peter and John, stiffened, their short pants, white shirts and dickie bows, a formality they were unused to. Mammy and Tom sat side by side opposite Angela. For all of 30 seconds there was a silence which I robustly broke.

'Mammy, Mammy, it is so good to see you,' I grabbed her shoulders, and she stood up, her bag falling to the floor. I held her tightly as she lay her face on my shoulder and wrapped her arms around my waist.

'It has been so long, Mary. So long. I hardly know what to say. '

'Is it Mary or Sister Cecilia?' Tom interjected with a smirk.

'Mind your manners Tom', James threw in, 'she is lucky she was not called Sister Eucharia.'

'I don't need to mind my manners. Come here Mary, give me a hug.'

Tom was carefree as ever and I loved him for it, especially in that moment.

'Do you remember the time we skipped Sister Eucharia's piano lesson and Daddy found out?' James quipped.

'Do I what?!' I replied, 'There was murder.'

'Everyone dreaded Sister Eucharia.'

'I don't remember that', Tom seemed crestfallen.

'You were still a garsún Tom,' said James 'Mary, me and Martha, probably the first time we dared to do anything bold. Do you remember Mary? '

'Ach sure I do, of course I do. I was so scared.'

'I lightened it for you. We went into Murphy's and bought a liquorice and shared it between us. Our mistake was to hide out under Jim O'Shea's shed at the bottom of Saint Joseph 's Road. We were spotted. We were spotted by that 'ould matriarch, Mrs. Linehan. What is this her name was?'

'Leonora Linehan,' my mother uttered with emphasis, 'the dreaded Leonora, anyone but Leonora' Mammy continued, then straightening up she mimicked 'Leonora, Leo after my father the vet and Nora after my mother...,'

'The trainer,' we all muttered together and laughed.

'Anyone but her, the 'ould bitch.'

'James! Remember where you are!' Mum giggled a little. Peter and John giggled too and looked at their mother in surprise. Angela threw James a withering glance.

'Oh, there are many stories we could tell, but Eucharia and Leanora stopped us all in our tracks for sure.'

'How did you think you would ever get away with that?' asked Tom.

'Innocence,' replied James

'Innocence,' Mammy nodded.

'How are you Mammy?' I asked as I sat beside her still hugging her.

'I'm grand Mary, grand.'

'It can't be easy Mam.'

'No, it's not, and it hasn't been!' James uttered in what seemed like exasperation.

'Mary, all that is for another time. Today, we are celebrating you, though what you are doing in this place beats me. Donal Linehan would have you any day. He fancied you something fierce.'

'That's all in the past Tom,' Mammy interjected. 'You are right, what a great day Mary, you can introduce us to some of your friends. You have not met Angela.'

'Forgive me Angela. It has been so long since I saw Mammy.'

'Please! I understand Sister Cecilia.'

'Mary! Please Angela. I feel I know you. You always send a card at Christmas and on my birthday and the letters you sent after dad died – I kept them all.'

Mammy looked startled.

'Thank you, Angela. I appreciate what you have done, and I know you make James very happy.'

'She does, does she?' James smiled, placed the palm of his hand on the top of Angela's head and tossed her fine blond hair.

'Well then, I have heard all about the Irish twins, Peter and John.'

'We are not twins!' Peter uttered, miffed. John seemed dumbstruck but a tall woman in a black habit and veil must have seemed very forbidding to a three-year-old. In my enthusiasm, I almost forgot.

'You're right Peter, of course you're not. I know you are the oldest and John is the baby but there is only eleven months between you, and we call them Irish twins.'

'I am not the baby!' John was over himself, 'Mammy is having another one.'

I had not noticed Angela's bump but now that young John had said it, I turned around and sure enough, Angela's petite frame had a nice, rounded bump beneath her pink Empire line jacket.

'Congratulations Angela and James.' I stepped forward to hug Angela, my spontaneity overcoming any religious scruples. Angela's back straightened. It was clearly more than she was prepared for or regarded as appropriate for a nun. I placed my hand on her shoulder instead. 'When is the baby due?'

'September', Angela smiled. 'It won't be long now.'

'Indeed, it won't,' said James, 'what is it about these Church of Ireland neighbours that keep their family small? Are they in on a secret we don't know of?'

'James, that's enough! You were always the restless one. You should be down on your knees thanking God for your little ones.'

'Okay Mammy, okay and if it's a girl we are calling her Martha.' He walked across the room, threw his arm around his mother's neck and kissed her forehead. Mammy's eyes filled with tears and the door I had shut blew open.

'Oh Mammy,' I cried and there we stood in a circle of hugs James, Mam, Tom and I, arms and bodies interlocked, and, in an instant, I was home.

***

A knock on the door announced that it was time to eat, and we made our way to the dining room where fine bone Tara china was spread across tables dressed in the finest linen. Those were the days of home baking and crustless sandwiches, considered a luxury in the nineteen fifties. There were ham and egg sandwiches. There was fresh oven baked brown bread and fruit scones with home-made strawberry jam and clotted cream. There were Madeira cakes, tea cakes and Victoria sponges – three layers, Sister Gregory's speciality. There was raspberry jelly and sliced vanilla ice cream for the children along with TK lemonade or hot tea from one of the many teapots.

Mammy was always a woman to meet the occasion. She shook hands with the parents of the six other newly professed daughters. I observed them chatting like newly found friends. Yet, the more she attended to her responsibilities, the more alone she seemed. While entirely sincere, it struck me that such seemingly effortless effort possessed the kind of intensity necessary to hide the sadness she must have felt. The chatter rose lightly into the air. As the afternoon was unseasonably warm, the doors were opened to the garden. John and Peter skipped out along with other children to play amongst the laurel bushes. Four sets of the parents spoke almost boastfully proud of their daughters. One lady, leaning across the table to Mammy, uttered quietly 'Isn't it great to have a nun in the family. It always helps.'

Mammy bristled, 'What do you mean?'

'Jim's sister is a Bons Secour. When Joan applied for nursing, let's say it wasn't to her disadvantage.'

Mammy remained silent. The woman continued, 'Still, it is a big sacrifice to rear them for another life I suppose.'

'You seem prepared for it,' Mammy replied.

'Oh indeed, Eileen is the third daughter of five and Michael is getting married in autumn. Where are they all going to fit? Our house is large, but don't you know they'll be having family soon and the one farm cannot support all of that. Besides, Willy is not ready to retire. He loves the land. He'll be in his grave before he does that.'

Mammy smiled, noted, but withdrew.

I had known Eileen for seven years. She struck me as a reflective woman despite what her mother had said or implied. I knew Eileen to be sincere in her vocation and I trusted that. I reminded myself that God's grace falls everywhere and works in all kinds of situations. I still believe this but my interpretation of what this means bears no comparison to my understanding on that day. Nonetheless, I felt utterly assured of my own decision to enter religious life and was glad and happy to be finally professed. I am not sure mammy was reconciled to it, but I put it down to her grief for Martha and for Daddy. I promised her I would visit before Christmas but as I had been directed to take up a teaching post in Saint Declan's and had theological studies lined up for the summer, it would be close, before or after the holiday.

Later that night, restored and centred by evening prayer and the chanting of the ancient psalms, I lay in my bed tired but unable to sleep. I was remembering Martha, my beloved sister. I can still see her blonde curls and her large brown eyes. She was a natural leader. When Mammy or Daddy gave us jobs to do, feeding the calves or collecting the eggs, she decided who would mix the feed, carry the buckets or the calves for which each was responsible. We just accepted it. James, though older, never questioned it. Even in play when we jumped from the hayloft to the ground below, Martha dictated the order. We called her *Boss* and laughed for she did it all with humour and affection. When I was off on one of my sullen silences reading a book or feeling sorry for myself Martha was peeling potatoes with mammy or setting the table.

They both had a great eye for style. They could take any old item and elevate it with the right ribbon or matching hat. They were close. I knew I was loved but sometimes, I couldn't shake off the sense of being an outsider.

***

Just before I entered, David Carroll asked Martha out. She met him the previous summer in town, in the office of his uncle who did the books for the farm. They chatted right under Daddy's nose. A bond was formed. The following summer he was back. She had completed her final school exams and he, his first year at Cork School of Music. He played the piano, the fiddle and accordion. He was tall with a sweep of sandy hair and hazel eyes. He struck us all as gentle. We decided that he would never survive a farming life, but we all liked him. Mammy was concerned about his university experience (which I now imagine was very little) and Martha's closeted life as a convent schoolgirl but when she told us he had composed a special piece of music for her, Martha was not the only one smitten. He played on the piano gathering dust in the parlour. It was a plaintiff and beautiful air. Martha glowed with the happiness of our approval. David left soon after. It was late summer. I entered the following week.

Martha died two years later. Heart failure Dr Walsh deducted. It is known today as Sudden Adult Death syndrome. She was twenty. That morning, she had been out in the early hours, between the milking and the breakfast, picking flowers in the lower meadow. They sat in vibrant colour in a little jug beside her bed where she lay entirely lifeless. It was an image James never forgot from the moment he found her.

2

Recollections of Martha

Those two years, the last of Martha's life, we had spent apart. My life was structured, morning and evening prayer, mass, reading, study for entry to university, disciplines of fasting and prayer. Marking out the relevant feast days. Lenten and Advent deprivation saw me lose twenty-one pounds in the first year. My teeth became pronounced. At times the winter cold was skin peeling, but I offered my sufferings for the sins of the world and to bring myself close to the sufferings of this God whom I so loved and so desired and to whom I was dedicating my life.

Every night I prayed for my family. I thought of Martha, James and Tom every day. In the first year each season brought images of James and Daddy before me. In late winter and early spring, I saw them sitting opposite each other at the long kitchen table discussing plans for the year ahead, the calving at its full height. I could almost hear the cows moaning, as we sometimes did in our growing years, from the large cowshed sturdily built across the yard behind the two red corrugated barns. It wasn't unknown to be woken from sleep, to hear the rattle in the kitchen in the deep dark of a January night, Dad calling 'James, James get up! Old Daisy is in trouble. We must help her.'.

I often crumpled up to a kneeling position on my bed and pushed my head between the curtains just in time to watch the flickering of lamps cross the yard to the sheds behind the red barn, Dad's higher than James, a boy, only a boy. Later that boy smiled, tired and elated, over his milky porridge to tell the tale of how he had helped Dad pull the rope around the birthing calf's forelegs and brought not one but two bull calves into the world.

'Two! Imagine! I wiped them down with clean straw. Poor Daisy wasn't able. Ned Baxter said he might need me to help him deliver

Paddy Nolan's calves when the time comes.'

Mammy, standing behind James, winked at me as she laughed quietly to herself.

'You sound a bit like Paddy Nolan yourself with your gibberish…'

'Stop right now!' Mammy cut me short regretting her furtive wink and deciding I was not yet ready for a conspiratorial role. Jealous of his glory, I did not like being corrected.

In that first year, all the memories came flooding back and I wondered how James now tackled his farming responsibilities. In May, I imagined him in the lower meadow and up in the seven-acre field cutting and gathering the hay with hired hands. Each morning as I walked from the first landing corridor to the chapel for morning prayer, I passed a large east facing window frosted at the bottom, its apex was clear and as I descended the first few steps, I observed a line of light breaking above the horizon. I knew James was rising to milk the herd with Paudie as our sister Martha slept, the heavy curtains blocking out the light.

At first, I found it difficult to fill in the details of Martha's days. In that first year I was still only sixteen and prepared along with the other novices for my Leaving Certificate. I imagined her making new friends and going to the odd party with David, away from the prying eyes of the house. She wrote to me eventually, her first letter natural and carefree. She had made friends with a girl from Cork Sunday's Well, Cosette, 'such *an exotic name!*' Martha enthused. 'Cosette *loves to paint birds and plants. She writes poetry too.'*

Mary, Cosette is a scream. She has huge hair which she ties up in a large knot. She carries a diary, always drawing as she goes. Her father is an architect. Her mother goes to Paris every spring. Imagine Paris! Goes on her own! Says she could not face the year ahead without her fix. Her father must be very patient. But he does not have a farm to run or a bunch like us to rear. Cosette is an only child. You would love her. When I met her dad, Jim, he had a large cigar between his teeth but still managed to speak 'the lady Martha is it?' said he, taking my hand and kissing it! 'My great pleasure to meet you. Cosette has talked all about you. Keep her on the steady road Martha, won't you?' He asked as he led me out the great glass doors called 'French doors' it seems (must be the Parisian influence from her mother's visits!)– out into a terrace overlooking the River Lee. Imagine that, Mary! I did not think it was possible to have such a house in the city. It is far nicer than Leanora Lenihan's house. And so is she! David thinks they're all daft, but we enjoy them.

She sent that letter to me in the early spring of her first year studying arts. I read it in the presence of Mother Superior who, having first read it, described its contents as 'entirely unsuitable; an unsuitable account of equally unsuitable behaviour.'

She had done her part and written to my parents who 'will undoubtedly take steps to rectify the situation.'

I was not so sure, and now, I must do mine. Again, the word 'unsuitable' popped up.

'As a postulant there are standards. We must not be afraid to hold our lights high Sister Cecilia. Do not hide yours under a bushel. This is the life we choose, a noble life. We leave the world to help the world. Do you understand?' I dutifully nodded, my eyes downcast.

'You will write a letter to your sister asking her to address you as Sister Cecilia from now on. You must help her understand that you have chosen differently. Sister Cecilia, do you understand?'

'I do,' I whispered.

'Why Cecilia then?'

'It is my mother's middle name. My mother loves music.'

'Indeed, but what of Cecilia's spiritual qualities? Surely you understand that it is Cecilia's spirituality you chose and not just a family name?'

'Yes,' I replied, pattering off my knowledge of Cecilia, 'she trusted in the Lord's plan and was fearless in the face of death.'

'She trusted in the Lord's plan, and you are going to have to do the same. You will both find it strange and difficult in the beginning, but the time will come when Martha looks to you in confidence and having clearly established the integrity of your calling, will look for the light you will offer her. You will inform her that while you are glad for her happiness, she needs to be wise in her choice of friends. You do not need to mention her friend by name. She will understand.'

That letter showed a socially confident Martha who was now choosing to major in philosophy. I knew our formal distancing would initially hurt her, but I also knew she was clever and would find ways to keep our lives connected. I did not receive another letter for a long time which made me suffer. Another kind of dying which I wholly embraced as necessary to my vow of obedience. In the last semester of the same year Martha wrote:

I am troubled by a conflict with father. (I immediately translated 'Daddy is raging with me'). I love philosophy. I hope to go to Paris one day myself and visit the Pere Lachaise and Montparnasse Cemeteries.

Exotic indeed! I hadn't a clue about any of it and had no idea whether or not this was fanciful or a possibility at all. She rolled off names I had not heard of: Aristotle, Plato, Socrates, Descartes, Hegel, Khant.

Daddy thinks it is the most impractical subject in the world – 'What are you going to do with that Martha?' he pleaded with me as we walked the lower meadow through the cocks of hay down to the chestnut trees. I don't want Daddy to worry or to be a burden on him or Mammy. They are very proud of you, and I found it hard to explain to him. Sister Cecilia, I have thought a lot about his question since. The thing is philosophy makes me feel alive. It helps me understand my own thoughts, my own restlessness.

Does this make any sense at all to you? And if daddy doesn't understand then Ballymac is going to seem like the smallest place in the world, a place I am not sure I want to go back to.

The letters were few and far between now and, apart from a Christmas and Easter card, it was almost a full year after Martha passed her second-year exams with flying colours that she sent me a short, excited letter:

I am going to go all the way with this. I promise you. I promise myself. I am going to teach in this university myself, whatever it takes! I am going to show Daddy that I made the right choice.

David is gone to London for the summer to earn his fees for his final year. I would love to go but dare not even ask. Roll on September!

When we were in school, we could not wait for the summer! It was plain to read how happy Martha was even if there was a conflict with Daddy. On the farm we understood the vagaries of life and knew Daddy, and truth to be told, Mammys' hearts were in the right place. I wondered what Mammy thought. Her bond with Martha was especially close. I guess she might be torn but she never mentioned it in her letters. Nothing.

Her letters opened: *My dear daughter, Sister Cecilia…* they contained only points of information such as:

Tom is going to St. Joseph's in September; can you believe it? - Or- James has met a lovely girl, Angela. She is well mannered and polite. Her aunt is

Sister Genevieve. Do you remember her? She was the small, bright woman in charge of Saint Catherine's ward where your grandmother was being treated for leg ulcers shortly before she died. Ran the place to perfection and always had a kind word for her patients. A Nazareth sister.

Indeed, I did remember visiting Daddy's mother there. We were young. She was somewhat forbidding and after initial greetings, we generally ignored each other as the adults chatted. I also understood by osmosis that reference to Sister Genevieve meant tacit approval of Angela. We were a loving family but ours was not an easy house for the stranger. That August a short letter arrived from Martha:

I have been given the honoured task of accompanying granny to the novena at Knock. Maybe I deserve it! Five days and nights of torture! Yes, we will be sharing the same room! Even Mammy says she snores for Ireland, her own mother! But I am keeping my slate clean and agreed. Besides I think I might need the prayers! Pray for me Sister Cecilia, won't you?

Last line apart, which struck me as plaintive given the letter's tone, I was surprised it was allowed after receiving it in its opened envelope, but I imagine the reference to Knock may have saved the day. I was also pleased by the trust in me it now suggested in the year that had passed since my first encounter with Mother Superior over the nature and duty of the vocational life. My responses to my family were formal enough. I followed the dictates. I understand now how pious and businesslike they must have seemed:

Dear mother, Dear father, may God bless you, I will remember you in my prayers, et cetera.

***

I had a summer filled with importance – all my own. I was in my canonical year, a closed year with no contact with the outside world and culminating in my first profession on August sixth, to which my family was invited. I was desperately excited at the thought of meeting my family. I was happy. I wanted them to share in my happiness. I was preparing to read French and English in Maynooth. A three-week retreat program, another three weeks in the Order's summer house in Kerry helping out with older members one of whom was recovering from a stroke and another in heart failure.

I never wrote about this as it was not allowed. It was understood as a vow of obedience, a communal sharing of responsibility. I assured Martha that I did pray for her, all the time. I wrote to her and told her. She sent back a brief note saying how happy she was for me and apologising for her lack of contact which she put down to busy circumstances. Equally, I assured Mammy that everything was going according to plan. On the sixth Sunday after Easter Sister Xavier knocked gently on my cell room door.

'Sister Cecilia,' she almost whispered, 'am I interrupting your reading this Sunday afternoon?'

'No, No, just studying for the exams.' Her gentle tone alarmed me.

Sister Xavier was challenging at any time, but Mother Columba was the Mother Superior. As I entered the room, I observed her take in my demeanour. Her eyes immediately dropped as she moved objects on the large mahogany desk before her. Lifting a black onyx paperweight from right to left she demanded that I sit down on the straight-backed chair, one of two that sat before her desk. My alarm was deepened by her efforts to conceal her agitation and the equally unusual behaviour of Sister Xavier, I felt the stifling words rise in my throat and managed to vomit them into the clarity of space between us: 'What is wrong? If I have done something...?'

'Please sister Cecilia! You can relieve your anxieties of any such responsibilities here. By all accounts, as Sister Xavier informs me, you are a most excellent candidate but those whose spiritual capacities are able are often challenged most and indeed, you will find what I have to say deeply challenging.' She paused, 'I received a call from Dr Walsh thirty minutes ago...'

'Dr Walsh? ... Is it Daddy? Is it Mammy?'

'It is neither Cecilia. There is no easy way to put this. I'm afraid it is your sister Martha. She was found dead in the early hours of the morning. It seems she died at home. A post-mortem will be held to establish the exact cause of death... But Dr Walsh suspects heart failure.'

She added words – *young* – *mystery* – *burden* – *sufferings* – *offerings*. They rose like a host of demons into the air. Disjointed. Unconnected. My stomach fell into my bowels. My vision, blurred with tears, glimpsed the large hanging crucifix behind Mother Columba's head as she spoke. The gentle, beseeching eyes of Christ met mine and I let out a visceral moan.

'Sister Cecilia!' Sister Xavier immediately corrected me.

'Sister Xavier!' Columba projected her left palm out as she rose from her chair. Xavier stepped back. Mother Columba sat beside me, I felt myself disintegrating before her towering presence. She placed both of her hands on mine. I bent my head and sobbed. I tried every control I possessed but my defences were shattered.

'Sister Cecilia, I know this is a terrible blow. We will talk together about it again. When you are ready, I promise. I need you to be strong now. I need you to hear what I'm about to say…' I looked up, my heart racing.

'Your father, your poor, dear father is with Dr Walsh. He is awaiting a return call. He wanted to speak with you personally.'

'Daddy, poor Daddy…' I could not think of mammy. I would not allow myself to do so. Those thoughts of my mother, James and Tom would wait until I returned to the privacy of my own room. I dare not think of Martha, of all that beautiful and hopeful life lost. It took every cell of my being to focus on the task in hand, but I understood it was necessary for Daddy's sake.

'Are you ready Cecilia?' I nodded.

The large black phone stood to the right centre of the desk before me facing Mother Columba. She beckoned me to stand beside her behind the desk as she turned the dial with her right index finger following the numbers she had written into the record book which lay open before her. Each number clicked in circular motion. I was barely able to stand. I felt suspended beyond time and space and again made serious efforts to concentrate. I could see Daddy sitting there.

***

I had only been to see Dr Walsh twice as a child that I remembered, once for tonsillitis and the other to collect mammy after Elizabeth had died. I barely remember Elizabeth. His house stood behind high walls at the corner of Main Street and Church Street. There was a short, gravelled entrance where daddy pulled in the trap. The surgery was entered through a separate door, a small, tiled waiting area and an adjoining room with usual medical paraphernalia. As sick as I was with a fever from tonsillitis, I remember the lovely window overlooking the lush greenery on the side lawn and a gulp of swallows sweeping and diving, which remind me now that it was Summer.

Collecting Mammy was different. Dr Walsh had asked that Daddy would bring James, Martha and myself along. I could not have been more than four. We did not go to the surgery this time. Dr Walsh's wife swept open the front door. 'Come in Jack. Bring those handsome children along.'

She had cocoa and fruit cake ready for us in her kitchen. We sat at the thick oak table set about six feet from the range. She hung her copper, brass and aluminium pots where Mammy would usually hang the clothes to dry in the winter. We lapped up the spoils but absorbed the strangeness of it all. Something wasn't right. It was six weeks since Elizabeth had died of scarlet fever. A pall of sadness enveloped our house and though we continued to play, we kept our laughter low and fell silent when Mammy and Daddy spoke softly to each other which was often unpredictable and unsettling. We were used to our 'get up and go' father. This gentleman, unusually attentive to Mammy, was a stranger come to visit and, though a kindly stranger, we longed to hear the odd irritation and Mammy's laughter or rebuke.

After some time, Dr Walsh came in, his three-piece tweed lending his natural charm an air of grandeur. He was a warm man. 'Your mammy is waiting for you. Make sure you give her a hug now, won't you?' he urged, his hands on his knees. I thought this was odd. As young as I was, I knew that I did not need anyone, not even Dr Walsh, to tell me to hug my mother. It annoyed me. We entered a room full of soft furnishings left of the main door. Mrs Walsh had late autumn Maple leaf in red, amber and yellow arranged in a vase. I had never seen that before. I thought they were beautiful. The grandfather clock struck four.

'We must be getting along now. It will be dark soon and we must get home for milking,' Daddy stood at the back near a tall window.

Mammy, a very pretty woman, tall and broad shouldered, sat hunched, sinking into the chintz armchair in her green winter suit and Sunday shoes. Having wiped her nose, she was returning her handkerchief into the handbag on her lap. I ran and threw my arms around her neck knocking the bag to the ground.

'Take it easy Mary, for God's sake!' Daddy sounded irritated.

'It's alright Jack,' Mammy interrupted, lifting me onto her lap and pulling me close to her throat. She put out her two hands for Martha and James. We clasped each other in a long slow huddle. Quite abruptly,

Mammy looked at Daddy and said, 'I am ready to go home now Jack.'

'It will be alright; you know that don't you Maeve?'

'I do Jack, I do. Let's go.'

***

And now, I could see Daddy sitting in the same room, in the same armchair as hunched as Mammy had been. He would have to go out to the hall to take the phone call.

Mary!' I could hear his voice at the end of the line. Sister Xavier left the room. Mother Columba held back. 'Mary, … I…. I…' he repeated.

'Daddy…' my voice broke. I could hear his muffled sobs. 'Daddy…' I repeated. We held a long silence between us. Mother Columba left. I heard the heavy door handle click. 'Oh daddy, Martha, Martha…'

'I know, I know Mary. It is a disaster. Your mother will never get over this. Never.'

'How is Mammy, Daddy?'

'How do you think she is Mary?' He sounded almost angry. 'Come home for God's sake, come home.'

'What do you mean Daddy?' I was distraught. 'What do you mean? For good?'

'I don't know what I mean Mary, I don't know anything.' His voice trailed off.

'I will Daddy, I will,' I spluttered without any idea of whether or not I could fulfil that promise.

'The sisters will surely let you home for a few days, Mary. Your mother needs you. I need you.'

Mother Columba had re-entered the room. I deliberately said, 'Okay Daddy, I am coming home. I will ring Fr Healy with the details, and he can let you know.'

'Good girl Mary. That's my girl,' he sobbed.

'I am going now Daddy, goodbye. Give my love to Mammy, James and Tom.'

'I will, I will….' His voice tapered off as Mother Columba firmly took the phone from me.

'Mr O'Brien my deepest sympathy for the loss of your daughter, Martha. Please ask Father Healy to ring me with the funeral arrangements. I will do everything in my power to make sure that

Sister Cecilia is in attendance.'

I was not privy to Daddy's response, but I imagine it was polite if curt.

'Good. Rest assured you are all in our prayers. May God console you Mr O'Brien. Goodbye for now.' She put down the speaker and looked directly at me. 'Cecilia, for reasons far beyond your understanding, this pain has been brought to your door. It will test you to your limits. Of this I am certain. But she is worthy who keeps her hand upon the plough. Remember this. In spite of the chaos, you feel now, you will find peace. May God bless you child. You may go. I will be back to you when arrangements are finalised, which should be very soon.'

***

I walked back to my room in a fog of stupor. Martha, our beautiful Martha – all her plans – I am going to go all the way, Mary – to teach in university – to travel to Paris – to enjoy the exotic Cosette– to make a future with David – this tender young musician whom she loved. No, she will lie in her grave in Ballymac. All her dreams laid waste. I sat in my room for a long time. My thoughts were fragmented. I longed to be with my family. I could not join the community for tea. A tray was sent. I did not eat. Rev Mother Columba arrived at my door and insisted I come to evening prayer. She accompanied me, suggesting it would console me. It didn't.

Later, in the deep dark hours of the night when no sound was heard throughout the convent, at three a.m., the time of crucifixion, I made my way to the chapel and lay face down, arms outstretched before the tabernacle. My forehead against the cold tiled floor I cried: 'Lord Jesus, I know nothing. Nothing at all. I feel I am no more than a feather in the wind. Help me, help me, help me.'

I lay there in exhausted reverie. The blue, ochre and brown shades of the floor beneath me were the very same as those that lined the corridor which led to my first classroom. Those same polished tiles stood before the May altar which I remembered with pain and affection.

'Oh Martha,' I cried, 'you are bringing me back home to Ballymac.'

3

Back to Ballymac

Trust is the word you don't fully understand as a child but a reality you take utterly for granted. I found it difficult to untie the laces on my new school shoes and then, to pull them off in a timely fashion, pull on my slippers firmly round my feet and put my shoes neatly into my slot. Mary O'Brien, printed in black and white across the top line, middle row, my coat hanger above. I was the last into the classroom. The bell ringing at the bottom of the corridor had long ceased. I was in a heightened state of anxiety as I sat on my little chair with its red metal legs, but I soon settled colouring patterns.

Nonetheless, I did not look left or right or for that matter forward. I kept my head down not wishing to catch the eye of the teacher who was doing, what I later found out to be, roll call. Deirdre Benson, Lucy Brennan, Bernadette Neary, Mary Nolan, Mary O'Brien –*Anseo*– I replied, imitating the others. I had no real idea of its meaning other than that it must mean *'I am here'* or, *'I turned up'*. Martha had warned me to say this. As my body began to relax, I felt my head itch. I inserted my fingers through the hair over my ears and loosened it for relief. By the end of my first day in school I was a sorry sight.

Striding the first mile down Convent Hill, Martha's hand in mine as she walked purposely along, all her six years clearly dedicated to her charge, my feet hardly touched the ground. My satchel popped up and down the shoulders of my plaid coat, the one sent by Aunt Nelly from New York. I loved it. Its soft lavender and grey tones, its boxed pleats and soft velvet collar and cuffs, its brass buttons. Martha 's coat was also from that box, plain camel wool with dark brown piping, no velvet collar, no brass buttons. Martha was more than disappointed that mine did not fit. It would've been her first choice. All our eyes lit up when Mammy pulled it from the layers of tissue paper spilling out over the open box along with the smell of mothballs. Decisions had to be made and my four-year-old self felt like a queen, the comfort, as I slipped my hands deep into the satin lined sleeves. Martha accepted. Lots of choices were made based on what was practical. We all learned this at a very young age. By and large it worked, and each of us at some stage was at the receiving end of joy or surprise. That is how it is on a working farm.

We cannot keep Lady's pups, especially the bold ones whose cute brown eyes seem to implore you as voices are raised over who left the box of messages on the floor in the back porch or, how *Brownie,* of all the pups, ever got in there! Amid all the raised voices, there is Brownie looking at you, seeming to say, '*hide me please, let's go to the lower field and play*'. And you catch him and whisper '*Be quiet*' you hold him close. You stand still offering no defence. It would be useless. You are ordered to take him to the outhouse where he remains apart from the litter, and you sit at the dinner in silence. In two weeks, he is gone, and you know that this is how it is, how it has to be. You have a second evening of silence. Daddy is cross with you for these silences. There is a kind of dying. Two mornings later, a colouring book and some pencils in a brown paper bag lie at the end of your bed. And so, it is.

And there we are at the bottom of Convent Hill; we turn into Saint Joseph's Road where James waits for us outside Saint Joseph's school. I imagine we were a pretty sight for, as Mrs Walsh pointed out, we were handsome children: James thin, long hands and legs, freckled-faced, brown eyes and a curly brown mop. Martha, Scandinavian blonde, same brown eyes though larger, cupid face, a beauty and me, black wiry hair, green eyes, knees permanently scratched. Elizabeth was my younger sister who died just before her second birthday. Mammy just seemed to disappear for a while. All the aunts came in. Now, six-month-old Tom cooed and laughed in the playpen near the stove while Lady sat beside him on her old rug on the floor, both in Mammy's eyeline. Sometimes at night I could hear him wailing in the distance as I turned over in my sleep and snuggled further beneath the blankets comforted by the warmth of Martha beside me.

James, Martha and I walked downhill through Main Street over the bridge and left on to the Kilshannig Road where soon the horse chestnuts swept their branches down over the low Stonewall edging Linehan's farm. We arrived happily home where Martha swept Tom into her arms and James ran out to the barn. Mammy knelt before me, and I collapsed into her arms. A dark exhaustion came over me and I shed a few tears. But I knew, like Brownie, there was no escaping my fate. All in all, while they were happy days, it was a place of survival. Survival is an important skill. I learnt to up my game, mix in groups, hold my own in the yard, make it to the classroom door in time for the bell, avoid the eyes of Sister Cletus when she was cross. Though I did not always manage this.

In May, flowers were requested for Mary's altar which stood in the corridor dressed with a white laced cloth and vases of fresh flowers at Our Lady's feet. She smiled upon us all with a crown of stars around her head and her feet firmly on the serpent. We all knew that was the devil. Flowers were brought in every day. There were delphiniums and peony roses, cowslips and late May tea roses in their pink, red and yellow hues. I decided I would like to bring flowers to the altar. I discussed it with Mammy the evening before. We had an abundance of bright yellow dandelions around the large laurel bush under which we played house.

'But Mammy' I insisted, 'they are lovely, all soft and yellow '

'I know Mary, you are right, but some people think they are weeds.'

'I don't care. Mary will like them, won't she?' Mammy sighed and smiled.

I picked a bunch so large before leaving for school that I had to use my two arms to hold them. It was a bit of an effort to avoid squeezing their soft stems and the sap dripped from the bottom of the bunch, but I managed. I was determined and enthusiastic and wondered why Mammy and Daddy stood at the edge of the grass with a look of concern.

I stood midway in the queue waiting for Sister Cletus to unlock the classroom door. I stood very near the altar below one of the grand windows which swept from floor to ceiling. It took some effort to manage my slippers and keep my flowers together, but they still looked good to me as I peered out over their soft heads. I heard whispers travelling down the row of girls. I saw heads turn. I was waiting for Sister Cletus to come to give her my offering. I heard the words *Pissy beds*. I knew it was directed at me, but I had no idea what it meant.

Then, it was repeated over and over. I felt my cheeks colour. I knew it was not good. What struck me most was not the words but the tone, a simple phrase snarled and spat between teeth from pigtailed heads and girls I barely knew.

Sister Cletus arrived, unlocked the door from the key on her belt and let the surge into the expanse of the room. She took my dandelions from me, opened the large sash window opposite the door and unceremoniously threw them out. I felt a cry break inside me but dared not reveal it. The May sunshine filled the room with light but the light within me was already lost for that day. I did not speak a word but somehow felt a kind of tenderness each time I passed that statue, her arms outstretched to me. Yes, survival is indeed the word, but love too, Mammy had jelly and ice cream for me that evening.

***

Summertime had a life of its own. There were the upper fields, and the farm leased over in Sullivan's Quarry to be attended to. There were churns of milk to be brought to the creamery every day. The corn field to be saved from the crows and harvested in the early autumn. Bosco, the prize bull, was brought in from Jim Maguire's farm for a week or two to 'do the business' as Daddy always referred to it. Saving the hay on the lower meadow was a rite of passage.

It marked the beginning of summer work for which the hired hands and neighbours came in. It was seriously hard work, but I have great memories of it. James, Martha and I were organised like a little army. Dad came into our bedroom early and pulled back the heavy curtains in the darkened rooms. We were always in a deep sleep and groaned.

'Out, out, come on! Paddy is coming today, and I need all hands-on board. We will start in the big field. Get your Wellington boots.'

We moaned, climbed over the bed clothes, dressed quickly and made our way, half dazed to the kitchen for breakfast. In less than thirty minutes we were out in the lower meadow already feeling the itch of the hay dust. Daddy and Paddy worked ahead of us cutting as near to the ground as possible in smooth half arches. We each had a pitchfork with which to catch and shake the loosely cut hay to prevent it from rotting and sweep it to the hay cocks dotted all around the meadow. It was solid work and though we had fun, the mornings were filled with a methodical silence as we each worked our way through the meadow.

That we had disturbed the occasional bird nesting in the long grass was evident but this attrition aside, nature burst everywhere. The last bluebells sat in under the hedge rows along with yellow cowslips and pink digitalis, we called them *Fairy Fingers*, lush green ferns and scraggly branches of wild white hawthorn edged the shrubbery that found a home near the stream on the southwest corner of the field.

We were hot, sticky and itchy under the late May sun and blissfully unaware of the happiness of our circumstance. Tom, still too young to work alongside us, arrived with Mammy with a basket full of hot milky, sugared tea, brown soda bread and jam. A feast for hungry takers. We'd sit on the freshly cut grass which, if dry, scratched the back of our legs. We brushed off the horse flies and sometimes, the wasps. We were rarely stung and happily listened to Daddy and Paddy discussing 'the old days' of their childhood or the latest news from town. Later we slept the sleep of the dead. In the meantime, we swung from the branches of the horse chestnuts out over the bank and back, played chase, fought, fell out, fell back in, and now and then, got ourselves into trouble for minor misdemeanours.

Once, as an older child, Mammy asked me to take the hot ashes from the stove out to the back to an open shed for cooling. I refused. I was feeling bold. Now I realise that at eleven I was probably on the cusp of adolescence and already pushing boundaries. I simply said, 'No I won't!'

My mother was shocked. We were not defiant children, and my brazen response was an affront. She called Daddy. I took my chances. The belt was produced, and I felt the strokes sharply across the back of my legs. Martha and James looked on, sympathy pouring from their glances. Tom cried. I then took the ashes out under supervision and was sent to bed without supper for the remainder of the day. My legs hurt but my pride hurt even more.

When Mammy relented and came in some hours later with a hot cup of tea and buttered toast, the smell of the toast was delightful. But I was stubborn and angry and immediately recognising their regret in this act of love, I refused to eat or drink. I was longing to take the toast but the taste of that sense of superiority was even greater, and I refused. The next few days in the house were quiet.

***

There was an ongoing conversation between my parents when Martha was twelve years old and in her final year of primary school. Would she go to the local school or would she board? No such considerations back and forth were considered for James. James attended the local boys' secondary school, Saint Josephs. It was expected that he would do his final exams, which was more than many of his classmates. Tom Murphy, with whom James swapped books and who was the best player on the football team to read the game, and the opposition, would be leaving after his Inter Cert to become a block layer and go into building with his father. That is simply how it was. Sean O'Keefe and Kieran Dooley would take the boat to England, or, if brave enough, to the States following in the footsteps of their older brothers along with at least ten others. Some had already left school. And Brian Hanley, who came to work on the farm during harvesting, or when extra hands were needed, was one of these.

And there was Martha, all a fret and a fuster, her usual confidence disappearing, wondering what the outcome would be. Her place in the order of things. It unsettled her and Mammy and Daddy's wavering only reinforced her unease. Five of her sixth class, daughters of the professional classes, already planned to leave and go to places she had never heard of. They had formed a circle of their own. She was no longer included. They had had many happy days playing tag in the schoolyard. Now it was all changing. Bernadette and Maura, of whom she was fond, were continuing in the local convent school along with most of the other local girls. Kate Neary and Anne Hughes were going to boarding school in Rossnagh, forty miles away, a place she barely knew. She understood that it was a tradition among the farming community, whether they could afford to or not, to send their daughters to this school. A kind of inverted snobbery, not unlike the playmates who had left her. She had heard some of the talk.

'Sean and Paddy are sending their girls to Rossnagh.'

'Rossnagh, Jack? The boarding school in Rossnagh? That's forty miles away!'

'Yeah. That's the one.'

'Joan sent Nancy there too. A long time ago.'

'Yeah, and look at how she fared? Married Seamus Leahy. He had a horse running in Cheltenham there last month.'

'He can have all the horses he likes. Ask yourself Jim, is that a happy marriage? Every time I see Nancy, which isn't much, she is thinner and paler, as if the life is draining out of her.'

'That's not the fault of the school. Besides, you don't know that it's true.'

'No. But it makes the point that outcomes are not always what we think they're going to be. I love Martha's company about the place. She's less solitary than Mary. With your long hours on the farm and away buying and selling cattle, it's not easy.'

'How do other wives survive?'

'I don't give a damn about Sheila Neary, Betty Hughes or Joan O'Shea for that matter. Martha will be growing up, you know, need the support of a woman around her. Need her mother.'

'And how do all the other girls survive? You have to be a bit tough for this world.'

'Ah, Jack, for God's sake.'

'Ah, Jack what? You're not from around here. You don't understand anything.'

'And you do? How dare you!'

Martha quickly retreated up the stairs as she heard the kitchen door slam.

'I'm sorry, Maeve. I'm sorry,' rang through the narrow, empty hall. But even Martha could feel the sting of 'you're not from around here' for our mother.

In the quiet of the house, she heard our mother's muffled sobs from behind the locked parlour room door. Anytime Mammy went in there alone, you knew not to enter. You knew it was serious. Still, it was the first real argument she witnessed between our parents. She knew her father would be gone for the day. Probably right now, heading down to take the cattle from the old field to the upper meadow bordering Linehan's. There was more shelter there and heavy rain was forecast.

Martha, sitting on her bed beside the open door onto the landing upstairs, resolved there and then that she would go wherever she was sent. She did not want to be the cause of any argument. She recounted it all to me three years later on the bus home for the summer as I finished first year and she third in the boarding school in Rossnagh.

4

Rossnagh

Both Martha and I surprised ourselves by adapting so well to the life of a boarder. Routine seemed to settle us. Everything had its place. My thoughts were often chaotic, my dreams wild, my unconscious goals too great. Order and clear instruction removed the anxiety of this turmoil. I was glad also to be with other girls sharing the angst-ridden dread of our changing bodies. When, every so often, one of us fainted, we all understood though none of us spoke freely of blood or pain or erotic sensation. On one rare occasion, we giggled furtively as we spied on Sister Aloysius, her bosoms bouncing under her flannel nightgown as she ran down the corridor overlooked by our dormitory to attend to one of the older girls whom it turned out had to be hospitalised with appendicitis. That stolen glance kept us going for a year. When I relayed the story to Martha, she was shocked at our boldness that we would do such a thing but then she laughed too. We were innocently exploring our emerging sense of our place in the world.

Sometimes, it was all confusing. We had a collective crush on Sister Maria. She supplied the hot water bottles when we fainted, the shoulder when we cried and the advice when it was needed. I now understand that she was probably not much older than us and maybe even lonely at times. She mentioned that she had younger sisters at home. She had dark eyes and cupid lips, and we had bets on the texture of her hair, curly or straight? She was likely no more than nineteen or twenty and was probably a postulant or more likely, in formation, given light teaching and supervision duties until she left to study for her degree. She was our dormitory mistress and accountable to the house mistress who ran the Junior house for first to third year girls. It was a small school of forty or so students each year. All in all, it had a familial feel to it.

We were not an exclusive school. Though in the heart of the country we did not have a grand entrance or tennis courts. On Sunday afternoons, after endless prayers and solemn mass, we entertained each other with walks through the small woods on the school grounds, looking through the graves of the old sisters or spending time in a corner of the old, draughty library playing draughts, Snakes & Ladders, chess or simply reading a book.

On Saturday afternoons we did 'mission' work. We looked through magazines such as The Far East. We helped Sister Brigid sort the postal stamps sent in from all over the country to support the missions. We knitted woolly scarves and socks to be sent off to some destination we could only vaguely imagine, not unlike the pictures in the Far East, places with palm trees, tea plantations, colourful clothes and sunny weather.

I could never turn the heel of a stocking. Poor coordination managing four needles at the same time I suppose. Instead, I was sent to get wool from the storeroom at the bottom of St Teresa's and to look for any extra knitting needles I could find. It was dark in that pokey room under the stairs. If I delayed, I was never asked too much about it. It was Saturday after all, and Sister Brigid was pretty easy going. I had to pass the small chapel on route and on an unsuspecting afternoon, I glanced in, the door ajar.

I was drawn to the lighted candles beneath the large, framed picture of a young pretty woman with pink roses and a crucifix in her hands: St Therese of Lisieux. I took to sitting before her smiling face for a few minutes every time I went to the storeroom. I tried to imagine her life. She did not look very Irish. I wondered where she lived, if she had brothers and sisters, what her parents were like. How she managed to become a saint and what her association was with those beautiful pink roses. I asked her to help me become just as beautiful and saintly. I think my desire was as much to be adored as it was to become a pure soul for Christ. Perhaps she was to my impressionable mind what celebrity is to today's generation.

The chapel was always empty except for once when I hadn't noticed the presence of Sister Aloysius in a pew to the back. I got up to leave.

'Come here child, come here.' I nearly fell out of my standing. I had been in a kind of reverie.

She must have seen my fright and said, 'I am sorry. I frightened you.'

I said nothing but my heart thumped. 'It's alright child. Do you like the altar of St Therese?'

'I do.'

'She was a French girl, you know.'

'Was she?' It all seemed so exotic and romantic.

'I will get you the book we have on her life.'

'Thank you, Sister Aloysius.'

'What is this your name is again? O'Brien, isn't it?'

'Yes sister, Mary O'Brien.'

'Ah yes, sister to Martha?'

'Yes.'

'You father is Jack, is that right?'

'Yes.'

'You have the farm in Bally Mac.'

'Yes, sister but only the locals call it that.'

'Ah but I knew it well. You Dad's uncle Mick is my mother's first cousin. St Therese it is then,' and she smiled.

I realise now I had left an impression A possible candidate. At the time I was just pleased with myself that I now understood Daddy's connection with the place. Our fees were manageable. Martha and I heard Daddy and Mammy discussing their overall satisfaction with the decision to send us to Rossnagh during my second and Martha's fourth summer at home before she entered into her final year. Daddy was more than pleased with Mammy's approval.

'The girls are really growing into lovely young women, Jack.'

'They're hardly women yet, Maeve,' he laughed

'I know that!' she said, throwing a tea towel at him. 'They organise their uniforms and all their books for each term without being asked. Fancy Tom and James doing that?'

'Oh, you'll be waiting!' he threw back as he headed out the door. We giggled upstairs.

All in all, those were blissfully peaceful years. That year of 1952 was to be a significant one for me. Sister Maria did not return as our dorm mistress for my third and final year in junior school. We were sorely disappointed. There was no explanation though there were some murmurings about her having gone to a convent in Dublin. We didn't ask. It was not encouraged. She was replaced by Sister Ligouri. Sister Ligouri was precise and punctual. She had no tolerance for the kind of excuses we might have given Sister Maria and only supplied the hot water bottle when you were virtually on death's door. Nonetheless, she was fair and never succumbed to the kind of favouritism we witnessed in Sister Aidan. We were also a little older and more able for the rough and tumble of boarding life. I felt sorry for the First Years, some of whom seemed quite lost.

***

That October two nuns visited us. October being the month of vocations, they were on what I now understand to be a recruiting drive. They spoke of the privilege it is to be called, of the tender love of God that this world could not know but the soul touched by its force wholeheartedly understood. I related to that. I was nervous too. They spoke of the value of service. They spoke of themselves.

Sister de Lourdes told us she used to be just like us, a happy go lucky young girl with three sisters and an older brother. She spoke of the table on the landing of her childhood home where pictures of her grandparents stood beneath the cross. In the month of October, her father led them in a decade of the rosary each evening for the souls who smiled out from each picture, among them was her beloved grandfather who used to call her the apple of his eye. In the month of November, the oil lamp was lit each day to remember them.

They were never forgotten. She told us that she felt the fire of God's love grow in her every day for the life she had chosen. The other nun, I have forgotten her name, explained that there were nursing orders and there were teaching orders. There were orders that carried out charitable works, there were missionary orders who served in the far-flung lands of Africa and the Far East and enclosed orders who never saw their families again. *They* were a teaching order, and they stayed at home. I thought of Therese's 'Little Way'.

Later that evening I lay in my bed, my head full of images. I had a clear sense of the invisible beauty of the world, of realities I could not name that I knew not everyone recognised. I had to own that I more than recognised, I felt. Felt connected to that reality which was at the same time core to my own being. To deny it was to deny myself. I could see Sister de Lourdes standing before the picture of her grandfather. I could see the light from the oil lamp and the communion of the living and the dead in that moment where there is no parting, where their souls are one, embraced by a love I could not name. I kept it all to myself but poured my heart out to Therese whenever I got the chance. I struggled for almost a full year.

5

The Road to Dublin

The following September I left home for the novitiate in the grounds of the mother house in Dublin and Martha began her final year in school. I was sixteen going on seventeen, she was shy of eighteen. I finally shared my desire to enter religious life with Martha the previous spring. We went for a walk together in the grounds of the school. It was my birthday, and she had painted a little watercolour during art class which she wanted to give me. We were exempted from study for an hour immediately after school ended. In the background was the lower meadow, just suggested, in the foreground a book in the right-hand corner and a dog in the left and in the middle two intertwined hearts with the letter M on both. I loved the painting. So much in such a small space. Home, Lady, the dog, our love of reading but most of all our filial love. It had all the sentimentality and freedom of teenagers.

'I love it Martha, I love it,' I giggled as I threw my arms around her.

'Do you really?' she asked.

'I do,' was all I replied. It was enough. We tucked our arms into each other and walked along the pathways through the woods of beech, hazel, ash and oak trees. It was a bright chilly spring afternoon.

'Martha,' I said, 'I have something to tell you.'

'Oh,' replied Martha before I had time to finish my sentence, 'it sounds serious!' She had already picked up on my anxiety.

'Well, it is. But you must promise not to tell anyone. Not until I am ready.'

'O my God. You have me frightened now. Are you okay?'

'I am absolutely grand Martha.' And then I spluttered it, 'I am thinking of becoming a nun.'

'You're not! Seriously Mary, you're not!'

'I am,' I could barely bring the words from my throat.
'For God's sake Mary…'
'Exactly.'
'Exactly what?!'
'For God's sake.'
'Really? Really Mary?'
'Yes, really.'
'You don't want to be like Sister Aloysius, do you? Really Mary. Think of all you will be missing!' Martha was shocked.
'I know. I am surprised too but I can't pretend…'
'Pretend what? That you want to live a life locked up in some dreary convent? You Mary, you? You jumped from the rafters without batting an eyelid. Look at yourself. You're gorgeous for God's sake! I don't mean for God's sake. I mean… you know what I mean.'
We were both struggling to express ourselves clearly.
'Look Martha, I will just try it out for a year to see how it goes. That's all. I don't know why but I feel caught up in this great love.'
'I don't know what that means Mary. I have love too. I know I do.'
'Of course you do. We all do.'
'So, what's different?'
'I just feel this great desire to understand God more?'
'Can't you do that in the books that you read?'
'No, Martha, I can't. It is more like a surrender.'
'A surrender?'
'Yes. If I don't surrender to this love inside me, this God, I deny who I am.'
'Okay, okay. I don't really understand but I can see that something is going on.'
I laughed.
'Oh Mary, what about Mammy and Daddy?'
'They mightn't be too surprised. After all, Daddy's aunt was a nun out on the missions somewhere and he often used to visit his friend in All Hallows.'
'All what? I don't know how you even know these things, Mary. Where is that?'
'I don't know really but it is some place in Dublin, I think. Which is exactly where I will be going if I decide to enter.'

'How do you know that?'
'Because that is where Sister Maria went.'
'The lovely Sister Maria?'
'Yes.'
'And how do you know that?'
'Because I asked.'
'I wouldn't even think of asking. I suppose that's the difference.'
'I don't know. I have been speaking with Sister Aloysius. Last week I received a card from Sister Liguori inviting me to visit the 'novitiate' is what they call it, where you become a nun. She invited Helen Carroll too'
'And where is that?'
'Dublin.'
'Where in Dublin?'
'I don't know but I will soon find out. We are going there for a weekend after the Easter holidays.'
'Helen Carroll! She is our best camogie player. The Easter Holidays? I take it you will tell Mammy and Daddy then?'
'Yes. Sister Aloysius will want to meet them. Three weeks' time, so not a word. Promise?'
'Poor Mammy! I promise but don't leave it any longer.'
'I won't.' We were both caught up in some introspective reverie. 'I won't change, you know that don't you, Martha?'
'I do. But still and all, there will be change.'

***

Mammy's response took me by surprise.
'Are you sure this is what you want, Mary?'
Yes Mammy, I think so.'
'You need to more than think, Mary. You need to know. Here in your heart Mary. If you can tell me that is where this decision is coming from, your heart, then I will find it easier to accept.'
Her query helped to clarify my own thoughts. 'It is Mammy. It is from my heart.'
'Then, I won't stand in your way, but you are young, and I want you to know, no matter what anyone else says, if you should ever choose to leave, I will be waiting for you. Do you understand?'
'I do Mammy.'

A single tear fell from the corner of her eye. She shrugged it off and smiled as she threw her arm across my shoulder and hugged me. Daddy spoke with me later that day in the parlour.

'This is a big decision, Mary. Are you sure it is what you want?'

'Yes Daddy. I'm fairly certain.'

'You were always special to me. You know that don't you?'

'Yes,' I replied indulgently.

'I remember from the time I first picked you up after you were born, I thought you were so like my godmother, Peg. I was very fond of Peg. She was always full of personality and so good to me growing up. She was good to my mother too after my father died. She had an easy way with her, and she was thoughtful. So, it isn't just your curly hair that reminds me of Peg. I will miss you; you know?'

'I know Daddy, but I am not disappearing.'

'You will for a while. You know that don't you?'

'Only for a while Daddy.'

'It is difficult to come out if you decide it is not for you. Sean Dooley's son left for New York after three years in the seminary. A *spoiled priest* is what they call it. Frowned upon by all and sundry. It isn't easy to come home.'

'Would you send me to New York Daddy?'

'No, not at all, but you might want to go yourself. These things are not easy to get over Mary. Judgement can be harsh.'

'I see.'

'Are you sure?'

'Yes Daddy, I am sure.'

'Then I won't stand in your way. You have spoken with your mother. Maeve is a wonderful mother, but all her geese are swans. She would walk through hot coals for you all, but life is rarely that simple.'

'Are you proud of me Daddy?'

'Of course I am! I have always been. You have given me nothing but happiness. I want you to be happy. That's all.'

'I know Daddy, I know.'

'I don't know why I would even question it. Auntie Brid is still in Tanzania. She works in a hospital out there. I haven't seen her in over thirty years. She will die out there and is by her own account doing great work and is very happy.'

'Is that the woman whose letter you read every Christmas morning?'
'Aye, that's her. So, who am I to question you.'

I wanted to tell him I loved him, but these words were rarely if ever expressed. I squeezed his hand.

'Come here,' he said and hugged me. We will have many a walk in the meadow between here and September.'

'We will, daddy. We will.

6

Martha's Wake & Funeral

Arriving at the house under the weight of such a tragedy was like no homecoming I had experienced before or since. The silence was all-encompassing. The house was full of people who did not speak or, if they had to, did so in deferential whispers, moving about with purpose and politeness. Swift feet disappeared around corners. Those with nothing to do either looked at their hands or stared into the middle distance. I could hear the occasional moan from Lady who hobbled on her arthritic limbs around the kitchen at the back of the house. A whispered, though audible voice was heard from the back of the stairs: 'Put that blessed dog out'. I knew this would not happen. Lady had been part of our family for fifteen years. A pup for Martha on her fifth Christmas.

I stood in the front door frame frozen to the spot. Aware of eyes upon me, I suddenly became deeply conscious of the novice's habit I was wearing. Nobody greeted or addressed me. I guess I was very different from the Mary they remembered. In truth, I was, but I was the same too. A child returned home. I was angry and sad in equal measure. I wanted to say, 'Look here John Murphy, look! It's me. Say hello and stop staring! And as for you Agnes Downes, take your hand down from your mouth and spit out what it is you're whispering!' But I didn't. I had a greater reality to face. I both longed to and dreaded seeing Martha. My dearest wish was to spend some time alone with her.

Tom appeared at the top of the stairs. He was pale and black under his eyes, his open neck shirt ballooning around his clearly thin body. He had grown. He zigzagged his way down through the neighbours standing on each step. He looked at me curiously, a little bewildered. But when our eyes locked, he was filled with tears. He quietly clasped my outstretched hand and led me back up the stairs. I could hear Betty

O'Dea repressing her sobs as she watched us climb together.

Tom, one step ahead, not letting go of my hand, I held on tight to the intimacy of that clasp. My twelve-year-old brother had thrown me a lifeline of solace in the midst of overwhelming emotion. I hung on also, watching my footsteps, managing my long habit, sweeping over the familiar territory of the now frayed red and gold carpet my grandmother picked out in Ryan's for the Stations a lifetime ago. My foot stubbed against the brass rods at least twice. The air was acrid in spite of the open windows. I was flushed by the time I reached the landing.

James stood waiting for me. He was formal. We did not hug. I understood the fortitude necessary to get through devastation and the desire to keep it together before watching eyes. I could not allow myself to feel anything except courage. I leaned in and whispered, 'She is not in her own room then?'

'No. The backroom is larger and cooler. We have every window in the house open.'

'Can I have some time alone with her?'

'You left it a little late for that. Last night was the night to come.' Though he spoke in hushed tones. There was an edge not just to his voice, but to his whole self, a tension I put down to the stress of the moment. 'Father Healy will be here in the next half hour to say the closing prayers.' He was softer this time.

'I'm sorry, James. I truly am. I just couldn't…'

'I know, I know.' He cut across me, 'you're a nun now, they decide, vow of obedience and all that.'

I felt truly tested, hurt and wanting at the same moment.

'Come in Mary,' Tom pulled me towards the door.

My head spun and I had to refocus as, although windows were open, curtains were drawn, the only light coming from the splashes of sunshine when breezes lifted the billowing drapes and two candles on either side of the bed where Martha lay. I recognized the same starched linen sheets Granny was laid out in. The sheets for the dead kept out of sight in an old blanket box. I caught sight of Daddy first. He sat against the far wall facing the door. It struck me as odd that Mammy was not sitting beside him. The pain was etched in the creases of his face. His mouth was drawn. He stood up and swept over to me.

But as if some other switch clicked, he stopped just short of me saying formally, 'Welcome home, Mary. You are here finally. That is all that matters now.'

I stepped forward. We embraced politely. I saw Daddy's eyes scan the room. He was doing what he felt was appropriate opposite his extended family. But I was wrenched. My eyes had not moved from the bottom of the bed. I turned to see Mammy. She did not move from her chair. For all the world, she looked like a mannequin. Her eyes were fixed firmly on Martha. Aunt Sheila nodded in my direction and vacated the chair beside her. I sat down and put my arm across her tense shoulders. I knew not to speak. I pressed my fingers firmly on her forearm. It was the only offering I had. I kept my eyes lowered and was genuinely grateful to those aunts and uncles who had the good sense to leave the room for a few moments. Not all did.

I raised my eyes to drink in the deathly pallor of my sister's face: a white, grey, blue lips, dark circles under her closed lids, her blonde curls soft against the pillow and the rigidity of death. A small holy water bottle held her jaw in place. Her pearl communion beads were wrapped around her young and very blue hands. She would have been seven years old when they were last intertwined around her fingers, probably posing for the family photograph. The absurdity of it all aside, two things struck me immediately. Even though I was looking at a corpse, Martha was much thinner than I remembered. Her face was contorted. She was not a peaceful corpse.

I don't know what I had expected or how I had hoped to reconcile myself to this. But I was disturbed by the utter torment of her expression. It cut through my heart. I bent my head almost to my lap in silent sobbing tears. I wanted to be away from the world. *Martha, did you suffer? Did you know you were dying?* My questions remained within. Mammy, though still fixated on Martha, sighed a deep sigh and caught my hand. That was it. Fr Healy had come. Voices were raised in the hall below. There was movement on the stairs and landing.

Father Healy entered, his breviary, beads and cross in his hands accompanied by Sister Xavier. They were followed by a swoop of those aunts and uncles who had left the room and any one from the landing who could occupy any available space. Father Healy, a serious and sturdy man, stood at the end of the bed. He beckoned to Sister Xavier, who responded by standing shoulder to shoulder with him. Even she could not hide her shock as she raised her eyes to look at Martha. Beautiful, dead, unhappy Martha. Sister Xavier's eyes diverted to mine. I understood she was observing me. I dropped my glance and firmly fixed my hands on my lap, still holding Mammy's left hand between my palms. I was rigid with the effort it took to control my emotion. The prayers began.

Father Healy read from the scriptures. Only those who did not have the space to kneel remained standing. I left my seat to kneel at Martha's bedside, my hips almost touching the bed cover. Mammy withdrew her hand the instant I indicated my intention. She stayed exactly where she was sitting, tight lipped and cross legged on her chair. There was a space before her, but she did not kneel. Daddy knelt to the left of Father Healy. Sister Xavier to his right, flanking his solemn intonations to the heavens. Five decades of the rosary were recited. The Glorious Mysteries led by Father Healy, then Sister Xavier, who quickly charged me to lead the third decade with one directive glance. I was angry. I was submissive. I recited each word in a stupor and was glad when Aunt Sheila immediately took it upon herself to continue the rhythmic prayers. At no time did I look at Martha. I understood very little, but I knew that to do so at that moment was more than I could bear.

***

Martha's coffin was placed in the same cart we used to so delight in being transported after haymaking. She left our home in Ballymac pulled by our old mare. This time, however, the cart was bedecked in the lush, dark green branches of the cypress tree. No wood was visible. A blanket of green received her. A simple bouquet of blue and white delphiniums tied by a white satin ribbon rested gently at the base of her coffin. We followed the three miles in our family trap. The young pony almost prancing. Sister Xavier had gone ahead with Father Healy in his Ford car. I insisted on travelling with my family. She did not object.

That evening, we left Martha before the altar at the top of the central aisle. There was a wrench in that for each of us. I imagined her there in the empty space accompanied only by the ghosts of many who had gone before her from this place and the promise of the living Eucharist in the tabernacle. She was present to an all-encompassing silence where only the Blackbird and Robin would be heard in the hours after dawn eventually joined by the sound of feet crunching the gravel as we arrived for her morning funeral mass, in Latin, no eulogy, just our simple tears and Mammy's stony silence.

As we left to take her to the adjoining cemetery, I was woken from my reverie by a conscious, unrelenting stare from a young man beneath a recess near the holy water font by the main entrance door. I raised my glance. My eyes met with David Carroll's. He stared directly and deliberately. I was quite shocked at his intensity. He had crossed my mind the night before, as I slept in our childhood bedroom. I recollected that I had not seen him. I thought no more of it as I was the late arrival and assumed he had visited earlier.

I was holding Mammy's arm. Daddy, James, and Tom were ahead of us, shouldering the coffin. I was stricken by his intensity. Unable to leave my mother's side, I resolved to meet him later. However, that opportunity never arose. I searched but there was no sign of him. I asked Mammy. She suggested that it was maybe too difficult for him. His grieving eyes hung on my heart. The house still full of neighbours and family, Sister Xavier approached to remind me that we had to catch the one o'clock train. Father Healy was waiting to bring us to the station.

Before leaving I looked for Daddy. I found him sitting alone in the hay barn at the back of the yard. Based on Daddy's formal approach the evening before. I stretched out my hand to say goodbye. He caught my arm and, drawing me towards him, stood up and wrapped his arms around me. I felt my heart collapse.

'Mary! Mary! Must you go so soon? What is happening to us at all?' he cried openly. I cried.

'Let that blessed Sister Xavier wait.'

I nodded, unable to speak. 'Do you remember all the fun you had out here, Mary? I often heard your laughter as you and James jumped the bales following Martha's orders. I used to get great suss out of hearing you all play together…But it's gone… it's over.'

'Oh, Daddy. It's never gone. She is here,' I sobbed pointing to my heart, 'and she is in yours too.'

'I would prefer to have her here chatting with us right now.'

'I would too,' I admitted, 'I have to go, Daddy. I have to go,' I sniffed, feeling the weight of time and the pressure of Sister Xavier's reminder.

'Do you? I know... I know. But do you?'

'Don't make this harder for me than it already is. Please, Daddy...I...'

'I am sorry Mary, I'm sorry,' he sighed, brushing back his thick, wavy hair. 'Come here. I want to show you something before you go.'

We walked deeper into the barn. And there, in a warmed dip in the hay at the back, was a litter of newborn kittens. Their mother was feral, so we did not go too near. Six fragile creatures, their eyelids still closed under her protective eye.

'Born while we were saying our goodbyes,' Daddy said. 'Isn't life full of contradictions, Mary?' We walked back to the house together, both of us exhausted. My bones ached. Mammy came to meet us. She threw her arms around me and held me in a tight hug. Just as we untangled, she lowered her head and sobbed unrelenting tears, almost losing her breath. I bawled. Daddy seemed alarmed.

'Maeve, Maeve!' he cried as he stepped forward.

'Don't. Please don't,' she whispered, 'I can't.'

I was thrown. I did not know what to make of any of it. I knew they were stressed and seemed alienated. A light had gone out in all of our lives but there was a darkness in both of my parents that I just could not reach.

Is this what grief looks like? I thought. Is this how Mammy felt after Elizabeth died all those years ago?

Daddy went for Tom. Both were back within minutes.

'I'd better go.'

'If it's Sister Xavier you are worried about, Sheila is keeping her busy, introducing her to all the neighbours', Tom threw in.

'Good old Sheila,' sighed Daddy while glancing at Mammy.

'It's not Sister Xavier,' I cried, 'if I don't go now, I won't go at all,' I collapsed into Mammy's arms.

'Then stay!' Daddy whispered into our silent huddle.

I could feel our hearts breaking. But those words seemed to act as a catalyst for Mammy. She caught me by the back of the neck and looked me straight in the eye. 'Be who you want to be Mary. Be true to yourself. Don't let anyone take that from you.'

Daddy instinctively put his hand across his mouth, had an intake of breath and stared at his wife but she kept her focus on me.

'O Mammy,' I cried throwing my arms around her. 'In that case...'

I stammered.

'I know, I know, I know my own daughter. You are making the one o'clock train.'

'Yes,' I replied. 'I am making the one o'clock train. I love you. I love you all.' I needed to hear myself utter these words. My resolve was wearing thin. Had I stayed much longer, I may have never left.

'We will see you in six weeks, Mary.' Mammy spoke gently, 'for your first profession.'

'Six weeks. Is that all it is?' Daddy queried.

'August,' Mammy said

'Yes, August sixth,' I replied.

'Let's go,' said Tom.

I slipped out quietly. I could not face goodbyes with the extended family being asked to explain what I could not, even to myself. I looked for, but could not find James, which I regretted but over which I had no control. We were already out of time.

As the train pulled out. I truly felt I had left home for good. I had overcome the greatest urge to stay. Just. I was grateful to my mother. Though I thought it was not possible, as the train picked up speed, my sadness deepened, as did my fortitude for I knew I was letting go. I closed my eyes, only to see Martha's coffin lowered into the heavy clay along with a piece of each of us.

7

The Crushed Reed

On the day of my first profession, I was already down a full-dress size since Martha's burial. I wore a white dress made of simple cotton. Three years since I left Ballymac and Rossnagh yet so much had changed. I spent the remainder of my schooling years in the novitiate in Dublin. After my Leaving Certificate, I had to commit to an enclosed year before taking my temporary vows. I understood that my world would be different from Martha's. I did not anticipate that her world would simply disappear, and my family's world was forever changed. I looked forward to attending university the following September. I had a great desire to learn and an even greater desire to be close to the memory of Martha. The whole context in which she had communicated with me was that of a woman come alive through her life in university. I wanted to experience some of that and draw close to the blossoming about which she wrote.

My heart was clear that the choice I was making was the right one. I trusted what Mother Columba had implied, that one day my family would look to me, that I might be the one to step into the breach of support or guidance where it was needed precisely because I had chosen differently. I would be free of prejudicial ties or the desire for what was material. I would be free of agenda. While later I was to understand that this thinking could lead to unfettered ego or spiritual pride, on that day my intentions were innocent, perhaps even naive but nonetheless pure. I loved my family. I prayed for them every day. Grief still lived in every cell of my body, and I understood, those of my family's, too.

They lovingly attended, did all that was asked of them: met Mother Columba, Sister Xavier, the other parents and left at the earliest opportunity. I now understand that they were just about able to get through it. Daddy had lost weight too. He looked haggard and worn.

I caught his eye on my presentation as a bride of Christ to the bishop who blessed and presented me with my habit. I suppose I was a picture of simplicity. Beautiful in my own way. Daddy's face cracked when I smiled at him. He lost his composure and put his head in his hands. Mammy placed her hand across his lap. I did not look at them again until the service was over. I could not. It is here that I lose the details. As the ceremony ended visitors rose to make their way. My family sat for some time huddled alone in their pew. We met in the dining room where families mingled. I hugged each in turn. Daddy was last and held on for a long time until Mammy reminded him that we were all in company. We sat together for tea; our brief conversations interrupted by

Will you have another cup of tea?

Are you very proud of her?

I am so sorry for your loss.

***

Mammy and Daddy put on a good show

No, no we won't have any more tea, thank you.

Yes, we are very proud of Mary. (Daddy never again referred to me as Sister Cecilia)

'We are proud of all our children, truth be told,' Mammy replied tartly.

Yes, our lovely Martha.

James and Tom said nothing at all.

'We must go Maeve,' Daddy hopped up, almost knocking his chair.

'Are you alright Daddy?' I asked, knowing full well that he wasn't.

'I will be,' he tremored.

'Okay,' Mammy quickly cupped her hand under his elbow and led him to the exit. 'We have to go now Mary; it is a long journey home.'

'Yes, two hours on a bad road,' Tom was throwing me a bone.

Mother Columba swept through and offered to see them out. They were gone.

For a second time I walked to my room in something of a stupor, lay in my new habit on my bed and watched small raindrops fall from the Silver Birch outside my window.

After many random thoughts, I imagined what it would have been like had Martha shared this moment. We would have hugged and kissed. There would have been laughter. But she wasn't and there was no laughter, only the heavy pall of grief. I aimlessly opened my bible, the nearest book to hand. I am not sure what I was looking for. Comfort, consolation, answers? The following line jumped out, it was the only line my eye fell upon: 'And Jesus looked at him and loved him…' I knew the story well. The rich young man who could not leave his possessions. I knew that I had given away all I had when I left Ballymac. I knew it again when the convent door closed as my family left. I needed that gaze of love upon me. I cried out.

There was a knock on my door. Mother Columba swept in and stopped as if interrupted. She sighed. There was a moment's silence. She sat on the only chair in the room, turning it around from my desk to my bed. I sat on the edge of the bed. She did not look at me but bent her head, her hands folded on her lap. She spoke slowly and deliberately. 'You are young Cecilia, and, in truth, a lot has been asked of you. What age is it that you are now? Nineteen?

'Yes,' I sighed, 'I will be twenty later this year.'

'Hmm,' she seemed uncertain. 'Your family today, they were….'

'Broken,' I whispered.

'Yes, I won't deny it.'

I could feel a single tear slip from the side of my left eye.

'You were very brave. You are young and you are brave.' She lifted her head and looked directly at me. 'I do not know what path is laid out for you Cecilia, but I do know this, you will meet the moment, don't doubt it. There are many your age who have not been asked to draw on such strength. When I consider the choices, you have made, I cannot help but reflect that your strength is rooted in your faith. There is a deep well being formed in you and I know in my heart that there is someone out there, perhaps even many, who will draw from that well. They will come to you seeking solace or guidance and you will recognise the moment when it comes. Jesus says many times in the gospels 'do not prepare your defence…' You will have no need of any defence Cecilia because your soul is already being formed. Right now, despite all your sorrow, it is bright.'

'How can you tell?' I asked in innocence.

'Because your love for your parents and your brothers today was clear for all to see and, I am sure, brought them much reassurance.

You were considerate. You were calm. Only a young woman who is at peace within herself despite her loss could show such presence. But it was the deep joy obvious in your expression and the clear utterances with which you made your commitments to this life you have chosen which painted the picture for us all.'

I remained silent trying to let those insights settle between the gaps of my chaotic thoughts.

'Do you understand Cecilia?'

I nodded. 'I think so.' But did I? Did I really?

'Come, come Cecilia. It is almost eight. The community is already gathering in the chapel to pray the evening Office.'

I picked up my breviary. That evening, I sat in the chapel for a long time after the Office was over and all had left. It was to be the beginning of a practice I kept for the rest of my days. It was here I whispered all my struggles. Here I dropped my baggage. Here I felt that gaze of love upon me. It never left.

***

Once I started my degree, not unlike Martha, I became consumed with my studies. I refrained from joining any clubs and generally kept relationships with other students cordial. However, two students in particular, Sean O'Loughlin and Una Muldoon, sought my advice from time to time as if the veil granted me some elevated maturity of which I was not at all worthy. We were the same age.

They were first cousins who had taken a year out as volunteers in Belize supervised by their uncle Dr David Muldoon who spent most of his adult life working with the native people of Belize. Apparently, he fell in love with this small country during his travels there as a student long before such travel began in earnest. Once qualified he made his way back and never left apart from visits home every second year, the years of the war apart. He regaled his family with colourful, often heroic stories, and when Sean and Una reached the age of eighteen, he convinced their parents to let them work alongside him for six months. They stayed for nine. And here we were. We became firm friends. They understood the ground rules. No socialising outside the academic timetable. I returned to the convent of the Sacred Heart for lunch. Despite the restrictions, we laughed a lot together. I found their company refreshing.

The first semester flew by. Advent was difficult but I managed, grateful for the opportunities this experience of education afforded me. Like Martha, I felt a quiet power growing within me, my own self. Studying English was wonderful. I fell in love with Thomas Hardy and George Eliot. The Brontes, however, were still favourites. I graduated from Jane Eyre to Wuthering Heights. I found a forlorn quality in many of their characters, plots and their description of the landscape. That sense of being set apart, an outsider, an observer, was something with which I identified. I found a similar sense of separation and observation in the lives of many of the saints that I have continued to read throughout my life. Wandering pilgrims, searchers of the love beyond all telling, mystics, you might even say dreamers. Perhaps in another life I would have been a poet, but I committed to serve.

My days were truly content but each night I lay down beneath a heavy sadness. I was saddened by the loss of my sister. On those evenings when we gently chanted the psalms, the silence of eternity seemed to open its doors. Music, unlike literature, accesses the heart directly. The experience was both consoling and raw. Certain lines stand out, still do:

He shall not crush the bruised reed
    Nor quench the smouldering flame.

Or

A thousand years is like a day
    Or a watch in the night
You whisk them away in their sleep
They are like the new grass of the morning

***

And so, Christmas morning in all its spiritual simplicity arrived. A newborn son, a little child that held the soul of the world, was celebrated. It was a peaceful if cold day. After breakfast we were given our Christmas post. I received a simple card from home. What struck me immediately was that it was non-religious, the first! A stone farmhouse with a red door on a snowy hillside. It evoked memories of home. It was also a statement of independence which I instinctively knew Mother Columba would have noted. Eileen's mother would have never sent it. Mine did.

I smiled to myself. I thought of James and Daddy up early for milking despite attending midnight mass. The usual ritual was warm milk when we arrived back home blowing on our fingers and a sliver of Christmas cake. Christmas Eve always marked the beginning of celebrations in our house. We were hushed promptly to bed while Mammy and Daddy placed little gifts beneath our paper decorated Christmas tree. Linen handkerchiefs with blue or pink sprays for Martha and me, plain for James and Tom. Simple Ludo games, a post office, a bag of brightly coloured marbles, a metal train set, a doll was among the magical and highly anticipated offerings.

This Christmas was different. We were all grown up now, even Tom, who had turned thirteen in my absence. I imagined him helping Mammy in her lonesomeness, collecting the eggs from the henhouse or peeling vegetables at the sink below the window overlooking the yard. It would all be low key and gentle. Their message was short

Dear Mary
We hope you have a peaceful Christmas. We all miss Martha, and we miss you. We are thinking of you.
God bless,
Daddy, Mammy, James and Tom.

At the time I understood their reference to 'missing' me was an expression of endearment and affection. I realised much later, that my vocation after the loss of Martha became another kind of death for them. I was not surprised at the brevity of the message. The handwriting was Mammy's. I imagine it was all she could do.

In the evening, those who wished were allowed to listen to the proms on BBC Radio Four. There were forty of us overall in the community. We were considerate to each other and there was a warm camaraderie, by and large, but there were differences also. We were organised no differently than the society from which we came. I did not question it. There were Choir nuns and Lay sisters. I was a Choir nun which meant that I was afforded the opportunity of an education and could hold office in the future. Lay sisters, on the other hand, were not afforded these opportunities and were assigned tasks related to the labour of the convent, the laundry, the kitchen, the garden. We had stepped away from the *trappings* of the outside world. Yet the social order by which it lived was fully operational within our community.

What I loved about Christmas Day and Easter Sunday was that we were all equal and did whatever was necessary to make the day special for each other. There were a few, such as Sister Xavier, Sister Cletus and Sister Assumpta, who did not surrender to such sentimentality. Though friendships were not encouraged, I felt close to Sister Mary Anne, an art teacher in the local school and to Sister Nancy, the gardener. Often in the early morning or afternoon, Sister Nancy and I would sit on the roughhewn seat at the back of the vegetable patch by the low stone wall. It was something of a sun trap and a gate nearby led to the rose garden. We shared stories of our childhood, discussed the herbs and sometimes walked among the tea roses. We had joined the community in the same year and had a dread of Sister Xavier in common in the early days. The laughter we shared helped us get over many a grievance, but we were never too critical, understanding that it was simply not allowed or worthy of a Christian soul.

On January 2nd, 1957, my head in my breviary as I walked beneath the arches reciting morning prayers Mother Columba approached me walking swiftly across the gravelled path. She was upon me before I knew it. Just as well. She led me down through the side door of the empty chapel. We sat before a side altar dedicated to St Joseph.

'Sister Cecilia, I know we have spoken of this in the recent past. I had not foreseen that it would be necessary to do so again so soon and in truth, I cannot imagine the burden you are being asked to bear, but I received a call from Fr Healy who is offering the most holy Eucharist as we speak for the peaceful repose of your dear father. He wishes to assure you that he will storm heaven and earth for you and for your family.'

'Daddy, is it? What are you saying?' I watched her falter.

'Your father, Daddy, as you call him, has been called from this world Cecilia. He passed away late yesterday evening it seems. I am unsure of the circumstances of his death, but I am certain and so very sorry that it is so. Your father is dead Cecilia.'

I felt the life drain out of me. I did not utter a cry or a word.

'I took it upon myself to ring Dr Walsh,' she continued 'but he was not available as he is presently with your family. His wife confirmed all Fr. Ryan had said.'

We sat in silence for some time. Mother Columba took out her rosary and knelt in whispered prayer. I did not move. My mind was blank, my legs dead weight beneath me.

'Come Cecilia, you have had a shock. You need something warm.'

I followed. Did exactly as I was told, grateful someone else was thinking for me. I surrendered to all she suggested. The cup of sweet milky tea, the glass of sherry after, the hot water bottle placed beneath my blankets which warmed my feet as Sister Mary Anne tucked me in, my teeth chattering uncontrollably. I fell in and out of a disturbed sleep, images of my father before me. After some hours I heard myself groan and Mary Anne reached across and held my hand. Only then did I become aware of her presence. She, Sister Xavier and Mother Columba sat in rota over a twenty-four-hour period. When I came through to some level of reality Columba was asleep on the chair beside my bed, the frost still on the grass as it had been the morning before when she first broke the news to me. I sat on the edge of the bed. Alert as ever, she woke rather quickly. She placed her arm across my shoulder. I wept uncontrollably.

'I must go home' I cried

She placed her hand under my chin and raised my face to look at her. She spoke directly.

'Cecilia, there is no question of you going home. You must understand, we made an exception for you to attend Martha's funeral due to her young age and sudden death, but we cannot do so a second time. I am afraid it is not possible. I am sorry.'

A heavy silence enveloped my room. I lay back without moving. For the first time I felt the sparsity of my surroundings. Bare white walls, my narrow bed, my locker with its reading lamp, my desk with its row of books, a small wardrobe in the far corner containing all my belongings. No images to bring comfort, no pieta or white winged angels, just a simple crucifix at which I refused to look. Not even my window, which overlooked the flat roof of a ground floor extension, could offer me the sight of a single tree or blade of grass. I was angry. I offered Columba no consolation. An epic conflict raged within me. *Is this the meaning of obedience? Am I being tested? What kind of God are you? Where are you, Daddy? Columba, don't you pontificate. Don't you dare! I don't want to hear your words.*

She left the room. I lay there for a long time staring at the ceiling, a heavy rock upon my chest. Once the tears escaped from the sides of my eyelids, I turned over, grabbed my pillow and screamed into it. Finally, I heard footsteps echo back along the corridor outside.

Mother Columba entered without a word. She was accompanied by Sister Anthony, our choir mistress, who opened a case and removed a fiddle. I had only ever seen her play the organ in our chapel. Her arthritic knuckles were plain to see yet, with the gentlest and most focussed of movements she played music so sublime that my tears flowed uncontrollably. I later learned it was a piece called *Meditations from Thais*. The sound filled the entire corridor and spoke to me of profound sorrow. When she finished, we remained in silence.

Eventually, she left. I had never heard that music before, but I recognised in its sharing an understanding of a troubled and grieving heart. The kindred spirits exposed in this gesture convinced me that, in spite of my gut-wrenching pain, I was in the right place. Nonetheless, for the entire month of January, I spent each hour of my evening prayer on my knees crying for my family's pain and crying for my father. I saw his thick wavy hair, his broad hand as he leaned on the straw to show me the newborn kittens. I realised some of those survived longer than he did. I hung on only by the thread of a sensitive woman's delivery of a piece of music telling the story of a troubled soul.

Once again, I was drawn to music and Sister Anthony proved a gem. She reacquainted me with my early music lessons in Ballymac. During the next two years I learned to read proficiently and enjoyed playing the piano in our community room. Simple pieces, some a little more complicated, all mellow and largely hymns. I was allowed thirty minutes three times a week. It helped me negotiate the darkness.

II

8

Ballygraigue

After graduating, I was appointed by the Superior General to Ballygraigue, a midsize town one hundred miles from the novitiate, with a school of two hundred girls in the heart of rural Ireland. I did not mind saying goodbye to the mothership. I felt liberated and ready. The convent chapel in Ballygraigue was small and intimate. Its rural simplicity appealed to me. I always sat in front of the side altar dedicated to the Sacred Heart. On cold winter nights the sight of the Sanctuary lamp burning felt like a homecoming. The love pouring from the image of the heart before me, the one who had given all, filled my own. I always felt at once humbled, grateful and with purpose.

On day one, after I met my first charge of fifteen-year-old girls to discuss expectations for the year ahead and introduced Shakespeare's sonnet *Shall I Compare Thee*, I felt my prayers had been heard. We succeeded in having a brief discussion on romance and the nature of love. I surprised myself. The girls were intrigued. Smiles all around. I left the room on a high. Later in the afternoon I took a senior French class, all six of them. Introducing Guy de Maupassant, I quickly realised their comprehension was poor and they were bored, even if curious, about their new teacher. I abandoned my class plans. It was like letting go of a lifeboat. I was petrified. Asking them why they chose to study French I learned: two because they wanted to get into a university of any description, one because Dermot Moloney whom she adored was going to UCG and she was going too, one because her family went to France every summer on holiday, one because it was a romantic language and one because her best friend convinced her to join her in the class. With five minutes to go to the bell I extolled the virtues of Paris, the Champs Elysee, the Eiffel Tower, the Louvre, the

Shakespeare and Co. bookshop. One of the girls, Elizabeth Foley, flatly asked, 'Have you ever been there, sister?'

'No Elizabeth I have not.' End of the hard sell, I was relieved to hear the bell and left the room deflated.

Every morning, I walked through the school doors crossing the convent garden with its manicured lawn bordered by rose bushes and surrounded by a high box hedge which separated it from the schoolyard. I seldom left the grounds. The convent required, if not permission, at least notice of my intention to leave. The need did not arise then. I entered the grey, square school building by a backdoor. I was armed with my books and meticulous plans over which I poured for hours each evening. I was busy. I was anxious but I was succeeding too. By the end of the first term, my English classes were up and running with vibrant exchanges among the students and thought-provoking written work being turned in. French fared better than my first experience. Juniors was a doddle teaching the basics of grammar and comprehension to ambitious girls.

The senior French class, small as it was, was still my challenge. However, I pulled a master stroke early on in the term when I spotted the descriptive talents of Orna, the holiday maker. I took her aside and asked her to tell us all about her trips and her impressions of France. She had to prepare it in advance and had twenty minutes to speak. She had us all in stitches with her stories of her first experience of French toilets, Monsieur de la Serna's strange ways sitting all day smoking his pipe and listening to organ music, and the French family they joined for dinner in the South of France who served rabbit on a large platter in the centre of the table with rabbit ears decoratively placed like the fish head is sometimes served with fish. Much to her delight there was a collective groan, but it piqued the girls' interest and once a month we had a storytelling session. While Orna spoke only English, the girls were only allowed to ask questions in French, and so the progress began.

***

I settled well into the community of twenty nuns. There were four elderly nuns. Sister Josie was almost blind but was visceral in her observations and retained a keen wit despite this affliction. I grew very fond of her. She and Sisters Bernadette, Augustine and Aidan were cared for by three of the four young nuns, Sisters Peter, Ligouri and Borgia, the latter with whom I shared a dormitory. They were incredibly attentive to their charges. I rarely heard a cross word from any of them. They were gentle souls. The eight youngest nuns slept in dormitories of four, each with her own locker, wardrobe and desk neatly placed on either side of her bed, with a surround plywood partition for privacy.

It was privacy that I missed most. In moments of frustration or sadness, the chapel was my only refuge and sometimes, if I wished to read below my night light, I avoided it in case I would disturb Sister Agnes beside me. I had already submitted to such privations believing them to be beneficial to spiritual maturity and evidence of my vow of obedience. My real test in those years was Sister Celestine, Deputy Principal of the school. She had a room of her own along with those who were there more than five years or as those rooms became available in that old Georgian building fronted by a square flower garden, all lying to the back of the school which was built on land originally attached to the house.

Celestine was my burden for almost four years. I now realise how ideologically opposed we were. My first disagreement set the tone.

'That one has notions above her station.'

'Who?'

'Marian Smith, who else?'

'She is only in second year. How can she have "notions above her station"?'

'Have you seen how she dresses? Two out of five days a week she is not in full uniform. Last Tuesday she came in wearing blue shoes. I stopped her in her tracks to ask her where she was going.'

'I am sorry sister', she says 'but the strap broke on my navy ones. Noreen, (the older sister), gave me these. She was a bridesmaid last year. She said they cost a lot. She said they'd keep me dry 'til I am sorted.'

'Well, you can't wear them, I told her. Any other dark colour might be acceptable but not blue.'

'But sister, I don't have another pair.'

'I brought her down to the locker room to see if we could find another pair. There were a lot of odds, but we managed to find a left and right in the same colour, but nothing would satisfy her. She complained because one was laced, and one had a strap. I tried to reassure her. Nobody will notice. They are navy. That's what matters. The she decided, "They smell rank." Rank! Whatever that means! She decided she'd be a laughingstock. "Mary Ellen Jones will torture me with the slaggin'." I reminded her that Mary Ellen was a well-mannered girl. And that she was wasting time. Then I get it.'

'Get what?' I asked

'Attitude. Attitude with a capital A and there's no fixing that!'

'Why? What happened?'

'"No!" She said, "No way." I couldn't believe her audacity! I was doing my best to solve the problem. She has to go.'

'You can't be serious? She has no mother to help her.'

'You're right, she doesn't and that's just the point. With nobody to guide her, she is a bad influence. Take it from me, this situation is only going to get worse.'

'But Celestine, surely there is a fund to help in these situations?"

'There is no fund or cure for attitude. Do you know what she did next?' Not waiting for an answer, Celestine rolled on, her cheeks reddening in temper, 'she stormed up the hall roaring. Yes, roaring! I do not say it lightly. Turned on me! Saying something like, "You will never be a bridesmaid." Then she invoked our Blessed Mother in her slanderous words! Suggested that because blue is the colour of the blessed virgin, the colour I didn't want, that not even she can help me. As if I needed that child to tell me what help I needed! "It would take more than a miracle!", she roared. Out she goes, slamming the door behind her.'

'Celestine, she may be a handful. She just needs some direction, that's all.'

Celestine slapped her hand against the table and pushed back her chair. The rising colour on her cheeks seemed to puff her face beyond the strictures of her whipple. She was ready to burst. And she did. Pointing her forefinger, I was accused of a lack of respect, lack of insight, judgement or necessary experience. She stood up and left her parting shot, 'Bad enough to have an errant child question me but to have a member of staff and of my own community! Its beyond belief!'

I knew I had made a mistake. I had stepped across a line not easily forgotten. I could feel the egg I had just eaten rise in my throat. My hands shook.

Sister Agnes, who was within hearing distance at the end of the refectory that evening, visibly took an intake of breath. She glanced at me sympathetically but quickly reverted her gaze to the middle distance. The following evening as I was about to leave the school the Principal, Sister Eucharia, asked me to come to her office for a few moments. I had an immediate sense of dread. Sister Eucharia and I had a professional relationship, one which up to that moment I didn't doubt.

'Are you happy here? …. Do you understand what is required to be part of a team? …. Do you understand what is required to be part of a community? …. It will work itself out… I'm hearing good reports.'

Her message was clear. I was duly chastened.

And so, days turned into weeks and very quickly the school term was complete. Marian always remained with me, however. She hung on my heart. Though her mother was dead, she, with the aid of her older sister, attempted to attend second level school, a privilege not afforded to her siblings or many girls of her time. That opportunity was so readily lost. For what? A pair of shoes or the frustration of a teenager up against the immovable object that was Sister Celestine. An attitude?

On a rare trip to the Main Street some years later to pick up some books from Pat Garvey, I met Marian coming towards me pushing a pram. I smiled and went to step forward towards her as we crossed a side street in opposite directions. She caught my eye but quickly averted her gaze. The words stuck in my throat. I knew there and then that I, and any woman in nun's clothing, forever represented that exchange with Sister Celestine. I was wronged but Marian was robbed. Robbed of an education which would help her open doors. I felt the bile rising within me.

***

By the end of my second year, I had started a small but promising choir. Fifteen girls had their first public performance following the May procession through the streets of the town. Every window was dressed in peony roses, delphiniums, foxgloves, tea roses and geraniums. Pictures of Pius XII, statues of Our Lady of Lourdes, Our Lady of Knock, Our Lady Queen of Heaven, along with the Child of Prague, were bedecked on cloth covered tables outside front doors. The whole town was out. Men with white gloves and sashes, the parish stalwarts, lead the way proceeding through the main street of the town to the canopy-covered altar set up beside the entrance to the convent. Once the monstrance was placed upon the altar the ceremony began and the full voices of Miss Nolan's choir swung into action with a rousing rendition of *Faith of Our Fathers*.

Negotiations took place between the town choir and the Monsignor. He insisted the girls should be heard by the people of the town. I think of him fondly for this, for though the girls were shy and anxious, he understood the importance of young voices being given the opportunity to shine. He often visited the school. He was passing through St. Anthony's corridor towards the back of the school to retrieve his car from the convent garden when he heard the girls sing the first verse of *Panis Angelicus*. They had been practising for weeks and on that fortuitous afternoon their rendition was sublime and beautiful.

Though a tall, broad-backed man with a towering sense of presence, embellished by the deference with which he was treated by all, so involved were we in the hymn's delivery that none noticed his quiet entrance from the side door of the school hall. Had he come in from the back it might have been different but as the final notes drifted into and hung in the cold March air suspended in some seconds of silence, we jumped with the sound of a rapturous clap which seemed to come from nowhere. I blush to think of it now, but I blushed then too. Though not timid, I was reserved, and the uninvited accolade surprised and delighted me.

'Wonderful, wonderful' he declared, 'Sister Cecilia, isn't it? The patron saint of music! And here we are!' I blushed to the gills. The girls became giddy. 'And who is the young lady with the angelic voice who sang the first verse?'

Siofra O'Grady's eyes immediately reverted to the floor as it was her turn to blush. All others turned towards her, some with delight, some with envy, all a little jealous.

'That would be Siofra,' I demurred, 'Siofra O'Grady.'

'That Sean's daughter?' He boomed across the hall and as he took his forward strides he continued 'your daddy Sean? The bank Sean?' Siofra nodded, Ach sure I know Sean well. Ace at the golf. I didn't know he had a soprano in the family.'

At this point I felt a creeping anxiety taking hold of me and was very glad to hear Monsignor Dooley acknowledge the voices of all the girls in the choir.

'My God girls, you would open Heaven's gates. I am so delighted that we now have a school choir. Ballygraigue is proud of its musical traditions. We have to get you heard outside of these walls. Is that Angela and Mary I see?'

The girls were moving and giggling with enjoyment and anticipation. Children were not often praised.

'But' I interrupted, 'we are only just beginning,' conscious as I was of Miss Nolan's reputation for a tight hold on the parish's highly reputed choir.

I immediately imagined all kinds of difficult scenarios. It was my second year in the school. I was new to the convent and town. I was making steady progress, but I did not want to ruffle any feathers. A choir strictly within the school was an achievement and more than enough for me, apart from that I could not imagine any opportunities for public performance in town outside of Sunday Mass and this was strictly the preserve of Miss Nolan. She had earned her right. She was there for over thirty years.

'You leave that to me,' Monsignor confidently intoned, leaving with a swagger.

And so, we found ourselves standing to the side of a main altar setup for Benediction outside the convent walls for all to see and given the closing hymn *Flower of the May* to sing. As quiet and respectful as the congregation was, they couldn't resist joining in on the final verse and on that sunny summer's day when all the hedges burst with green, the notes swooped and dived out over the small townland and into the meadows beyond.

9

Prima Donna

I regarded the choir as my own. It was the activity to which I committed with the most passion. This did not always serve me well. My vanity was enhanced by the praise and success of its first year. The choir was well received in the community. Miss Nolan, far from being threatened, used it as a source of talent to enhance her adult choir once the girls left school. She was the perceived Prima donna, but I eventually saw her looking at me in the mirror.

Three years in, my fourth in Ballygraigue, joining the choir became something of an unspoken though not unexpressed status symbol. Students stayed after school on Monday and Wednesday for a two-hour practice and on Saturday mornings for up to three hours in the run up to Christmas and Easter pageants and end of school year concerts. Membership became so popular that a selection process was put in place and the second Monday of the opening term saw many girls line up outside the old school hall. They sat between coat racks, not very comfortable, and for those who missed the space, they stood, sometimes for almost two hours.

I sat in the old draughty school hall with my tuning fork and piano. While initially I gave five minutes to each applicant, in the third and fourth year, she was lucky to get two! In the beginning, I looked each girl in the eye, had a warm, personable conversation … *'you're Nora's sister'*… which I later discovered they hated or … *'what lovely curls'*… which they loved, was reduced to… *'next please'*… while they entered with my back to them, my eyes on the keyboard, pendulum or tuning fork. Once I vibrated the tuning fork and asked each to sing the scale, I felt I knew within seconds those who could sing and those who would improve with much attention and work which I was not prepared to give as, I now understand, I was in pursuit of perfection.

Only the perfect voices for the perfect choir.

I failed to consider the charged atmosphere which I had created and its effects on the more sensitive girls. Once put through their paces, many girls left hurriedly with smiles on their faces exiting by the upper door near the stage and away from the cloakroom, but their entire demeanour revealed the result. Their step was light-hearted, and the door swung quickly and heavily as the next candidate entered from the bottom of the hall rather more quietly. If a student sang out of tune, that was it. No second chances. On one such occasion, Nuala Minogue burst into tears. I had just listened, my eyes closed and then down to put a line through her name on the list. To my shame, I had failed to notice her distress until I heard her stifled sob and the tears flowed. I sighed in frustration as we were already overtime and fifteen more waited to be heard.

'For goodness' sake Nuala!' I heard myself utter, 'it is just not for you.'

'But sister...' she stifled her words through her tears, 'Mammy said I have a good Soprano voice.'

'Does mammy say that Nuala?'

'Yes...yes, she does. She will be so disappointed.'

'Why does mammy say that Nuala?'

'Because I sing *Marble Halls* at all our family gatherings.'

I knew this was not an easy piece and required a degree of accomplishment to deliver.

'Alright, alright! But quickly go again and without further ado!' sounding the note on the turning tuning fork with little regard for Nuala's heightened state of anxiety. She simply croaked and folded. I sighed again. 'Do either of your parents sing Nuala?'

'Daddy recites poetry.'

'But does he sing?'

'No,' she whispered

'You have other gifts I am sure, but a musical ear is not one of them.'

'Next!' I uttered loudly and with some irritation.

Two years later, I, along with three other sisters, was given permission to attend the sung Easter morning mass in the town. I was anxious to compare my choir with Sheila Nolan's. The altar was ornate with marble arches, lighted candles and fresh flower arrangements. No details had been spared. The incensing of the undressed altar filled the space with the scent of mystery and after six weeks of fasting and prayer I felt ready to receive the joy of the risen Christ. I felt my strict discipline and often gnawing hunger prepared me. I was about to be rewarded.

The centrepiece of the side altar to the left was a sensitive sculpture of the Pieta. A mother holding her dead son. It was beautifully adorned, all purple coverings gone on that Sunday morning in early April. We were moving from grief to joy. Having read the scriptures in advance, I knew this morning's gospel was that of Mary of Magdalene meeting with the risen Christ whom she did not recognise until he spoke her name, 'Mary', my own before Cecilia. It always struck me as such an intimate encounter. She was too blind in her grief to see him stand before her, but she immediately connected with his presence when he named her.

I still love that gospel, but on that Sunday morning I was once again stirred by my own rapture. It was in that state of mind and spirit that I listened to the sublime delivery of *Be Thou My Vision*, the first verse:

Be Thou My Vision
Oh Lord of my heart
Not be all else to me
Save what thou art.

It was sung tenderly and slowly by a Soprano voice from the gallery loft at the back of the church, supported and enhanced by the full choir for verses two and three. After the closing ceremony, once the silent solemnity of the inner vestibule was exited; voices rose in excited and uplifting chatter.

People were making their way home for a Sunday morning breakfast after the long fast of the night before. No doubt there would be many rashers fried on a hot stove that morning. Bacon rashers were always in good supply and very welcome after the endurances of Lent, one meal (fish if possible), and two collations, usually black tea and dry toast over six weeks. And so, it was in the midst of the rising chatter that I stepped quietly out as I pompously thought *befitted* my vocation but not before discreetly asking the name of the soloist.

'That is Nuala. You must remember her? She would have finished with you last June. Joan's daughter,' proffered Nancy Doolan, Legion of Mary aficionado.

Nuala? Nuala who?' I asked knowing in my quaking spirit that there could only be one.

'Nuala Minogue, wonderful, isn't she?' Nancy flourished on.

I was immediately transported to the school hall three years before. To Nuala's tears and trepidations, to my own deaf ears. I was immediately confronted by my own arrogance. As Nancy chatted with Sisters de Sales and Ligouri, I fell into a solitary reverie. That Easter Sunday morning's epiphany brought me from the joy and beauty of the Easter Garden to a descent into hell. I could barely eat the boiled egg and soda bread prepared for breakfast and in the hours between that and the later solemn Easter feast, I retired to my room to consider my thoughts.

That it was the sublime music of another that had opened the doorway to my inner self was not lost on me. The very subject that held my passion became my teacher. I remembered the anger, a righteous anger, I felt towards Sister Celestine describing her exchange with Marian Smith. What I regarded as her arrogance and her blindness and, upon remembering, I immediately recognised my own. Far from maturing in spirituality, I had regressed. The shock of this realisation hit me profoundly. As I knelt in prayer, filled with shame, I could not formulate any words at all. I could only hear David Carroll's plaintive tune as it was released from our piano at home and rose to touch each of us, our hearts blown open. I remembered David's gentleness and immediately understood his nearness to God, to love.

'Where are you, David?' I asked myself, 'what became of you?'

And then I thought of Martha. Of her lost potential and the potential, I had been given and was in danger of wasting. I wept.

***

The deaths of Daddy and Martha apart, that simple revelation on that Easter Sunday morning represented a real spiritual crisis. It took all I possessed to get myself through the remaining eight weeks of the school year. I structured and planned with abandon to avoid my inner turmoil. The vision of the powerful woman I so rejected and was becoming, honing an authority born of arrogance and not compassion or service, haunted me. I found it extremely difficult to live with myself. Well in advance of the summer holidays I asked Mother Agnes, to be absented from all communal duties and sent on an extended retreat.

'Sister Cecilia, the nature of your request suggests that you are either self-indulgent or troubled,' she glanced above her glasses, her soft, watery eyes looking directly at me. 'Neither insight is encouraging,' she said rather sharply, waiting for me to reveal the nature of my ailment. She left the silence hanging probably for a moment, but it felt like ten. I said nothing.

'Very well,' she sighed, lifting her large girth from her soft leather armchair. 'We will make do. I will make some enquiries and get back to you. However, I insist that you do three days in Lough Derg in repentance.'

'Yes, Mother Agnes,' I replied. Repentance at that point was my modus operandi. 'But if I may be so bold, wherever in your wisdom you choose to send me, please know that I am seeking good spiritual direction.'

'You are, are you? Hmm! This sounds serious, Sister Cecilia. I will do my best. But know this, I cannot guarantee the quality of direction you will receive. This is something you would have to pray for. Pray fervently. By all accounts it seems you need your prayers answered.'

'Yes, Mother Agnes. Thank you,' my voice trembled, 'I have one other request.'

'Yes, you do, do you? What exactly?' she sounded exasperated

'I would like some time with my mother. Just a few days.'

'I will give you credit for your bravery or perhaps it is audacity Sister Cecilia. This is out of the question.'

'Is it?' My heart sank but I immediately understood that she had no idea of the impact or reality of the circumstances of my family's grief. She was aware of the loss in name only and life was tough for many. I had no idea of her circumstances. We were not encouraged to think in those terms, and it seemed to me to be a long time since Mother Agnes had done so.

'Sister Cecilia, remember it is your responsibility, and should be your desire, to draw close to the sufferings of our Saviour. I recommend that you read *Of the Imitation of Christ* by Thomas Kempis. I will see that you get a copy from our library. You may go.'

***

I thought of my mother. I longed for her. I found that loneliness difficult. I was troubled by the way it took hold of me that late spring and summer. The fact that I had not attended my father's funeral, not touched his hand, not kissed him goodbye, not held my mother in her loneliness, made the whole experience surreal. I did not see my family anyway and their correspondence was often brief. I sensed they found writing to me an onerous task as if I was forever a reminder to them of all they had lost. How was I to reconcile my desire to be true to myself and to be present to my family?

I tried to imagine how it must have been for Tom, he was so young, but he never approached the topic of his inevitable sadness. He wrote only of the seasons on the farm, the odd local news and at seventeen his intention to study maths at university. Now he was about to graduate from UCD. A graduation I would miss just as I had missed James' wedding. He didn't even ask me. He married within a year of Dad's death, and I suppose understood that if I was not allowed to attend my father's funeral, there was no question of my attending his marriage celebrations.

I was beginning to realise how easily I had accepted all that. I had mistaken strength for some notion of spiritual martyrdom and an ego driven authority. I did not like who I was becoming. This cold, ambitious creature needed to be stopped in her tracks. The demons were all inside me now. I began to question everything.

10

Retreat

Despite my trepidation this was to be the beginning of a deep and lasting spiritual journey. In the end Mother Agnes, after consulting with the Superior, gave me the option of a directed or silent retreat. I chose the silent retreat as I felt I had fundamental issues to sort out within myself. Consequently, I found myself in the monastery of St Benedict occupying an old stone room with a simple bed, reading lamp, chair, writing desk and a small shelf of reading material: *John of the Cross, Augustine's Confessions, The Life of St. Clare, The Book of Hours, Christ in Renaissance Art, The Monasteries of Ireland, The Power and the Glory.* That collection intrigued and excited me. They suggested an openness with which I resonated and until that moment had not named.

What attracted me most was a small arch window, its iron frame painted white, which opened by means of a latch to the left side so that when opened, nothing interrupted the view. It was a little picture in a recess opposite my bed on the far wall. The light poured in early in the morning and as the day progressed it was all shadows and light as the sun's rays projected through the branches of a large lime tree, its leaves almost alight. Below the window a soft path meandered through the woods my room overlooked. The only sound was the occasional pheasant or hawk always coming from the direction of the sweeping field to the right of the Woodlands. I had been instructed to spend the entire month of July there.

From the first full day, I rose each dawn and attended all the services: six a.m. Matins and Lauds (morning prayer), nine-thirty, mass, noon, Sext (midday prayer), six p.m. Vespers (evening prayer) and eight thirty p.m. Compline, (night prayer). The monks sang and prayed from the ancient texts. Their solemn chants began to shift my racing thoughts until all, school, community, family, the torrents of my heart began to still. After four days I approached the Monk on confession duty that day. Facing my own darkness was hard. Publicly naming my vanity and pride in front of another was harder but once done, I knew there would be a letting go. Father Ignatius took me by surprise. A small, bony and pale man, he spoke with great gentleness.

'So, in your rush for perfection you missed the voice of an angel?'

'Yes, father but…' I hesitated, 'she did not just have an angelic voice, she was a young girl who felt so intimidated by my presence, my hurry that she could not perform!' I was ready to sob!

'Yes indeed.' He offered no consolation. 'Why were you in such a hurry?'

'There were other girls waiting to be heard. Two hours had already passed.'

'So, you were in the third hour?'

'Yes father'

'Do you often find yourself in situations rushing from one task to the next?'

I hesitated, 'probably'.

'So, not only are you in search of perfection but you take on too much.' I was taken aback. 'That is a difficult combination. You can see the odds are stacked against you, can't you?' My head began to throb. 'Lots of demands and the pursuit of perfection are two opposing forces. You have left yourself nowhere to go.'

'I have not ever thought of it like this.' I spoke quietly.

Again, he remained silent for some time. I felt decidedly uncomfortable. Had I already received absolution, I would have left. But I was not so bold. As I considered my options, he leaned forward toward the grid and asked, 'What is it that you are running from?'

I was stunned.

'I am not running from anything Fr…' I was angry and defensive. How dare he! Had he any idea of what I had accomplished! 'I just do not want to become one of those… those awful…'

'What exactly?'

'Those, those…institutional voices.' I spluttered: 'It would be so easy. Everything is clearly defined. 'I have the authority; you do as I say. Nobody would question it. But I could not live with myself. I am no hero, but I chose a different path because I understand the tender love of Jesus not because I want power or glory for that matter,' thinking of the title of that book on my shelf.

'Oh! but perhaps a smidgen of glory, no?'

I was flushed. I did not answer but was beginning to regret coming at all. He continued.

'Yes, yes indeed. I have met many people of self-appointed authority within all kinds of institutions. But I have met the others too. What you had was a moment of self- awareness, profound and painful and necessary. You were on the cusp of an evil path. Give great thanks that you were given the grace and insight to avoid it. None of us likes looking at our own darkness, at the evil we are capable of, at our casual indifference. But you have had an experience of redemption. My dear child, let your heart be filled with gratitude rather than anxiety.'

My eyes began to sting with tears. I felt the warm embrace of this aged and wise man take hold of me. A wound was being lanced and we both knew it. What I did not understand was just how deep that wound was. I sighed. More silence.

'How long are you with us sister?'

'For the remainder of the month Father.'

'Good. But do not come here to the confession box. Come to the guest house.'

'The guest house Father?'

'Yes. There are rooms there. We can meet, just you and me and of course, the Holy Spirit. Do you think we have a deal?'

Coming full circle I said 'Yes'.

'Alright then. I am coming back to that question, 'What is it that you are running from?'

I was immediately regretting my yes! 'Please Father, I...'

'Just let the question sit with you awhile. Regard it as your penance.' Then he suggested, 'there is a wooden seat at the turn of the stream, a nice walk into the wood. Very peaceful but the water is heard, soothing as it passes. A good spot on a warm afternoon. I will see you at eleven on Saturday, before lunch. Give it a shot. Let's see where it takes you. Now absolution.'

I was left both uneasy and relieved. I had a restless sleep pondering what it was he felt I was running from. Far from focussing on the question, I felt somewhat aggrieved. I talked a lot to myself: 'I have made a deliberate choice. I have paid a price for it for God's sake. I won't ever have children like James or Martha, had she lived. I didn't get to Daddy's funeral. Or to see Mammy recently for that matter. I have to put up with Celestine and her likes lauding it over me. Am I not doing enough?!'

Self-pity was one enemy I needed to lose. I returned armed and ready for battle should I feel put out again. I had to make him see the sacrifices I had made. This old man with his big heart whom I both feared and admired.

***

'Well Sister Cecilia, how are you today?'

'I am fine, thank you.'

'It is great to be fine on such a lovely summer's day.'

'What is your name of birth Sister Cecilia, the one your parents gave you? Don't worry, I understand and respect the significance of your chosen religious name.'

'Mary.'

'Well Cecilia, tell me all about Mary.'

'What do you want to know Father? There isn't a whole lot to tell.'

'Let me be the judge of that. You are no different to the rest of us and we all have a story. A beginning if you will. Even the Lord himself had a beginning.' He continued, 'John the Evangelist tells us 'In the beginning was the Word and the Word was with God, the Word was God' and even he came and "pitched his tent" among us. His tent?... Joseph and Mary in Bethlehem... So, Cecilia, what tent did you emerge from?'

It was clear to me that Fr Ignatius was no bible thumping hacker of God's word but his flourish into scripture left me feeling he was either slightly mad or absolutely brilliant. I thought of Mother Agnes' words, pray fervently and I had, so I decided to take a chance but not before I established my lack of credentials.

'I cannot compare myself to Christ Father…'

He laughed. 'Nor I… but he did become one of us Cecilia, he became human. Don't you see? It is all there.'

'What is Father?' I was exasperated

'The first and only place we begin our journey is in our human story.

You are here because you love God, correct?'

'Yes.'

'You are distressed because you feel you have in some way betrayed that love by your actions?'

'Yes,' I whispered

'Then you have been given great love indeed. A young girl called Mary travelled the journey of childhood before she entered and became Cecilia. Who is Mary?'

And so, I began three weeks of the most profound sharing: my place in the family, my mother, my father, James, Martha, Tom and even Elizabeth; memories of the farm, neighbours. It had been a long time since I had travelled back down so many roads. I laughed a lot. I shed many tears. On the third or fourth occasion, I began to realise that Martha was never absent from our sessions and Daddy wasn't far behind her. That realisation, though now it seems obvious, hit me like a stone.

'I seem to constantly speak of Martha,' I sighed. We had already been through the chaos of the grief surrounding her and Daddys' deaths. 'It's not as if I rake over it every day.' I was almost apologetic. 'I am way too busy for that.' I did not want him to think my grief made me incompetent.

'Yes indeed. Which brings me to my original question. What is it that you are running from?'

'Martha? But Martha's dead.'

'Exactly. Martha died. She was, as you describe her, beautiful, young and very talented. And you lived. Can you forgive yourself for living?'

It hit me with force. My stomach collapsed. My heart was pounding. 'Why didn't God take me? Why? I had already left my family. I would have accepted it.'

'Would you? What about your potential? Are you not worthy of a future?'

'But Martha was worthy of a future. She was in the third year of her degree. She had plans. She had a man who loved her. My parents needed her. I was gone.'

'Not yours to choose Cecilia.' Silence and tears. Then very gently he asked, 'Can you give yourself permission to live?'

'To live father?'

'Yes, just to live. You do not have to be the best. You do not have to be the most perfect. You can stop running. Give yourself time to hear an angel sing.'

'Ah!' Something in me collapsed. I went to lean forward in my chair and nearly slipped off. I knew I could not stand up. I was exhausted.

'Take some time out Cecilia. Rest. Sleep! What are you reading at the moment?'

'Thomas Kempis'

'On the Imitation of Christ?'

'Yes.'

'A classic text but you can put that away for now. Not the time Cecilia. I have some recommendations. We will discuss it all soon enough. Meanwhile go out over the next two days, hear the birds sing, bathe in the sunlight, let yourself be loved. You might even walk across a meadow like you used to do. And write. Do you write?'

'A very sporadic diary'

'Now's a good time to fill some of those pages.' His small, wrinkled face beamed and belied a spirit so generous it swallowed all my guilt, the irrational guilt of having lived. He took my hand and patted the back of it as I rose to leave.

'Choose the little way.'

I was immediately transported to the boarding school in Rossnagh and the time I spent sitting before the image of Therese of Lisieux. She desired no more than to do what she could within the circumstances of her life. I felt affirmed in my decision to become a nun even if I had not anticipated what it would cost.

***

I closed the door behind me. I spent many afternoons on that seat in the woodland of lime and chestnut trees, their leaves fluttering in the summer breezes as I sat bathed in sunlight listening to the water ripple in the stream before me, its current hastened by the small rapids, one a hundred yards or so above where I sat. Its soothing dipping sounds washed over me. I brought neither journal nor book with me, entering fully into the healing presence of the world around me. I became as the crane beyond me who occupied her nest on an inaccessible recess of still water beside the bank on the opposite shore.

I disappeared just as quickly each afternoon in writing and prayer for the remainder of my time in the monastery. I knew it would not be possible to return in this manner again. Though I did return twice over the next decade. Once overnight with special permission to attend the Easter vigil. On the second occasion to pay my respects to Fr Ignatius, attending his requiem mass, giving thanks for our fortuitous encounter and the blessing he had been in my life. I wrote to him several times seeking his counsel which I always found direct and tender. I realised over the course of that month just how rooted in wisdom is the spirit that can challenge the struggle without breaking the speaker. I loved him for it.

11

The Bliss of Solitude

The following school year was my best in Ballygraigue. Having observed the success of the school choir and its popularity amongst the girls, music was added to the curriculum and the order appointed a music teacher with responsibility to teach all incoming first year students. Thus, music became identified with St Declan's, the beginning of a proud tradition in the school.

Sister Rita was the teacher's name. She was a tall, thin woman with a long nose and long fingers which exaggerated the movement of her hands when conducting the choir. Unlike me, she had entered at twenty-three and was sent on rudimentary supervision and teaching duties in the nearest school to her novitiate. She had completed all scales in piano and completed her Leaving Cert before joining the civil service. She attended music lessons privately in her hometown from a young age. As she chose a teaching order, it was a natural progression for her to study for her degree in music having completed her canonical year two years after entering. Thus, by the time she was appointed to St Declan's we were both the same age.

Though taken by complete surprise when informed of developments in August of that year, I was delighted to have a colleague with whom to share my love of music. We did not always see eye to eye, but I quickly got over myself and we became firm friends. Timing is everything and Fr. Ignatius' wise words were a real source of support throughout that time. By the end of that year, I had more or less conceded all choir duties to Rita. I was glad of my newly found freedom and found a great liberation in letting go.

The year after that was my final in Ballygraigue. I had come to love the marrow and bone of this rural community. I seldom had reason to meet their parents but experienced the life of this place through their lively and spirited children I grew in confidence of my own judgement and sometimes desiring the open road, I slipped out the back gate, walked half a mile out of town and slipped down a maze of small boreens away from all activity. I was no revolutionary, just a seeker in all I did. So, about six times a year in the late afternoon I walked alone, keeping it to one hour. I was always back restored and well in time for supper.

I soon realised that home was still in me. I had a pattern, autumn a few weeks after the school term began, and late spring, at the end of Lent or post Easter when my spirit called to the solitary vibrant beauty of the hedgerows. The cowslips, banks of moss and primrose, wild violets, the red and purple lanterns of the woody fuchsia rising above my head granted me a canopy of beauty and solitariness which nourished my very soul. In spring, the pink cherry blossoms followed by the white hawthorn and the leaves unfurling often from stark, rain-soaked branches were delightful. In autumn two large chestnut trees which I passed on return from the final boreen back to the road always reminded me of James, of the boundaries that swept the road of Lenihan's farm on the way to our own, but they reminded me of more too. The majesty of their sturdy trunks, sweeping branches, their leaves of green, yellow and burnt amber, the glossy brown speckled chestnuts, the hoary, green fleshy shells spoke to me of a beauty, a reality which flourished beyond me, my perceptions, my very existence.

There was a beauty and a life force here which was entirely independent of me yet capable of transforming me, of lifting my spirits, of recognising the hand of the great artist not just at work in the majestic tree before me, but painting the colours of my own heart as I drank it all in. Always after these little escapades my spirit sat quietly before the altar of the Sacred Heart and experienced the same connection. I came to recognise it as a kind of radical love. I knew while walking those roads, despite the frustrations of community living and the demands of work, I had chosen this life, and I was fundamentally happy in doing so.

Each time of I turned from the main road down the first narrow boreen, I met Paddy O'Sullivan, an old man tending to his cottage garden with its lilies, delphiniums, foxgloves, sweet pea, clematis and honeysuckle all in bloom in their season on the corner between the road and the boreen. To the back he tended to his tomato vines, pea shoots, blackcurrant and gooseberry bushes. Paddy lived alone. On the first occasion he smiled shyly as I passed. After four years of these sporadic forays, we knew each other well by stealth and recognition and in that final autumn he stopped me and without a word passed me a cup of blackberries and gooseberries.

'For the journey, sister, a woman after my own heart.'

Lost in reverie, I was startled, outside my comfort zone really. Once recovered, I understood we were kindred spirits. I smiled but had no words for this unexpected gesture of goodwill. On return to the road, determined to rectify the situation, I stopped and called:

'Hello, hello.'

'Is that you, sister?' Paddy emerged from the open front door

'I, I just want to return the cup you so kindly gave me.'

'No need at all sister, sure it's cracked, no good for the tay.'

I laughed. 'Good enough for the sweetest berries though. Sister Cecilia.' I stretched out my hand. 'Paddy, Paddy O'Sullivan.' He took my hand.

'Thanks Paddy', I withdrew and hurried back, the hour almost up, and Paddy's warmth singing in my soul.

The following spring we stood on that corner and chatted, he inside the low stone wall, me outside leaning against a large jutting stone, my feet resting sacrilegiously on a carpet of bluebells which edged the grass bank by the road. I learned that Paddy had lived alone in that carefully tended cottage since his mother's death fifteen years before. His brother Jim had left at sixteen to fight in the Great War. Joining the British Army even for a good cause was frowned upon.

'We had a great time growing up roaming these fields, but Jim was always a bit wild, a bit of a revolutionary too. If he had not joined the war effort, he would have been ready and waiting for the black and tans when they came. But there is no point in trying to explain that after the fact.'

Paddy was a bright spirit, but his words revealed an ocean of sadness.

'He left a boy... and came home a broken man. Mammy and daddy had a terrible time trying to quieten him. He shook all the time and cried a lot. They didn't ask anyone for help, didn't know how. Private people, you know?'

'Yes Paddy, yes,' I whispered.

'Well, all privacy was gone when he ran stark naked to the woods in Curraghveen and ended up kneeling and crying beside the Lusma River. By the time we got to him, he was waist deep in the river. We all agree he was trying to drown himself. Ended up in the Redbrick. I never saw him again. Poor Jim.'.

'I am so sorry, Paddy.'

'Ah whist! That was a long time ago. The parents took it hard. Never went into town. The comments, you know! Mammy went in on Mart Day about a month after. She was still raw. As she tells it, Mary Powell, a good sort, says to her something like this "Ah Mags I'm awful sorry. I remember Jimmy, a dotey young lad with a big head of curls, a bit of a rogue but an innocent for all that". Of course there is always the one with her ears pricked. Sheila Healy had been listening and threw in her tuppence worth. "What do you expect from a man who betrayed his own. He got what he deserved." She turned on her heel and walked away. Mammy dropped her messages and was unable to move. Mary's brother, also Jim, brought her home in his trap. She thanked him, closed the gate on her garden and never left, not until she was taken out in her coffin.'

'People can be very cruel.'

'Aye, they can…. They're all gone now.'

'You never married Paddy?'

'Ach no! Just as Mammy closed the gate, so did I. There was no point. We had a few kind neighbour's but in general we knew we were not wanted. We were happy here in our own way. Daddy had regrets. He was very strict, you know. Strict on Jim. Jim reacted, ran away to the war.'

The silence hung between us.

'That's a heavy cross you carry Paddy and all I see is the life and colour of your garden and your freshly painted house.'

'A man has his pride.'

'For sure.'

'Ten years ago, I was contacted by a cousin of mine. She comes to see me every two months or so. Her three children are mighty, love the garden, love the life but Margo won't come to live here or to her home place. She likes the invisibility of city life; besides, her neighbours are good. They don't judge her.'

'Why would they judge her Paddy?'

'Back from England without the husband!'

'I see.'

'He was not a good man, sister, not a good man. I will leave it at that.'

I just caught his hand.

'Do you know sister I have not spoken in years and why would I now, to you?'

'And why not Paddy?'

'You're a woman of the cloth. I never had much regard for the collar or the cloth you know. Have not been inside a church door since my mother's funeral mass. Fr O'Connell kept praying for my mother's sins, for her release from purgatory. Well, you know sister, she lived in purgatory here. She was the kindest, mildest woman I know ... but, if we had purgatory here, we had heaven too', he said pointing to a sunny enclave to the left of the front door.

'She'd sit there for hours undisturbed, just smiling. Sometimes I would sit beside her and hold her hand for a while.'

'Oh my God Paddy, the time!'

Painfully aware of what I had just said, coupled with the urgency of being back on time to slip in unnoticed, I made my excuses and left. Overwhelmed by Paddy's revelations I parked the conversation knowing I had serious demands upon me the following day. I vowed to come back the following late afternoon if I could manage it at all.

I did, but Paddy's front door was closed. I walked those homespun country roads flooded with the conversation of the day before. Paddy's pain was visceral. He was reconciled. He had chosen to remain apart, yet he had joy and tenderness in him. I thought about it all that afternoon. What is it that makes the sum of a life? I now understand that all pain is connected. The tears flowed as I thought of Paddy, of the young boy Jim, of his parents, of Daddy, Martha, of Paddy's cousin, Margo.

That day the fragility of our humanity lived in my marrow. I saw neither the light flickering through the leaves, nor the bursting primrose banks but I understood that as universal as suffering is, so is our experience of the natural world as a benevolent and beautiful force, in faith where God is to be found. Paddy saw that in me. I saw a man who found struggle, purgatory, peace and heaven in the natural rhythm of his garden and the love of his family. But I never saw Paddy again.

***

Within the week I was summoned to meet Mother Agnes and Sister Eucharia.

'Sister Cecilia,' Mother Agnes began, 'you have settled in well here.'

'Yes, I have.'

'Sister Rita is doing well.'

'Yes, she is. She hopes to direct a musical here next year. I believe we are ready. It is going to be great. We are already considering possibilities.'

'Well maybe not you.' I was taken aback. 'Sister Eucharia can explain Cecilia.'

'As you can imagine Cecilia, I am in touch with other principals, particularly those in our own order. I have many chats with Sister. Paul Lacey, principal of Scoil Mhuire, Carrigeen. She is tired and ready to rest. But she won't be retiring. She will go back to teaching maths. However, as and from the end of August she will no longer be principal. Mother Agnes and I have discussed it along with some others but the end of it all is that we are recommending you for the post.'

'I don't know what to say. Scoil Mhuire?'

'Yes, Scoil Mhuire is a nice little school tucked into the hillside facing the Atlantic Ocean. You will like it Cecilia. It is not too onerous. A small but busy school serving three or four townlands on the Carrigeen peninsula.' I heard the hard sell. I also felt entirely unprepared.

'I am not sure I am ready.'

'On the contrary, both Mother Agnes and I agree that you are. Your time here has borne fruit, and you are well liked but none of us is invincible Cecilia.'

'Indeed,' I replied, 'I am sure there is someone with more experience than me.'

'That may or may not be so, but you are capable Sister Cecilia. You have built a choir from scratch, have upgraded French and by all accounts, your English classes are enjoyable and achieving good results.'

'Quite different to running a school.'

'A microcosm, no more. You have initiative and ambition. Scoil Mhuire requires both.'

'Well Cecilia,' Mother Agnes intervened, 'if it is your young age that concerns you, our youngest principal was two years younger than you when appointed and ran a tight ship, God be good to her. You are not breaking new ground.'

I could feel my heart beating faster as one objection after another was removed. I was dealing with two formidable women. Finally, I said 'I will have to pray about this.'

Mother Agnes quickly intervened. 'Oh, indeed you will, every day, whether you are tending a garden or running a school it is your duty to ask the Lord's hand to be in it and then trust that it is.' She was leaving me no wriggle room. 'I will see you in a few days when you have had more time to come to terms with this appointment. Gratitude is the only way forward Cecilia. To be considered is an honour.'

'Yes, Mother Agnes.' I left her office both fearful and excited. A little school, I thought. Maybe it will be okay.

Later that evening I made my way into the library and pulled out a book titled *The Maps of Ireland*. There I found the Carrigeen Peninsula, and its townlands of Carrigmoss, Carrigbawn, Lochmore and Trábeag. It was one hundred and fifty miles west of Ballygraigue and about two hundred north of Ballymac. As a child, and a farmer's daughter, I had rarely been to the sea. There simply was neither time nor inclination but one very hot summer Aunt Sheila insisted she take all three of us down to Kerry, to the Maharees for a long weekend. Now that I think about it, it was the summer after Elizabeth's death. She was probably giving Daddy and Mammy some time alone. She was shocked that we could not swim and threw us into the sea for hours on end over the four days. We had great fun and got terribly sunburnt. Each evening soaked in calamine lotion, the salt of the sea still in our hair, we were treated to doughnuts and ice cream.

'The only rule here is to have fun,' Sheila laughed.

***

I was given four weeks to prepare. Once certain, I rang Mammy to tell her. I found it hard to gauge how she felt. She insisted she was coming to see me. I did not drive. At that point there was no possibility of it. Neither would the community justify the use of a driver for the sake of a home visit. Mammy and James came to me before I left Ballygraigue to settle in Carrigeen. We had tea in the convent parlour which I think they found stifling but it was the general atmosphere of sadness which defeated us all.

I had been excited at the prospect of their visit. They had a three and a half-hour drive to Ballygraigue. All three of us hugged warmly full of proud chat as to my appointment as principal at such a young age. The high spirits were interrupted by Sister Dolores who insisted on pouring the fresh, hot tea and would be returning in minutes with a second pot after which she left us. The air became flat. No matter how we tried, we could not rescue the greyness that enveloped us. We ate, we drank, we spoke of local neighbours.

Then Mammy said 'so you are going to the Carrigeen Peninsula? Peter showed it to me in his school atlas.'

'Yes Mammy, I am. I had to look it up in an atlas myself,' I smiled.

'You weren't far away enough?' she said plaintively. And there it was.

James intercepted, 'Mary can be anywhere Mammy. The nuns decide that. You know that. We all know that. That's the deal.'

I felt my heart sink. Though it remained unspoken, we all knew that this was grief. Circumstantially, my first profession was book ended by the deaths of my sister and my father. There was no getting away from it, my vocation was regarded by my family as a loss. No achievement would ever bridge that gap. Nonetheless it was Mammy who wrote a long letter twice a year, at Christmas and on my birthday. I would always be her child

***

The remaining time was hectic. I had little to pack but had notes to prepare for my incoming replacement. To the best of my knowledge, she too was a newly professed young woman. I would not get the opportunity to meet her. We received our degrees, and we taught. There was no training. I wanted to leave her enough to give her some kind of buffer against the freefall sensation of being dropped into a deep ocean when first confronted with the reality of teaching. Sister Rita and the choir had prepared a parting afternoon to which all the school was invited and around which there was a lot of preparation. There was a thanksgiving mass and a special dinner with the community

However, Paddy, that gentle soul in his lovely cottage a mile or so off the road at the back of the convent, hung on my heart. Four days before I was due to leave, I made my way out the back gate. I was aware that

Sister Eucharia was looking for me to consider readings, but I disappeared for one hour. I walked briskly keeping my head low from the misty rain. I held on tightly to a letter in my pocket. It was a small offering which could have got wet or lost in my hurry. His front door was as I had previously found it, closed! My heart sank. I swept in past his wooden gate, my habit sweeping the edges of his drenched borders. I knocked on his door without reply. I did not hear a sound. This reassured me. I looked around and in the absence of a post box, found a heavy stone, placed the letter on his mother's seat and covered it with an empty planter.

My letter was simple. I wrote that I thought of him every day. That I understood how honoured I was to hear his story. That I shared the pain of loss. I laid out my story. That I was leaving but would remember him wherever I was. I hoped it would be enough.

III

12

Principalship & Friendship

Mick, our driver, and I travelled west in his Ford over badly surfaced, narrow roads winding through drumlins and sand banks. The sea peeped and disappeared over the horizon. The only other vehicles we met were donkeys and carts, some ponies and traps, and two Ford Astons, one of which I later learned was Dr. Larkin's, the resident doctor on the peninsula. The only other car I would see in our local parish was Fr. Ryan's Volkswagen. At that point, the convent of ten sisters did not possess a car. We did however have access to one from John Delaney of the next townland of Trábeag two miles up the coast. He made his services available to the local communities in the event of emergencies and to the sisters throughout the year. Much like Mick did in Ballygraigue. The truth is none of us knew how to drive. John was the driver for the Bayview Hotel, transporting visitors to and from their destinations. Summer was his high season. Though more sporadic, the locals kept him going for the remainder of the year. The year was 1967. The world was changing fast, but Carrigeen was a world of its own.

Though I arrived in the first week in August, I did not have the most salubrious of introductions. As I stepped out of the car, my veil was almost whipped off my head by onshore winds so strong that I kept my mouth shut for fear of losing my breath. Mounting stone steps, one hand on my head and the other firmly holding my case to the side, I slipped in behind large double doors avoiding opening them too widely. I was greeted by a rattling, empty hallway with terracotta floor tiles and a poorly painted sweeping stairwell. The place had a general air of neglect or, as I quickly reminded myself, perhaps it was the wear and tear of the salt sea air.

A door opened at the end of the hallway to the right of the stairs.

The heavy smell of broth emerged into the cold air. A small older woman stepped brightly forward.

'Oh Sister Cecilia! We were not expecting you so soon. You must have been on the road bright and early. Sister Paul,' she stretched out her hand. She had the wind-swept look of the sea about her and immediately reminded me of farmers I had seen on Mart Day like Dinny O'Keefe, small, wiry and resilient. Dinny was the kind of character who applied himself in a crisis. Though an assumption, my first impression of Sister Paul was similar. I wasn't wrong.

Immediately on her heels was Sister Monica who was already observing me as Sister Paul spoke. Her eyes narrowed.

'This is Sister Monica, Irish, English and religion teacher.'

'Hello Sister Monica,' I offered her my hand.

'Dia dhuit,' Monica took my hand as a matter of form but there was no clasp, and she quickly withdrew both hands placing them across her chest, inside the panels of her habit.

For warmth? I thought but quickly concluded, no there is no warmth in Sister Monica. My card was already marked.

'Come along Sister Cecilia. Lunch is almost ready, and the others are looking forward to meeting you.'

'Paddy followed behind me, placing a box of books which I had brought with me on the floor under the half-moon table inside the door.

'Mother Agnes has sent some gifts,' I protested. 'The box is still in the car.'

'Time enough,' Sister Paul insisted as she led me and Paddy into the dining room; a large impractical room with high ceilings and four separate rectangular tables. The Formica tables were neatly set with placemats, cutlery and napkins, salt, pepper, sugar bowls and glasses for water. Behind the door, stood another table set against the lime green wall with cups, saucers, teaspoons, a jug of milk and three jugs of water. Sparse but enough.

I was determined to make a good impression and stepped forward to meet five other teaching nuns. Sister Goretti, Science (later I was to learn this meant biology only), Sister Elizabeth, Art, Sister Benedict, Home Economics, Sister Kieran, Music and Geography, Sister Sienna, English and Irish. The exchanges were perfunctory.

'Sister Claire, with whom I share maths, is on retreat and sisters Francis and Anthony will serve lunch shortly,' Sister Paul explained.

'I would like to meet them.'

'There will be enough time for that after lunch. The kitchen is busy right now.'

***

The remaining weeks of August were a whirl of activity. Sister Paul wasted no time and the very next morning I found myself in the school building. It was more dismal than the convent. Grey is the only colour I remember from my first impressions. Grey walls, floors and ceilings, the outside built of granite. Though small, Scoil Mhuire was authoritatively set on a hill with a sweeping driveway. It struck me as ludicrous asking children to walk up an exposed path in wind and rain.

No more than Ballygraigue, I learned how to pick my battles and what was worth fighting for. Getting more children on that pathway was more important than eliminating it. Our student numbers vacillated between two hundred and thirty and two hundred and fifty for the whole peninsula. An area with the circumference of about twenty miles, three small parishes, Carrigmoss, the largest and most populated at four hundred and four including its townland according to the last census, Carrigbawn, seven miles further down at one hundred and twenty including its hinterland, and the historical parish of Tobarbron in the townland of the almost deserted Trábeag and the townland of Loughmore, mainly isolated inland clusters of houses beneath the shadow of hills sheltering from the raw gusts of the Atlantic Ocean. In spite of poverty, most people made the best of it.

I found preparing the timetable one of the hardest tasks. I was grateful to an innovative and well organised school secretary, Peggy Muldoon, and to Sister Claire for their invaluable help in working out the computations necessary. Core subjects, choice subjects, options, facilities available, teachers available. In truth, parental choice was not something we understood in those days. In a good year we had the timetable finished in three weeks. In other years we were still finalising options at the end of six weeks. In that first introduction, Sister Paul had it all well in hand.

I wished to make a strong and supportive first impression. After the very first visit I asked Sister Paul if we had money in the budget for a lick of paint.

'Paint?' she said. She seemed disappointed.

'Yes, paint.'

'There are greater priorities Cecilia.'

'Yes, no doubt but is there any floating cash at all?'

'Do you not think it would be wise to consult with the staff before making any decisions?'

'I won't be doing anything major. Besides, I imagine as an incoming principal, there are times when I am going to have to trust my own judgement.' I decided to clear the decks. 'Did you not find it so Sister Paul?'

'Yes, yes, I suppose there were times when I did.'

'Do you think you can trust me?'

'I hope so.'

'Well then?' I smiled, 'otherwise, what are we at?'

'Alright, you make your case,' she pointed her finger at me and smiled also, 'you have twenty pounds, no more.'

'That will do me nicely. Thank you.'

'What do you have in mind?'

'Let me surprise you.'

'You have me worried now. We have an account at Morgan's hardware store in Kinoulty. You would have passed through it on the way down.'

'Yes, that's the town with the wide main street and sharp right turn to Carrigeen?'

'That's it. You have to organise the transport.'

'About thirty miles away?'

'Yes. You are sure you know what you are doing?'

'I think so.'

I knew I didn't have time to waste. I was still unsure of how I was going to achieve my ends. The following day Sister Paul brought me to the home of Peggy Muldoon. I thought this unusual as I would have expected to meet the school secretary in the school office.

'That is not how it works here Cecilia. This is a small community. We all know each other for better or worse. Peggy is an approachable woman, closed the door to the office four weeks ago and is not due back for another two. So, I have no intention of bringing her onto the school grounds. She is looking forward to meeting you.'

***

I stepped into Peggy's warm kitchen, a red geranium in the centre of the table, Peggy bent over taking scones from the oven. I don't know what I expected but Peggy surprised me. She was a tall woman with receptive brown eyes, sallow skin and brownish red wavy hair. She stood back observing me. She put out her hand. Her grasp was strong. She did not say too much. In truth, I found her very refreshing.

Her house was painted with lime wash with pale blue windows and doors. It was full of light. It was full of colour. The red geraniums apart, she had an odd collection of eclectic-coloured cups and saucers, none matching but all harmoniously living together. On her floor my eye was drawn to a rug of natural blues and greens. Books, some opened, sat in the deep window recesses. Among them I noticed Graham Greene's *The Power and the Glory*, the book which I had started reading and never finished on that retreat some years before. I felt my heart soar. It was clear that a reflective woman lived in this house.

After preliminary conversation I was taken aback when Sister Paul revealed my proposed project to Peggy. I was unprepared. I had not had time to work out all the logistics involved not to mind choosing a colour.

'So, you are painting, Sister Cecilia?', Peggy smiled, 'you are brave. What colour do you have in mind?'

'I…. I still have to choose the colour, but it must be bright.'

'Good for you!' she said

'What colour do you suggest?' I asked instinctively

'Peggy is into painting you know,' Sister Paul offered

'Not very much Sister Paul,' Peggy seemed to withdraw. I knew immediately that Sister Paul regretted her remark. There was a brief silence before recovery.

'I don't know much about your painting Peggy but looking at your kitchen I would value your opinion. Your colours are full of life.'

'Thank you, Sister Cecilia,' Peggy almost whispered.

'You are too modest,' Paul suggested. 'Look here at this' she pointed to a painting set above a door to the adjoining room.

My eye was drawn to the foreground of delicate seagrass through which one could view the crashing waves. Paul was right. Peggy was talented, but it was clear on that day that Peggy did not wish to share her gift. We discussed the school and agreed that we would meet the week before opening day in September. We said our goodbyes and excused ourselves, but I was looking forward to getting to know this woman.

'I messed up', Sister Paul confessed. 'Peggy is sensitive about her paintings. She paints in the lean to off the side of the house, but I have never been in it. Dr Larkin has. He encouraged her to exhibit, but to no avail.'

'This place is already proving interesting,' almost out of relief, I threw my arm around Sister Paul's shoulder and removed it just as quickly. I did not wish to come across as needy. I wasn't. I simply felt she had already grasped a lot about me. She was sowing the seeds of possibility in my head. This wise woman would be missed as a principal. It was too soon to ask why she had chosen to step down. Too soon and too impertinent. I knew she would tell me in her own time.

Later that evening over a supper of a halved boiled egg, ham and brown bread, Sister Monica inquired as I poured her tea, 'How did your visit to school go?'

'Fine' I replied, 'I am looking forward to it.'

'Well, you won't be pouring tea there. It will take more than that.'

'I don't understand Monica, more than what?'

'It is going to take a strong hand, not necessarily a warm hand to run Scoil Mhuire, a big dropout rate after third year.'

My egg was now smelling bad, 'why is that, Monica?'

'They all leave for the boat to England or New York.'

'But these are children who want to be educated.'

'Do they? Maybe the odd one but that's it.'

'Then we have to convince them,' I was already playing her game.

'Good luck with that!' she sniggered, 'you haven't met Seamus Kelly yet or Thady Muldoon?'

'Anything to Peggy?'

'Her cousin. Father of eleven, wild and dangerous and thinks he has an in because his cousin works in the school. I'd have them all gone.'

I offered no comment. Monica smiled. She already knew she was inside my head.

The following morning, I woke from a troubled sleep. Determined not to give in to anxiety, I abandoned breakfast after mass and made my way down to a sheltered strip of sand that I had spotted the day before, a kilometre or so beyond the convent. The tide was out, the sun had risen nicely from behind the hills to the east and I could feel the warmth coming into the day. Once I descended into the cup of seagrass, sand dunes and washed-up stones, all the village life disappeared. The only sounds were the wash of shingle and the cries of the seagulls swooping and diving over a washed-up carcass further up the strand. Sandpipers were my nearest company or so I thought. I walked for a long time before deciding to turn.

Feeling better, I decided not to leave the day pass without putting my plan to paint the staff room and the two first year classrooms in motion. I bent my head to look at a rainbow-coloured shell lying in the sand. Lost in my thoughts, marvelling at the sheer beauty of a random shell just lying there, I was quietly approached by Peggy.

'Morning Sister Cecilia, I knew it had to be you.'

'Oh, hello Peggy. I didn't see you at all. Why? How did you know it had to be me?'

'Because I have never seen any of the sisters on the strand before.'

'Sister Paul, no?' I uttered, revealing my ignorance of her movements, and the novelty of a nun walking the local strand in her heavy black habit.

'Oh no, she walks the roads and climbs the occasional hill.'

'I just assumed: she has that lovely weather beaten look about her.'

'But the strand, in that habit! A bit of a task I would have thought.'

'Yes, I suppose it is. I didn't consider it really,' I said realising that I had gathered up my heavy black habit while negotiating the sand dunes on my way down, that I had decidedly picked the drier parts of the beach to walk in order to prevent the possibility of sand or water slipping into the sides of my heavy black laced shoes, that I had picked a time when I had hoped I would not meet another soul. So, I had considered it, almost unconsciously.

'Well, you'll have the windblown look soon if you keep this up,' she smiled. 'Have you chosen your colour yet?'

I smiled. 'Did God send you my way this morning?'

'I wouldn't think so. God hasn't communicated with me in a long time.'

'Oh, I don't know about that! One look at that painting above your door tells me you have a beautiful soul and the gift to express it. I think you must make God smile.'

'I never thought of it like that. In any case, the colour?' she moved along quickly.

'I was thinking about the colour of the sun.'

'I like that,' she smiled.

'A warm yellow.'

'Hmm. An ochre maybe.'

'Not orange.'

'No, a warm yellow! Isn't that what you said?'

'Yes.'

'And a soft white for the skirtings and doors.'

'A great idea.'

'Where are you thinking?'

'The staffroom and first year classrooms.'

'O my God. The staffroom is the dullest room in the building stuck in the back corner of the west wing. In the winter it gets rightly cranky in there.'

'Really?' I laughed

'Really,' she replied dryly. 'I am going up to Kinoulty this afternoon with Helen, Dr Larkin's wife. She collects medicines and stuff for him from the pharmacy there. Would you like me to have a look in the hardware?'

'Fantastic! See you were sent. I had no idea how exactly I was going to work this out.'

'You'll get used to it sister. We have our ways and means of managing things around here.'

'So, you'll pick out the colours?'

'Sure, if you don't mind.'

'Don't mind! I would be delighted.'

'Suddenly sounds like way too much responsibility,' she was witty and wary.

'I'll take the responsibility; don't you worry about that, but you have a maximum of fifteen pounds to spend.' I wanted to keep money for labour. 'Do you know anybody who would paint it? If I must roll up the sleeves myself, I am prepared.'

'That would make for good gossip. New school principal is up in the school painting the walls! Some would love you for that and others would regard it as beneath you.'

'You're right.'

'I'll ask Jody and Mick to do it. I'll keep an eye on them.'

'Jody and Mick?'

'Relatives, they're a bit wild but they're good natured and hard working. They have to know you trust them. They'll be chuffed to be asked by the new principal. I'll manage them.'

'It's a deal,' I said, taking my chances, with Sister Monica's voice rattling in my head.

'A new day,' I thought to myself as I climbed back up the sand dunes onto the deserted road to walk back to the convent. I would be keeping this to myself.

13

The Good, the Bad

That first year was a whirlwind. The bright colours were well received, and the staff took the initiative to reorganise the layout of the staffroom. Old books and records that had laid there for years were burnt by Tommy, our caretaker, in a big bonfire out on waste ground at the back of the school. The first-year pupils, not knowing any difference, settled in well. The art teacher, Sister Elizabeth, created a competition based on the seasons of the year with the winning poster placed on the grey wall immediately opposite the entrance door. By the end of October, a poster filled with the colours of autumn took pride of place there, only to be replaced by a tender nativity scene as Christmas rolled in. So keen was the interest that the Wise Men made their way to the crib under a bright star on the wall adjoining the stairs to the upper floor. The shepherds watched from the walls on either side of the front door and Peggy completed the scene with a swooping angel attached to the railing above. All in all, it was a good start but in truth only dressing. There were more serious issues to address.

Among them was Sister Monica who took every opportunity to gripe. The walls though ochre and soft white were 'too yellow' and made the place 'look like a circus'. Unhappiness is one thing, when it translates into devious behaviour, grenades can detonate in any context, none more delicious for Monica than the staff meeting at the opening of the academic year, my first as principal.

'Education is a serious matter not given to frivolous decor. How much did it cost? Has the leak in the roof of the Home Economics room been addressed?' she asked with the energy of an engine getting started.

'What leak?' I asked with some dismay

'Are you not aware of it, Sister Cecilia?' An uneasy silence.

'Clearly not,' I answered.

'If I may,' Sister Benedict intervened, 'I only noticed it yesterday morning, Sister Cecilia, when I opened the Home Economics' room to prepare it for the coming school year. There was a very heavy shower with the wind blowing from the east which seems to have created leakage between the roof and wall due to a damaged gutter and a leaky downpipe.'

'Is it not true, Benedict that the downpipe was leaking last year?' Monica was quickly in. I observed Sister Paul rubbing her eyes and sighing.

'Yes, but there was no threat to the internal wall at that point.'

'No matter. It will be addressed immediately. Benedict, I will meet you with Tommy after this meeting.'

'The painting project?' Sister Monica was not for turning

'Eighteen pounds and sixpence including labour.'

'Who carried out the labour?' Sister Sienna asked in a manner which suggested she already knew the answer as did everyone in that staffroom.

'Jody and Mick Muldoon.'

'Are they not minors? Why not Sean Devine?' she continued.

'Sean Devine is tied up in a big project at the Bayview,' Sister Paul was in like a shot. 'As you well know Sister Sienna, Jody is sixteen and Mick is thirteen. There's many a young lad working on farms around here or out on the boats working for the food they eat.'

'That's as may be but why would we encourage the brothers of Millie Muldoon who behaved so badly towards members of staff?' Monica quipped looking around her for support.

'Specifically, towards you, you mean Sister Monica. I don't recall incidents with any other member of staff.'

'Well yes! But surely there are consequences which underline respect for all members of staff at any time?'

'Indeed. That matter is in the past and long settled,' Sister Paul seemed to pale from the strain. At that point, I knew we were overdue for a long chat as to her real reasons for stepping down as principal.

'Well, I don't think there are any complaints about the outcome. A cursory glance at the skirting boards and the coving is evidence of the care to detail that was taken here.' I attempted to close this line of conversation.

'I agree,' Sister Elizabeth said with a firm tone. Nothing else, but it finished the matter. We moved on but once again, my card was marked, and an uneasy air hung over what would have otherwise been a very pleasant gathering.

However, if I thought I had adversaries in Sisters Monica and Sienna, Fr Alphonsus Ryan, the Very Reverend, as he so often reminded anyone who was forwarding correspondence to him or addressing him publicly, was on a different scale. I have often tried to understand his behaviour and many times on my early morning walks I ruminated as to his exact motivations. Power of course explains much of it but there was more. The only word I can think of is *entitled*. Fr Ryan had a serious case of entitlement and all who crossed his path were forced to endure it. It would be wrong not to acknowledge that the system which trained him, cultivated him and appointed him as parish priest is the real issue here. But there we are and there I was as a young principal of thirty and he, in his late fifties.

***

During that first winter I became increasingly aware of young boys with very little or no education at all. Largely it was a matter of lack of opportunity. Those boys who went on to take the Leaving Certificate were invariably from wealthier families and sent away to boarding school. We had one local writer who sent his sons to Blackrock. Other lucky boys went to the nearest diocesan boarding school in Ballymoyle where they were afforded an education in lieu of training for the priesthood. Many did go on to the priesthood. Others did not. The fees were simply reasonable. As for the others, even those who could read and write and had passed the Primary Cert, they had nowhere to go. I thought of Tom Murphy, the brightest boy in James' class who left school early to work on the buildings with his father. He had emigrated to New York and fallen from the third floor of a wall he was constructing. That fall left him with life changing injuries.

Kinoulty had a small vocational school. Scoil Mhuire served three parishes and once national school was complete many disappeared back to their small holdings and coastal homes not to be seen on school grounds again. I became acutely aware of it six months later when I discovered that Jody Muldoon, apart from his name, could neither read nor write. Mick had some grasp but as Peggy explained their childhood was disrupted by a father who moved back and forth from England to Ireland with his wife and children in tow. After their mother died, he did not go back to England, but five of his eleven children had already left for New York, Boston or Camden.

There was an advantage to isolation. Though my life was busy, the school was small. Sister Paul as deputy principal and Peggy as an efficient secretary, made sure my weekends were by and large free and welcomed for their rest. The following autumn I offered to take the boys for some tuition on a Saturday morning for two hours. I had grown fond of them and knew they were ambitious for a life beyond eking out an existence. Jody wanted to read the letters his brothers and sisters sent. They had already lost contact with Seamus, the eldest. My goals were practical. Help Jody to write a basic letter and to improve Mick's reading skills by introducing him to books that might interest him. The only people who knew about it were Sister Paul and Peggy who asked them down from the rolling hills that lay between the sea and Loughdubh in the townland of Loughmore, a journey of three miles. She convinced there now alcoholic father that there might be jobs going on the boats or casual work at the hotel. Sometimes there was and Jody missed the occasional class. But he was always grateful for the interest. I was grateful to those who trusted me.

We never discussed it but instinctively knew it was better kept under the radar. Each morning as I left, the other sisters assumed I was going for my morning walk. I am eternally grateful to Sisters Anthony and Frances in the kitchen who looked curiously at me the first time I asked for two scones or rock buns and a small bottle of milk on the second Saturday before I left, exiting by the back door across the narrow pathway by the field to the adjoining grounds where the school awaited. After that they were ready and packaged and offered without a word.

So, my heart missed a beat when Fr Alphonsus Ryan walked into the room. We were making progress, into our eighth Saturday. Jody had managed five. He was copying out the first line of a typical letter which we had spent some time reading. He was delighted when he managed to read a paragraph. They had just finished a warm scone and shared the milk. We had chosen a small room off the library out of the way of prying eyes if lights were noticed. Tommy walked behind Fr Ryan. He raised his hands in dismay and mouthed 'I'm sorry.'

Fr Ryan's colour rose, 'for God's sake man, I only asked you to let me in, not to follow me. Now go!' As Tommy shut the door behind him, he continued 'What is the meaning of this?'

I felt my legs weaken and leaned towards a shelf.

'Can we discuss this in private please Fr Ryan? You can come to my office.'

'I don't need to go to anyone's office. Frankly, as chair of the governing body, I am appalled. This is a secondary school for girls run by your order and accountable to Bishop Bourke.'

'I am well aware of that. We are finished for today boys. You may go.' They looked at me and left silently.

'You need not think you can come back,' Fr Ryan raised his voice. 'This ends here.'

'You understand what you are doing here father? Destroying the chances of two young brothers from your parish. Do you even know their names?'

'I understand that what I am doing here is not sullying the reputation of this school. No good Catholic school will have mixed education!'

'There is no question of that. How many pupils do you see around?'

'Not the point, not the point at all! This is the thin edge of the wedge. If this is allowed and word gets out, we will have every rag o' muffin looking for help. You're a bit naive sister. But that's what comes of appointing someone without the relevant experience.'

'How dare you Fr Ryan!' I screamed in my head. My blood was boiling. Equally, I was on the verge of tears. The pendulum of my heart swinging between these two points, I held my council not willing to let him spot any vulnerability.

'I have no doubt that the women who made that decision are wise women and did so for their own well-founded reasons.' Though at that point in time even I was questioning my appointment. My pride got the better of me however, I was not prepared to let him see that my hands were shaking.

'I know who they are alright. Thady Muldoon's offspring. Never inside the church door.'

'Jody and Mick.'

'What?'

'Their names. Jody and Mick.'

'We fight for our own. Do you know if they are even baptised?'
'There is no reason for me to think otherwise.'
'No reason indeed, but you have not asked the question, have you?'
I did not answer.
'I believe their aunt works here in the school.'
'She is not their aunt, a cousin.'
'Seems she has some kind of background. Oh, she came highly recommended. It is not often you get references from The Clarence Hotel in London, especially out here. Why would anyone want to come back? But it has been suggested to me that she left Carrigeen under some kind of cloud.'
'I am not aware of anything'
'Perhaps there is a lot that you are not aware of Sister Cecilia.'
'Perhaps,' I conceded
'Let this be the end of it and I will leave sleeping dogs to lie.'
'What do you mean?'
'I won't investigate Peggy Muldoon. Quite the artist, isn't she?'
'She is a sensitive and talented woman.'
'Takes one to know one I suppose,' he smirked. Was this some effort at placation? I did not know.
'I am off now. We have an agreement. Yes?'
'Yes,' I said resigned to the clear threat to Peggy.

He was gone in an instant without a backward glance. I heard his confident strides as he walked down the corridor and made his way out the front door of the school. As I struggled to lock the heavy library door, my hands still shaking, Tommy appeared.

'I am sorry Sister Cecilia. He took me by surprise. Arrived up at the house knocking furiously. I thought someone was dead. One of Sean Murphy's men drowned at sea, maybe. But no, he was furious. He had been down at the school; he said and couldn't get in though he knew you were in there.'

'He said that did he?'

'Yes, sister but how I don't know! I didn't know nor do I want to sister, it is none of my business, I say. If you wanted me to know, you would tell me.'

'I would Tommy, but I am sorry too.'

'No, no sister, he was in a rage and ordered me to open up and leave him in. No one crosses Fr Ryan, no one.'

'Don't worry about it Tommy,' I attempted to smile. He noticed the shake in my hand

'I'll lock up, sister. Get yourself a sup of tay.'

'Thanks Tommy,' I left quickly but in some distress. I made my way down two halls and exited quietly by the back door, the wind nearly taking my veil.

'Sister, sister, you okay sister?' The two boys were hunkered down in a shed at the back. I gathered myself.

'I am fine boys, really.'

'Is this going to cause trouble?' asked Jody

'I don't think so.'

'He is one cross man sister, and we know what cross is. You should see our ould man when he gets going,' Mick was on a roll

'Enough,' Jody cut across him, 'just checkin' in, that's all sister.'

'Thanks for that.'

'Will we see you next Saturday sister?' Mick looked almost pleading. I sighed.

'Ah, what do you think Mick, for God's sake? It's alright sister. Thanks for tryin'.' Jody caught Mick by the shoulder and went to go.

'Hold on,' I said, 'I will do my best. We will work something out,' though I had no idea what or how, 'I will be in touch. Peggy will let you know.' And they were gone, scampering across the dunes, they disappeared.

I quickly made my way back to the convent. Apart from Francis and Anthony in the kitchen preparing dinner, no one seemed to be around. I made my way down to the chapel where I found Sister Paul praying the Office before the main altar.

I sat beside her only to feel a hot tear falling. She looked at me alarmed.

'Come on, we have an hour before dinner, let's get out on the roads.'

We threw on heavy rain jackets and made our way down the hill in the face of south westerly winds rolling in from the sea.

'How did he find out?'

'I fear he will have his eye on you now. He is a formidable man. You don't need this.'

'No, I don't,' I was filled with self-pity now.

'Monica or Sienna. It has got to be one of them.'

'But they know nothing about it.'

'It's a small place Cecilia. I heard Monica make some remarks over breakfast two weeks ago. I should have paid more attention.'

'What, what remark?'

'Oh, something like, *I am not sure it is walking she is*, she stopped as if I had interrupted a conversation. I clearly had. She must have been watching you.'

'I was careful. I never saw her.'

'You do not need to justify yourself here Cecilia. We follow the gospel, or we don't. And yet, I feel you are on difficult territory. Fr Ryan will put the worst possible interpretation on it, and you are aware of all the fuss in Carraroe and the possibility of mixed education in rural areas. The Presentation sisters have been under serious pressure.'

'I don't need this.'

'No, you don't. I am afraid Jody and Mick will have to find some alternative arrangement.'

'What? There isn't anything!'

'We will just have to be creative. We just need to stand back a little. But I am warning you, do not let Monica or Sienna see any weakness in you today. Eat your dinner, all of it, in front of them.'

'I actually feel nauseated.'

'I know, that's what stress does. Believe you me, I have had fifteen years of Monica and ten of Sienna. Handling personalities was the hardest part of being principal. The logistics were fine. The teaching was fine. The parents are usually grateful. They want their children to be educated. The children are just that, children, eager to learn. But the self-opinionated are a difficult cross. Monica and Sienna don't have the power except over their charges of course, but the Very Reverend Fr Alphonsus Ryan does. Be careful!' She sighed.

'This is no easy territory, Cecilia. My life was made more difficult with Fr. Ryan's appointment. As chairman of the board, he has power, and he uses it. He may have heard that Jody and Mick got that painting job. Small as it is he would have his own man. I did not think of that. He checks in with Monica every so often as to the goings on in the school. Any misdemeanours, any little mishaps. She delights in his attention and the power she receives by association. I have been principal for a long time, but these are the most difficult kinds of issues to negotiate. I just got plain tired of it all.'

I knew in that instant that I needed to get some steel and deal with Monica. I had to find some way to suggest she move. She had the withering glance of Medusa. Right now, her snakes were tight around my heart. Maybe Fr Ryan had done me a favour, maybe I had been naive, but no more.

'Come on, we have twenty minutes, no more talk, just let the sea air in, and the sight of those rolling waves. You're in the garden of Gethsemane Cecilia. Stay alert lest they come to take you and listen for the voice of He who has been there before you.' She squeezed my hand and off we strode back as the snakes loosened on my heart only to be replaced by a clear anger flowing through my veins. I had planned to visit Peggy that afternoon, but I knew I was too emotional, so I decided to wait.

14

The Ugly

The following Monday I approached Peggy, 'Can we meet after school for an hour or so?'

'What's this about?'

'I had a visit from Fr Ryan on Saturday.'

'And?'

'Saturday morning at the school. He ordered the boys out.'

Peggy, who I already surmised was not prone to drama, put her hand across her mouth, 'I was wondering why the boys didn't call on Saturday, but I did not think too much of it. I was kind of glad because I was finishing a painting. Oh God.'

'Yes, there may be trouble on the horizon, but I assure you Peggy, nothing we cannot sort out together.'

'Trouble? What kind of trouble? Jody and Mick are good lads.'

'He referred to something in your past of which he is not sure.'

'In my past is it?' her voice faltered. Her face was white. She sat behind her desk with her forehead in her hands.

'What is it Peggy?'

She did not answer. After a moment she heaved a heavy sigh.

'Peggy, you have me worried now. Is there anything I need to know?'

'You're all the same…' she spat the words out, 'that bastard!'

'Please Peggy, I cannot allow you to refer to Fr Ryan in this manner,' I heard my unbearable, officious tone.

'You cannot allow it! You cannot allow it! Why the hell did I come back here at all? I should have known that the so-called do gooders would get their claws into me.'

She headed for the door, 'To hell with all of you,' she uttered through gritted teeth, the crack of pain across her face as she glanced at me before storming out.

'Please Peggy, please,' I implored but to no avail. In an instant she was gone.

I lay my head back and took a deep breath. As I exhaled, I felt an internal collapse. The blood rushed to my stomach. It took serious effort to stop the warm tears which began to flow. I hopped up and closed the office door. The pressure of responsibility prevented me from allowing the full force of the torrent of frustration and despair I felt within to seep out. Class was in mid-session; the silence of the corridors gave me some reprieve. After ten minutes of staring into space re-orienting myself, I began to assess my situation which I knew I had to rescue before losing control entirely. I checked Sister Paul's timetable. Now in maths, she had forty-five minutes free and three other classes to teach throughout the day.

Swinging into action, I identified Sister Elizabeth, Sister Claire and Ms Howard, our newest addition to the staff, as approachable. They would free up Sister Paul. I would make no explanation other than a line about 'heavy administrative duties. This was true. My brief was written before me on my desk: roll call figures, follow up on school repairs with Tommy, another leak in the cloakroom beside the hall, preparation of the BOM agenda for the following week. The latter would be important.

Significant changes were ahead with the introduction of free education and transport. It was only early Spring, and we were already receiving the occasional enquiry from families living further down the coast. We had a lot of work to do. I knew the board would be open to receiving new pupils. It would require a lot of planning. They would probably not be receptive to mixed education. I did not know them well enough yet.

I clearly knew Fr Ryan was not. I had to carefully steer the ship as Fr Ryan was holding the chair. He was erratic and unpredictable. I was also well aware that I now found myself in this situation without a secretary but more importantly without a valued colleague, undermined because of his threat to Peggy. He threw the grenade and I, unwittingly, pulled the pin. I had to get Peggy back. I had already made up my mind to take off the following day.

Paul and I briefly chatted. We rolled up our sleeves and got on with it. The day threw up its shares of the usual unpredictability. Mary Kelly arrived crying at my door altogether unable to face the next lesson. Sister Sienna put her standing at the back of the room for over an hour because she had been unable to spell. Mary was a bright girl suffering from what we now understand as dyslexia. Neither of us knew this but we did know that she was tired and humiliated. I sent her over to the convent to Sister Anthony with a message to give her a cup of warm milk and a bun. She returned when she was able, about another hour later for her favourite subject, art. Every day would be a struggle for Mary, but I was not ready to take on Sienna yet. Other priorities called.

***

The following morning, I opened school as normal and after an hour, I slipped out. I returned to the community chapel and prayed fervently for guidance, for the divine spirit of wisdom to be with me in all I said and did that day. Thus, by noon, I found myself on that sunny Spring morning at Peggy's door. Peggy looked directly at me, half accusatory, half curious. A disturbed silence lay between us. Then, as she was about to speak, I raised my hand:

'Get your coat Peggy. Let's get out of here.' She stood there without moving.

'You understand that you have hurt me.'

'I do.'

'Deeply…' she lowered her head.

I reached forward and caught her hand, 'I am truly sorry though I do not fully understand the wound I have touched. Please Peggy let's get away for the afternoon. I have arranged with John Delaney to bring us to Kinoulty for 'school supplies. It suits him. He is collecting medicines from the pharmacy for Dr. Larkin, and he wants to visit his mother-in-law. So, we have a few hours without drawing attention to ourselves.'

An hour later, after negotiating the hilly dune-locked roads from the coast to Kinoulty, we made our way to Mrs Murphy's tearooms and sat in a quiet corner at the back, away from the main door. Though I wore my veil, I was relieved of my cumbersome headdress the previous summer after a discussion had taken place at our chapter meetings, the result of which concluded that those who no longer felt it necessary could swap the wimple for a simple veil. I had not imagined myself being so grateful as I was, in that moment, for the Second Vatican Council.

We ordered vegetable soup, bacon and cabbage. Peggy had the soup but barely touched her dinner. Her face was drawn. She was in deep thought. I was anxious and filled some of the strained silences explaining what arrangements I had put in place in her absence. I knew to stop when she sighed and rolled her eyes. 'I am a bit more than the sum of my parts, Sister Cecilia.'

'Meaning?'

'More than a school secretary…I.'

'Well, I know Peggy' I gushed, 'you clearly are a talented artist. Dr Larkin thinks you should hold an exhibition during the summer months when the tourists are around.' I had broken a confidence, but to no avail.

'Don't sidetrack me. What was your name growing up?'

'My name? Mary,' I obediently surrendered

'Did you like your Da.'

'I did. I loved him dearly.'

'He's dead then?'

'Yes'

'He was good to you?'

'Yes, yes, he was.'

'Well, you see this is what all you do gooders don't understand.' I resented her comment and her easy judgments. I could feel the hair rising on the back of my neck, but I held tight. I had not experienced this dark, angry Peggy before and found it hard to integrate her with the sensitive, creative and wise woman I had experienced since landing in Carrigeen. Her trouble was deep. Even her voice changed.

'My dad was a low life.' She breathed the phrase out with some difficulty. Her voice began to tremble. 'I will tell you my story, once and once only. I never want it referred to again. I want it revealed to no one.'

'Peggy,' I said, 'It's a mild day. Let's take a walk. We have about two hours. We'll find some place a bit more private than this. Let's get out into that lovely spring sunshine. And we need never go back there again.'

'Okay.'

We chose a promising route out of town. The white buds of the ash were beginning to bloom along the hedges. The banks were strewn with primroses, cowslips and small wild violets. We walked for a mile in silence. I thought of home for the first time in a very long time. I thought of my lovely Daddy and our last encounter in the barn. We stopped at a small lane leading to an old holy well and sat on its low stone wall.

***

'My Da was a damaged man. All charm and darkness. Living with his mam out there on the edge of the world in Carrigeen with nothing but the Atlantic before him, when he met my mam.'

I heard Peggy settling into the reflective voice with which I was more familiar.

'She had taken a summer job as a chambermaid at the hotel. She liked to walk the long strand in the late afternoons after all the beds were dressed. He was hauling in lobster pots. He was a handsome man Cecilia, in that rugged sort of way and I have memories of him carrying me on his shoulders. In the early years we had days of real happiness, but he never allowed friends to come home to play. He could be violent you see but only after he had gone on the tear for a few days. He did not want anyone to know. He was ashamed. He'd be missing. Sleeping out in barns and stuff, wherever he could get his hands on the drink.' She sighed.

'They say Mam died of cancer. But she was worn out from trying to make ends meet and Da happy. I had a brother, Brian. He died a cot death. Daddy blamed mammy and gave her a beating. It suited him not to make the connection between those beatings and his dead son. Seems to me, no life is given a chance in these situations. Two years later she was sick. She died the summer after my ninth birthday. Apart from the sheer misery of losing the only person who sat with me drawing pictures after school, and sang to me in my sick bed, the only moments I remember about the day of her funeral was my father scolding me about the ribbon in my hair. "Tidy that ribbon, it is crooked and sloppy, like your hair. Tie it back. We don't want to disgrace your mother now, do we?"

'No daddy,' I whispered. I loved him, I hated him. I was scared of him, but he was all I had left in the world. As locals came to sympathise and shake his hand, I stood behind him, even in the church pew. Every so often he put his hand on my shoulder to check that I was still there. I hate to admit this, but it was strangely reassuring. I watched him hugging the sympathisers, crying at his great sorrow as they looked with pity at me, but few called to see us after, those who did were run out of it, even if they brought dinner or tried to help in some way. He'd find a way of turning their efforts into judgement:

Don't you think I can cook for myself and Peggy?

What are you bringing this for?

I can provide for my own house,"

A few months later we were alone. By the time I was ten, he was a raging alcoholic, and I was the only female left in his life.'

'I saw school through that year but by the end of the following summer, he decided I did not need to go any more. I was needed to wash and cook. To be fair, Sister De Sales, headmistress of Scoil Padraig came twice to the house. I did not like her very much when I was in school. She was all rules and regulations but now that I think of it, she had to walk a good distance to reach our house. She always came alone, and she was brave. When he roared at her that I had finished my schooling, she replied "She is a good girl and a good pupil and deserves her chance." Hiding behind the door, I grew about ten inches taller. I repeated her words to myself every night before falling to sleep for a long time after that.

"Aye," he said, "she is good, and she is doing fine here. Do not come here again." He closed the door shut and looked at me, winked and laughed as if it was all very funny. I just felt sad.'

Peggy looked hard at me and then her eyes dropped. I noticed a slight tremor in her hands which she attempted to control by interlacing her thin fingers.

'I was eleven when he first came into my room. Mammy was dead about eighteen months. He had been away for some days. I enjoyed those days. I took out the colouring pencils Mam had stored in a biscuit tin in our hiding place under the sink in the scullery. Anyway, after the first time, he cried and said he was sorry. I was just terrified, confused and very sore. He soon got over his regret and, despite my pleas, came a few times a year, always after he had been missing for some time. By the time I was fifteen, I was pregnant.'

It was my turn to put my hand across my mouth. I was truly shocked. Her recent anger aside, nothing in Peggy's demeanour to date would have suggested such trauma. I did not know how to respond.

My immediate instinct was to rescue her, so I leaned forward as if to put my hand across her shoulder. Peggy immediately stiffened. Taking my lead from her, I withdrew. I didn't feel chastened or rejected. I understood that this was Peggy's space entirely. She was taking control describing circumstances in which she had absolutely none. I got it. Once boundaries were established, she continued.

'My feelings had been dark for a long time, and I had been plotting to run away but I had no idea where to, or even how. One morning when I just didn't care anymore, I threw open the front door and left it swinging to the wind. I was past being afraid. I had made up my mind that if he came after me, I knew exactly where the pitchfork was between that door and the gate to the road. I swear I would have killed him. I walked two miles to the sea, down to Trá Dhúbh. You wouldn't know it; it is the other side of the headland. I knew the waters were rough there and if I decided to go in, there would be no turning back. I sat on a black rock with the wind blowing through me, watching the salt spray shoot up and crash down over the rocks. I looked down at my swelling belly and repeated Sister De Sales' words to myself: 'She is a good girl…' I cried: 'Mammy where are you?' she sighed and waited. I listened.

'I don't know how long I was there. It could have been an hour, it could have been two, when I was approached by an elderly man I did not know. He sat down beside me. "Don't be afraid wee girleen." I suddenly became acutely aware of my dishevelled appearance and wrapped my arms around my belly in a desperate attempt to hide my condition.'

'You Jim's girl?'

'Yes,' I whispered, 'how did you know?'

'You may have your mother's dark eyes, but you have your father's red locks. Not hard to spot. Besides there are not too many young girls living on these small roads that either lead out to Trábeag or end here in Trá Dhúbh. What did they call you?'

'Peggy'

'Ah, Peggy, after his mam, Margaret. I'm real sorry about your mam. She was a gentle one.'

I didn't know he knew my mam. I suddenly had this connection. It felt as if mam was with me after all.

'Only met her the once, at your parent's wedding. I'm your granduncle, Patsy, brother of Jim's mother. Ach, I left a long time ago. That wedding was the last time I was back until now. Maybe I am getting soft in the head, but I am looking for a place to spend my old age. I have always loved the sea. Can't ignore it when it's in your blood.'

'Where do you live now?' I asked

'London.'

'London!' I suddenly had a different picture in my head imagining this city I had never seen. I asked him what London was like. He said it was great when you are young, but he was ready to come home.

'And I am ready to go.' I sobbed. He leaned forward to put his arm around me when he noticed my bump.

'You poor wee girl, you poor wee girl,' he seemed very shocked.

I hung my head between my knees and wept. I felt so ashamed.

'I knew from day one that he would never be a good provider. He is refusing to help you, isn't he?'

He paced up and down the strand in front of me, cupping one hand into the other and occasionally wiping his mouth.

'Please,' I begged him. 'Please, don't make a fuss.'

'You're afraid of him? Of course you are.'

'No, no, it will only make things worse.'

'Could they be any worse?'

I knew they could. I knew my plan to take my life, but I didn't tell him, at least not then.

'I don't know what I am doing on this side of the headland. I don't know why I thought I would find any place to stay here but I am here. And I have met you, my sister's grandchild and you need help. No coincidence I would say. But this is my last day. My ticket is booked for tonight's sailing. I am due back to work in two days.' He was now speaking his thoughts out loud. 'Where is he now?'

'He was asleep when I left the house. Please don't go near him.'

'I won't but I need you to go back and get a coat or some sort of protection against the elements. Can you do that?'

'I think I can if he has not found the opened front door,' I was petrified. Petrified at the thought of him waking and finding me gone, arriving back to a slap or more. Petrified at the possibility of escaping and not escaping.

'The opened front door?'
'Nothing. I can do it.'
'Good girl. Don't pack a bag or draw any attention to yourself. 'Here,' he put five pounds into my hand, 'the bus leaves in an hour and a half. I'll be on it. You come straight but if anything happens that you don't make it, make sure you get the next one in three days' time. Get yourself to Dublin. I will have somebody waiting for you.'

***

'Well, I made it but not that day, three days later but that's another story. One of the scariest moments was searching his trousers for loose change to buy my bus ticket. A five-pound note would draw the attention Patsy asked me to avoid. No one presented a five-pound note for a bus ticket, that would have been talked about. I dressed very carefully and put on my mother's scarf, shoes and took her handbag. I looked older. I kept to myself. There were about ten people on the bus, but no one seemed to take any notice of me at all. By the time I got to the train station there was only one other person from Carrigeen who got on another carriage. I was met in Dublin by a small, neatly dressed woman who introduced herself as Mary O'. She was Patsy's next-door neighbour and lifelong friend. If I were religious, I would say she was an angel. The rest is history. I never came back until eight years ago.'

I was keeping an eye on the time. Peggy had spoken for over an hour. We needed twenty minutes to walk back to our taxi rendezvous in Collin's square at the centre of the town. I struggled to keep my thoughts clear after such a devastating recollection. She was right. I had, had a privileged childhood. I just didn't know until now. My legs shook but Peggy was washed out.

'Peggy, I don't know what to say.'
'Then don't say anything.'
'But you came back?'
'I did.'
'Your father died?'
'No, he was gone a long time. Clearly, I did not make it to his funeral. The truth is I knew nothing about it, but I would not have come anyway. At least, I don't think so. I came when I was ready. Once I had settled in London with Mary O' in her fourth-floor council

flat in Peckham I never looked back. She was there when I gave birth to a baby girl. I did not name her. I knew that if I did, I would watch part of me go. I asked Mary O' to hold her and oversee her delivery to Nazareth house for adoption. She had done all the research and decided that my baby would have reasonable prospects with the prosperous couples waiting for a child to love who had registered with them. I feel sure she has had a better childhood than I did and that is all I need to know.'

'Mary O,' I repeated, 'Mary O.'

'But of course, the older locals talked when I returned like a ghost from the past. They could not understand it. I had not come to any family funerals. I had dropped off the face of the earth but had the unforgivable audacity to return without explanation. What's more, I moved into the wee cottage set on the nicest site overlooking the sea. I later realised it had become a subject for discussion among a few prospectors hoping to build their own fine home. I hesitated when I received notice from Madison Solicitors in Kinoulty notifying me that Patsy had left me the entire property. They had enclosed a confidential personal letter. I wept when I read it, but it also gave me great consolation that Patsy had experienced many happy days there in his old age. He wrote of the green light over the sea in the early winter mornings, the deep orange sunset on very cold days, the jewels that sparkled on the surface of the water under summer sun, the sounds of the seagulls' cracking shells on the tin roof above him. Come *home Peggy, come home*, he wrote, *every corner of this house is blessed with love for you and if you want to paint, this is your place.*'

She closed her eyes as she said this. It was clear she knew the words by heart.

'You were painting then?'

'Yes. Life was easier in the fifteen years before I left London. Mary O' got me a job as a chambermaid in *The Clarence Hotel*. She was a housekeeper there. I worked my way up to receptionist after I attended secretarial courses by night. I became proficient in typing and shorthand at *Mrs Tatler's School for Young Women*.'

Peggy now spoke with a plum accent. I smiled.

'It had a reputation for the best. I was admitted only after interviewing due to my lack of education. We had classes in etiquette and dress and all else needed to impress. There were days when I came home thinking it was all nonsense and days when I was grateful. In the meantime, Mary O' was on the lookout for opportunity as it arose in The Clarence. She was a trusted member of the in-house staff, and they took me on her recommendation provided I proved myself within six months.'

'Which you clearly did, with flying colours no doubt.' I observed the tiniest of smiles for the first time. The mood was a little lighter. We started walking but not before I hugged her without a word exchanged between us. This time she readily accepted.

As we walked, Peggy continued as if viewing a film script: 'I joined an art class in *Camberwell College of Arts*. My tutor was really good. She encouraged me a lot. She offered me private tuition in return for babysitting duties on the odd Saturday. I really started to improve. She asked me to start building a portfolio to consider a degree in art and design.

'And did you?'

'Did I what? Do the degree? No. I came home but I have the portfolio!' she almost blushed as she heard herself boast a little.

Peggy was a woman of great integrity, but it struck me that she was hardest on herself as if getting a second chance at a decent life was something she had to prove worthy of everyday. Pale as a ghost, she slept the whole way back to Carrigeen. My thoughts were racing but I was determined that Fr Ryan would never be a threat to her.

***

Though we had a stormy board meeting with various views expressed about the role of the school in a changing Ireland, and though Fr Ryan may as well have been Moses coming down from the mountain, so great was his authority, an authority he relished and would surely use, I need never have worried. By the following August, Fr Ryan was afflicted by a progressive ailment for which there seemed no cure. A young pastor, Fr Leo Spillane, was sent to assist him and the whole life of the parish turned around. By Springtime, Fr Ryan had lost his ability to speak.

However, not before damage was done. About a week after our return, Jody disappeared overnight just as Peggy had done. Fr Ryan had suggested the possibility of Mick being packed off to Braghnateel Reformatory, an industrial school for wayward boys. His waywardness? Lack of attendance at school. The irony of his case was lost on no one.

Dr Larkin and I spoke and put a plan of action into place. We shared our plan with Mick on a Wednesday evening in Peggy's house.

Mick would go to the technical school in Scabhan, sixty miles away where he would continue his reading and writing and become skilled in a trade. He would stay with John O'Sullivan, bachelor brother of Helen Larkin. He lived on the homestead farming sixty acres. Mick was very quiet as we spoke with him. Timid and on the verge of tears. Every so often, he looked at Peggy for reassurance. She sat holding his hands. Jody, it seems had promised him he would never return. He had lost his closest brother and was now being asked to lose his home. Sean Larkin was accompanied by his wife, Helen.

'Mick, I promise you, John is a good and very kind man. He will take good care of you. In return for a hand on the farm, he will give you what you need. He told me he will be very glad of the company.'

'I will call to see you Mick. I promise. Take the chance, it beats a reformatory any day,' Peggy was urgent in her tone.

And so, Mick took the bus the following morning from the Carrigeen peninsula to Kinoulty where he was met by Helen's brother. There was no time to waste. Fr. Ryan had already secured a place in Braghnateel and the following Friday morning called to his house to collect him, only to discover he had already left. He eventually got over his fury. None of us opened our mouths.

I met Mick by chance ten years ago on O'Connell Street in Dublin. What are the chances? But there we are, and there I was, having just stepped off a bus from the Mater hospital where I had attended a medical appointment. He spotted me first as I stood outside a coffee shop hoping to get a bite before getting the bus home from the quays.

He smiled, 'Sister Cecilia, is it?' In two seconds flat, I had him. He was grey haired and sporting a neat beard but the tilt of his head, the way he held his hand up, forefinger on his chin awaiting an answer just as he did as a child, and his warm open eyes brought me right back to those days in Carrigeen. He had eventually made it to New York.

'Joined the boys in blue Sister Cecilia. Oh, I was so broken-hearted after Jody you know…'

'I do, I do indeed.'

'But I was well able to read and write. And that began with you… and the escape plan yourself and Peggy hatched. Come here,' he said and wrapped me in a tight hug. I had not experienced such simple affection in so long. I delighted in the freedom of this man's spirit.

'Jody still breaks my heart… like Seamus… we never heard from him again.'

We both thought of the boy with a bit of an edge; lanky, blonde, freckled, fiercely protective and yet, a little lost. There are experiences that leave a crack, and you draw a blind, this was one of those.

15

The Tree of Knowledge

If there were years when I began to hone the steel within me, it was those years on the Carrigeen Peninsula. Despite his despicable abuse of power, I felt deeply sorry for Fr Ryan in his obvious, and very public, decline. He was ill equipped to cope. The possibility of any kind of misfortune in his life never seemed to have dawned on him. He was cranky to the end, and we supported him. Sisters Anthony and Frances attended to the delivery of his meals each day and his regular changes of bed linen. Nonetheless, he required full nursing care by the following March.

He insisted on coming to the convent chapel in his wheelchair where, aided by Fr Leo, he concelebrated his final mass sitting to one side, uttering an occasional sound. Though inaudible, such utterances came at very specific moments; the consecration, the great amen, the final blessing. We understood. This leave-taking was difficult, not in spite of our chequered history, but because of it. Yes, I had been angry, but this anger was now replaced by a great swell of sadness for the possibilities lost. Each of us briefly stood before him and said goodbye. I felt overwhelmed as I stood there for a few seconds.

'May God go with you Fr Ryan,' I said, 'you are going to need him.'

He looked at me strangely and with great effort raised his hand and let out a cry. In that moment I recognised his dying ego, his regret. When the door closed behind him, I felt a relief of sorts, but I felt a humility too. I found it hard to name it all. I spent an hour in silent prayer.

The relief did not last for long. Later that evening at supper Sister Paul alluded to the contributions made by Sisters Anthony and Frances, and all that they had done to support Fr Ryan in his illness.

'Indeed,' Sister Monica announced, 'Fr Ryan will be sadly missed.

He always had the interests of the school at heart. He had standards. Standards are important to the reputation of a school.' I could feel myself bristle and had already entered the arena of her game playing. Emboldened, she continued,

'I'm not sure about this Fr Leo who seems willing to take anyone, but what would you expect of a man who thinks it is alright to play church music using a piano or, God forbid, a guitar?'

'Indeed,' replied Sister Sienna, 'a guitar? Sister Boniface, God rest her, must be turning in her grave. Do you remember her magnificent organ playing Sister Monica?' She went on, 'no doubt you approve of him Sister Cecilia, Boniface was before your time, I don't expect you have anything to compare.'

The floodgates were open, I did not hold back.

'Oh indeed, there are those in Ballygraigue, who would refer to my contribution to music there just as you refer to Sister Boniface.'

'Is that so?' asked Sister Monica, 'did you play the organ then?'

'No, I did not. I set up the choir for which the school has become reputed.'

'Oh indeed,' Sister Sienna warmed to my obvious and silly vanity. 'Then why have we not got a choir in our school?'

Sister Paul looked at me curiously. She spoke very calmly.

'As you are aware, the music teacher prepares the students more than adequately for all our services throughout the school year.'

'Yes, the choir is another matter altogether. It would be a wonderful addition to the school. How about it, Sister Cecilia?'

'As principal, I have too many distractions, and too much work to do.' I heard my defence to an audience who had no particular interest in anything I had to say other than realising that they had succeeded in provoking me. I felt foolish.

'Oh, you never know, Sister Cecilia, yourself and Father Leo might join forces and surprise us all,' Sienna giggled at her own remarks.

Later, I lay in bed, quite disgusted at my own foolishness. I fell into a troubled sleep conflicted as to whether I should accept and offer up the suffering these experiences caused, offer the pain up for Peggy, for the lost souls, for Jody or should I deal with their bullying ways? Was God testing me, burning the gold in the fire for greater tasks ahead or was I avoiding the poison in the root? I missed the guidance of Fr Ignatius.

By the following morning, I resolved to confront the poisonous powerplay of Sisters Monica and Sienna. The case of Mary McGregor overtook me.

***

Mary presented in the school seven months before, in the middle of April. She had arrived in Carrigeen from Scotland. The family's circumstances had changed due to the accidental death of her father in some kind of farming accident. Her mother and two younger sisters had lived on the edge of Glasgow. Teresa, Mary's mother, decided that the west of Ireland would provide peace for herself and her daughters. Without much thought or planning she found herself in Carrigeen after purchasing one of the coastal cottages about a mile from the school with the compensation provided after her husband, Bobby's death. She was from Donegal, and they had come to Carrigeen fifteen years before, staying two nights in the Bayview on their honeymoon. Clearly the memories were good. In Teresa's mind an idyllic place where her heart could rest in loving memory of the husband she had lost and so clearly longed for. Her grief was palpable even under the circumstances of our first encounter where anger swept the dust from every corner of the room.

I was finishing up in my office. Peggy had just left to get the last post. Sister Paul was down the hall in the lobby taking down the missionary posters and preparing for the November *All Soul's* display upon the school's return. Mid Term break would begin in three days' time. Tommy was out the back gathering wet leaves.

Teresa McGregor swept into my open office door.

'Where is this Sister Monica? Has she ever heard of the rights of children?'

I raised my head, startled. 'Sister Monica, is it?'

'Yes, Sister Monica.'

'I am afraid classes are over.'

'Well, they will be for her if I have my way.'

'Mrs McGregor, isn't it? Mary's mother?'

'Yes, I am Mary's mother, and this Sister Monica is accountable to me.' She bent over the large desk resting her hands towards either end.

'Please sit-down Mrs McGregor. What is this all about?'

'I will stay standing. Your Sister Monica humiliated Mary in front of the entire class in school today. Told her she had the oppressor's accent. That she would be better off going back where she came from. That her foreign and pagan ideas were not welcome. She suggested to the other children that their forefathers had fought and died to get rid of the kind of disgraceful ideas she was bringing into class. Imagine, she actually used the word *disgraceful!* She suggested that their parents, as God fearing Catholics, would not approve. All the while Mary stood facing the class having her palms slapped with a cane.'

'Indefensible,' I thought to myself but as I opened my month, I heard myself ask, 'What ideas was she talking about exactly?'

'Does it matter?' she almost spat at me, 'Adam and Eve. Mary suggested that the story was a myth. Sister Monica was on her like a ton of bricks before she had a chance to explain what she meant. "Who told you that?" she shouted at her.' Teresa McGregor stood up and gathered herself in.

'Her teacher in St Alban's told her it was a mega narrative. I remember because we had discussed it when she came home from school. She used to have those kinds of chats with her father. Mary tried to explain but was so frightened she got her thoughts mixed up. Sister Monica commanded her to come up and stood her in front of the class. "A what?" she asked her '

'"A mega narrative, like a founding story," Mary cried so hard here because she thought she was being given a chance to explain.

It was at this point that she was told that she could not *come in here* with her *foreign ideas*. Mary said Sister Monica's colour rose as she slapped her palms, twice on each, and then mentioned *the serpent* something about *the serpent in the garden of Eden being alive and well.* She left her standing there and made her way to the back of the classroom. Mary said the worst was when she looked at her school friends. They all had their heads down. Not one of them was brave enough to speak up for her. That was the worst of it for her, I think.'

'They are only children you know. Just barely fourteen.'

'Exactly! Exactly right! So, what are you going to do about it?'

'I can assure you,' I replied tight lipped, 'Sister Monica will reflect on her actions…'

'Reflect! Reflect, is it? She will have to do more than that sister. She will have to go. She should not be teaching children at all, full stop.'

I heard myself trot out a mealy-mouthed defence: 'Sister Monica has over twenty years' experience. This is the first complaint.'

I saw the faces of some of the girls I had seen in tears waft before me, some of whom left and never came back. God knows how many lives she had stunted. Remarks had been passed but here was the first parent demanding action. 'I assure you, we are, and will, take it seriously.

'Seriously, is it sister? What does this mean? That woman with her veil and her prayers destroying my wee daughter! A wee girl whose heart is already crushed. I have seen her cry after her daddy. Lose sleep, lose weight! They read books together and he disappeared from her life! But I never saw her sob! Are you hearing me sister? Sob, as if her heart was broken into a thousand pieces. How dare she!' Teresa Mc Gregor's fist thumped the desk between us. I almost jumped with it.

'Imagine coming all the way out here for a bit of peace and this! Makes you wonder if there is a God at all!' All the energy seemed to drain away from her.

Sister Paul gingerly entered the room, 'Please sit-down Mrs McGregor.'

'I don't want to. You are not going to fob me off.'

'You are pale,' I suggested, which was true.

'Would you like a cup of tea?' Paul asked

'No, no I don't want any tea. I want action!'

'I know Mary, I teach her.'

'You do.'

'Yes, maths. She is a bright girl. Probably top of the class.'

'She is bright, an independent thinker, I would say. She is like her daddy. Comes from reading all those books together but he always taught her the value of respect. He'd say "Mary, everyone has a story."' Her voice trailed off.

'Indeed, he taught her well. Mary is a most polite student,' Paul replied.

Teresa Mc Gregor's tears began to fall.

'Then why, tell me why that Sister Monica would want to treat her so badly?'

We all took a breath. I came out from behind my desk and sat down opposite Teresa. Paul propped herself on the edge of my desk.

'Right now,' I almost whispered, 'this is how we will proceed.

We will establish all the facts.'

'For God's sake, have I not given them to you!'

'Yes, but we need to hear them from Mary's point of view. And in the interests of justice, we need to record Sister Monica's account.'

'If it's justice you are looking for, she should be gone. Her account is likely to be self-serving.' We all knew this to be true.

'That be as it may, we have to do it. Will you trust us to do this?'

Teresa did not reply, her forehead was deeply furrowed. I continued.

'We have three days until mid-term. Why does Mary not take some time off to rest and give you some time together while your other daughters are at school. What do you think?'

'What do I think sister? I think my daughter is losing time at school while the person responsible carries on as normal. Where's the justice there?' Her tone was even.

'Okay, I hear you.'

'Do you sister, do you really?'

I reached out and caught her hand, 'I do.' She looked directly at me. I did not flinch. 'I insist that Mary has tomorrow off but you both come to see me at two thirty. She has nothing to fear. I want to reassure Mary of her right to be here and of our support.'

'Yes, she has to be reassured. It's going to take time. Her confidence has been shaken.'

'It has but I will do all within my power to see she does not lose it altogether.'

The three of us spoke about her life since coming to Carrigeen, about the wonderful summer she and her children had enjoyed free from strife, building sandcastles and strolling on the often-deserted strand. The children didn't mind the westerly winds or the roar of the ocean. They loved it. As a family they often hiked hills any opportunity they got. Their dad had taught them how to use a compass and read maps. They had gone camping on occasion. The outdoors suited them. All in all, she was happy with the decision she made to bring them to live on the Carrigeen peninsula. But Sister Monica's actions had sullied it.

Well over an hour later we left. This was my fourth year in the school, and I felt completely exhausted.

'I will miss you when you retire next year, Paul.'

'I won't miss it. I am ready but I will always be here for our walks on the weekend.'

'So, you are staying here?'

'Ah yes. The population is growing around these parts. There's talk of establishing a boys' school. I know most of the locals and I like to help where I can. Joan Morgan is retiring from Vincent de Paul. I might give a handout there. Besides, I often thought I would like to visit the old people living alone and isolated in these parts.'

'You're not going to disappear then?'

'Far from it!' she paused, 'you know, I should have confronted Sister Monica a long time ago. I truly regret that I didn't.'

'Well, here we are now, and we are going to have to deal with it. I will start with a call to the Mother Provincial. She is new to the position. She won't appreciate this dilemma.'

'I had a great relationship with Mother Augustine, I am not sure what this recently appointed Mother Ignatius is like, though she has a good reputation. Let's hope so. We are going to need her.'

***

Later that evening during our communal gathering, which our vow of obedience obliged us to attend for an hour regardless of any other obligations, we met in the drawing room, the only comfortable room in the house. Some embroidered, did needlepoint or rug making for the missions. Usually, we chatted about topical issues or listened to the radio on special occasions. Ironically, on Christmas Day we always listened to the Queen's speech.

'Did you hear what happened today?' Sister Sienna had everyone's ears pricked.

'What Sienna? What happened,' Sister Anthony asked in her innocence.

'Imagine a student who questioned Adam and Eve. Suggested it was a fairy story! The sacred scripture!'

'Oh dear, oh dear, what is the world coming to at all when the mind that questions God's word has found its way to Carrigeen,' Sister Anthony put her hand across her mouth and shook her head.

'Well, what would you expect from a child exposed to the paganism of the English. They questioned the pope and now they question God himself!' Sister Monica played to her audience. She and I knew she had a more nuanced grasp. She was great at creating scenarios to cover her tracks.

'I don't believe it was quite like that,' I intercepted.

Monica was taken aback. 'Really, what do you know of it? You were not there to witness such sacrilege.'

'Indeed, I was not, or it may not have unfolded as it did. I heard a full account from the student's mother.'

Monica went pale, 'you did?'

'I did. This is really not the forum to discuss any of it. We will talk tomorrow.'

A tense silence settled in the room. There were times when I resented the burden of responsibility and how easily others presumed upon it without ever having to deal with the consequences. This was one of those. I would like to have been the one bringing the joy into that room, laughter, carefree amusement but I think they would all have fallen off their chairs. I felt weary and angry.

I found my way to the altar of the Sacred Heart and the burning sanctuary lamp. I sat beneath my farmer sowing the seeds, though he was invisible in the dark, I could see him clearly in my mind's eye. I thought of home for the first time: the calloused hand dropping the seed, the rich clay soil, the heavy boots, the smell of rain on the branches, the red streaked sky beneath the snow moon on a damp early spring morning, later breaking into a bright day as Paddy Lenihan continued his sowing across the brow of the hill. As I sank into the images before me, I prayed to see my mother and brothers again.

'Lord, I want to go home. It is October, early in the school year, I have so much ahead. I am already tired. I have this deep longing for comfort, for my mother's arms around me.'

I closed my eyes, leaned back and sighed. Call it grace, call it what you will but I immediately felt the response grow within me.

'You are home Mary; you were always home. I in you and you in Me. Trust in the love I bear you so that we may be one.'

I understood in that moment that the intimacy and protection I sought would not be found in any place, in this convent or another, in the home of friends or my family home but within myself where it always had been. I was immediately brought back to the child who felt a benevolent presence lying in the sweet meadow grass looking at the clouds moving in the sky above while listening to the rough chew of the cud, the cow's tongue on the other side of the fence. Of the many moments I felt apart, conscious of my solitariness even in play. An observer of my world. I was passing through. I knew it to be true. I recognised it. I sank back into that love and could have wept with gratitude.

The experience brought clarity too. I thought of Mary McGregor, of her mother in her anger and grief, of her strength. I thought of Monica, of her unhappiness, for all her manipulation and cruelty and her savvy ability to spot another's weakness, she lacked any self-awareness. Self-righteousness had taken its place. I recollected Rumi and blessed Pat Garvey, the bookshop owner in Ballygraigue who had introduced me to his work some years before. That recollection made me smile. This inoffensive man who saw me looking through the poetry section on one of my few visits and suggested I might be interested in his work. I was. I am. Thank you Pat Garvey, thank you. Then I left my thoughts return to the Sufi mystic, as I often do:

Even if they're a crowd of sorrows,
who violently sweep your house
empty of its furniture,
still treat each guest honourably.
He may be clearing you out
for some new delight.

I prayed solemnly for all three and for the encounters that lay ahead. But I prayed, *if I am being prepared for some new delight, please let it come soon.*

Later, I slept soundly.

16

The Little Ones

Mother Ignatius was brief and to the point:

'Report back to me once you have spoken with Sister Monica. She is entitled to her defence. It would have been wiser if you had placed your call after this. It would give me a more balanced account upon which to make a judgement. However, corporal punishment is frowned upon in more enlightened schools and is certainly not behaviour with which I want any of our schools associated. Interpretation of scripture is a moving feast right now. Literalism is no longer tolerated in academic circles. How long did you say Sister Monica is teaching?'

'To the best of my knowledge, over twenty years in this school. I am unaware of her previous experience.'

'You need to gather as much information as you can so any conclusions drawn will be just. I expect a call from you in two days, Sister Cecilia. God bless.'

I put the phone down chastened. Now for Sister Monica. She was not for turning.

'Have we reached the point where any parent can come into this school, without appointment I might add, and demand that a teacher be reprimanded? It is altogether a disgrace!' Monica sat squarely on the chair opposite my desk, her large figure imposing.

'It is more than a reprimand that is being asked for. It is your removal.'

'This is outrageous.' Her colour rose.

'Do you wish to meet Mrs McGregor, Monica?' I looked directly at her.

'I have no intention of doing so,' she pushed the nearest object on the desk in front of her, 'and you have the authority to stop all this nonsense.'

'Times are changing Monica. Caning a child is no longer an acceptable form of discipline in this school. For many, it never was. Neither is sarcasm.'

'Sarcasm, is it?' Her pitch rose and she leaned forward, 'How dare you! I was defending the scriptures.'

'Then give me your account Monica,' I threw down the pen I was holding and leaned back.

'I accept I lost control and used the cane but only across the hand.' She sighed, 'many another student has taken it without complaint and with positive outcomes.'

'Are you sure about that Monica?'

'I am. Indeed, I am.' She leaned forward resting her elbows on the edge of her chair with both hands clasped and her chin pointed forward. 'Well brought up children who understand the difference between right and wrong, who know it is for their good. This is the first complaint of its kind. Of course, the child knows no better coming from a Sasanach.' Monica sat back.

'Her mother is from Donegal. Has it ever crossed your mind that those children that do not complain are afraid.'

'Afraid, since when did a little fear do any harm? Kept us all in line.'

'As a methodology it is going. Progressive educational thinking rejects it outright. It might have been tolerated in the past. It was never encouraged. It has to stop.' Without thinking of the irony of my statement in so far as I had corrected Monica for thinking in terms of *an outsider*. I confidently observed, 'perhaps it takes the outsider to spot the obvious.' Monica did not seem to notice. She was picking another argument from her arsenal.

'So, you stand over a child undermining the account of Adam and Eve? The story we have all grown up with?'

'That is a different matter.'

'It is central to this conversation.' She felt the arrow hit the mark.

'Yes but…'

'No buts, it is either central or it isn't!'

'What is central to this conversation Sister Monica is your fitness to continue teaching. That is what is being questioned here and that is what is at stake.'

'According to who? I will have no interloper coming in here and questioning me after all the years of service I have given to this school.'

'It is no longer just Mrs Mc Gregor you have to be concerned about. Mother Ignatius wants to be kept informed.'

'She does, does she! And who was it that informed her in the first place?' She narrowed her eyes.

'I did,' Sister Paul immediately intercepted, 'and I should have done so long ago when Brigid Noonan left. There have been many Brigid Noonans since then. It is time.'

I clearly saw that Paul's Brigid Noonan was my Marian Smith. Oh, the regrets!

'Time for what?'

'Sister Monica, I must have an agreement from you before you leave this office this morning that you will never again use corporal punishment. I want all canes in your possession handed in at close of school today.'

'I never used a cane on Brigid Noonan.'

'That is right,' Paul declared, 'your words destroyed her.'

'That brings me to what was said to Mary McGregor.'

'I said very little and nothing that wasn't true.'

'You told her that she had *the oppressor's accent*'

'Well, she has!'

I continued: 'that she *would be better off going back where she came from*. That her ideas are *foreign and pagan*; that other children should avoid her because their parents would not approve.'

'Her ideas are pagan.'

'Just stop Monica. Please stop.'

'As principal of this school, it is your responsibility to protect its Catholic ethos.'

'Have you ever heard of literalism, Monica?'

'I am well aware of its meaning.'

'Then you should know that the literal interpretation of the Old Testament is no longer accepted in Catholic thinking. You do understand what Mary meant by the founding story?'

'Of course I do! As a teacher of literature, I know that the best myth embodies truths and beliefs about how we understand ourselves and make meaning of the world.'

'Then why did you belittle Mary McGregor?'

'Because she has notions above her station. What fourteen-year-old talks about myths? She had the other children confused, thinking it was only a fairy story.'

'An informed fourteen-year-old talks about myths. The children were not confused, they were afraid.'

She looked at me nonplussed.

'We will talk again.'

'Do you expect me to go back into a classroom and teach after this interrogation?'

'It is not an interrogation. It is a frank and clearly long overdue conversation. If you wish to take time out for the rest of the morning, do so. Do whatever it is you need to restore your equilibrium, but I expect you to be in class by two this afternoon.'

I could hear the strength in my own voice. I spoke evenly and was glad of that. I knew this situation was a disaster, worse than I had feared. Decisions would have to be made.

***

Mary McGregor was a thin, tall, gawky teenager without any sense of her own beauty. She was nothing short of Nordic looking with broad shoulders, chiselled facial features, very blond hair and steel blue eyes, which she found difficult to raise when she came to see me the following day. I instinctively felt that her beauty may have been a contributory factor to her treatment at Monica's hands. She was on the edge of potential. Monica was watching hers disappear. It is not that Monica did not have potential, she did. The potential to be kind, engaging, to read, to study, to choose happiness. But she did not have the possibility of being a teenager on the road to adulthood again. She was unhappy. The bitter heart is squeezed. Once poison enters, it is difficult to eradicate.

Mary wept copious tears, her nose running, her eyes downcast refusing to make contact, her left hand pulling at the nails of her right hand. She barely uttered a word. The damage was evident.

'Thank you for coming Mary. Can you tell me what happened in Sister Monica's class on Tuesday.

'Mammy has already told you,' She whispered.

'Yes, yes, your mother has outlined the situation, but I would like to hear it from your point of view.'

'I can't, I just can't,' she whispered again.

Teresa Mc Gregor shot a furrowed glance at me over the bent body of her daughter. I struggled to find my next step. There was a moment of silence, even hesitation.

'What can I do to help you, Mary?'

She looked at me for the first time. 'I don't want to go back to Sister Monica's classes, but I don't want to be separated from my friends.'

'Have any of them contacted you since Tuesday?'

'No', she wailed.

'I see'.

'Well maybe you don't, to be fair only two days have passed, and your friends are here in school Mary,' her mother offered, 'they all have distances to walk home. Brid is the nearest girl to us, and she is half a mile away.'

'Yes, and she hasn't come near me. Maybe her parents won't allow her.'

'I doubt that', her mother asserted but clearly could not be fully sure.

'I doubt that too, Mary. Brid is a good-natured girl, full of common sense.'

'But Sister Monica warned them all off having anything to do with me.'

'The October break is almost here. I have no doubt whatsoever that Brid will call to see you.'

'Do you really think so?' she asked in earnest.

'I do.'

Teresa Mc Gregor threw me another glance. I have since reflected how the brightest of girls are often the most innocent, their survival instincts not keenly honed. Brid was rooted and would be armour for the sensitive soul who sat before me.

'You do not have to go back into Sister Monica's class tomorrow, but it would be in your own interest to join the class as normal after midterm.'

'I can't'

'You have to. Show your friends that you are strong and that you have nothing to hide.'

'We can talk about that over the break,' her mother intervened. I was not at all sure Mary was ready for school the following day. As they stood up to go, I remarked on Mary's Nordic looks.

'Ah, she's the head off her father. I see him in her every day.'

Mary about to exit, dropped her head into her hands and sobbed. I quickly closed the door. Her grief was overwhelming.

'Maybe it has all been too much, Bobby's sudden death and our move to here,' Teresa whispered to me over her daughter's bent head.

'Perhaps a visit to Dr Larkin is in order. It won't do any harm.' I was concerned at Mary's inability to speak even though she was encouraged to do so.

'I have met him already. He is very approachable.'

'I think so.'

The following morning, I sent for Brid. It would be dishonest of me not to pretend that coming to the principal's office was not intimidating for any young pupil. I asked Sister Claire to let her out discreetly under some pretext. Brid stood before my desk looking perplexed.

'Sit down Brid.'

'Yes sister.'

'You have no idea why you are here do you?' I heard my own stupidity.

'No sister.' She also kept her eyes down.

'Look up at me, Brid. I know you are kind and a studious girl. Sister Paul says you would be nothing to your parents if you weren't.' She smiled.

'You are friendly with Mary McGregor, right?'

She looked uncertain, 'I am.'

'Good. It is very hard for Mary coming from so far away. She has to be lonely sometimes.'

'Especially after her dad,' Brid added again looking down at her clasped hands.

'Exactly,' I responded with some relief that she was aware of this. 'Call to see her over the midterm break won't you.'

'I will sister. Is she alright? She wasn't in school today.'

'That's great, Brid. You will be a good friend.'

'Is that it, sister?'

'Yes Brid, that's it!' She stood up to go. 'Oh, before you go.' I put my hand into the drawer below me and pulled out a small packet of Scots Clan. Chocolate sweets were rare outside of Christmas and Easter. 'Bring these when you are going.'

'Thank you, sister, but I don't need them. I was going to see Mary anyway. Now I will have to explain where I got them.' I felt foolish at her admonition. She was right. So was I. I wanted Brid's parents to understand how fully supportive I was of the girls' friendship.

'This is not a bribe, Brid. Tell Mary I sent them so you can both have a good chew.'

'Okay Sister Cecilia.'

'Enjoy the break, Brid.' She left without a word. I felt uneasy.

***

One month after midterm, a school inspector, Mr O'Súillebháin landed on our doorstep. He wanted to visit the Irish classes. I was given twenty-four hours' notice, no more. Twenty minutes into Sister Monica's class he announced he was going to give Sister Monica a break and take the class for the remaining time. He quietly asked Monica to leave.

He spoke both Irish and English with the class. He asked them what they liked to do in their free time. They mentioned, getting the sheep off the nearby hills, gathering seaweed from the shore, helping mammy with the cooking or walking the babies, reading, picking flowers. He got the picture of earnest young girls with limited free time. He joked and laughed with them.

Five minutes to the bell, he asked them if they liked learning Irish. The laughing subsided into an uneasy silence. 'Okay', he said 'show me where the canes are.' No one moved. 'You are not in trouble here. Let's just get rid of those canes once and for all. What do you say?' Some heads looked at him sideways but then there was the creak of a desk. Brid pushed the books in front of her, walked straight to the radiator below the maps of Ireland and pulled out two canes from behind it. She handed them to the inspector without a single word and sat back down.

Fifteen minutes later he was in my office, the two canes laid firmly across my desk. I looked at them startled, 'But she had given me her bamboo cane.'

'That she may have done but she did not surrender these, did she?'

'No', I felt the full force of his anger and my own shock.

'This will be addressed. You will receive my report within days. Decisions are going to have to be made.'

'Yes, yes, I accept that'.

'You have no choice but to accept it. We have the evidence here before us.'

'Indeed.'

'I will be in touch.'

'Mr. O'Súillebháin, I have your tea ready in the parlour.'

'No thank you. Another time perhaps. I will make my way to The Bayview.'

I felt summarily dismissed. I was raging with him, with myself, with Monica. My thoughts were racing:

Who does he think he is, coming in here and making such immediate judgements?

Are we so contaminated that he wouldn't even take a pot of tea? For God's sake!

And then I heard myself coming back. I was making him the scapegoat just as Monica had done to Teresa Mc Gregor. I was filled with loathing for myself.

The only people failed here are the children. I failed them. Only my own self! I did not go down to the room and check for more canes. I took at face value, a woman whom I knew to be self-serving. My anger shifted to Monica:

You knew. You knew you had two more canes, and you did not respect me enough to accede to my request. You thought you would get away with it! You have had free reign for far too long! Well, it's over! It's all over now!

I collapsed into my chair. I knew the next few weeks would not be easy. I looked at the canes, one rounded, thick, painted in a tricolour of red, white and green. The other, thin and flexible. I thought of the children at the receiving end. I knew I had to meet the hour.

IV

17

There's a Change a Coming

No one wishes for enemies, but life inevitably brings them your way. I remember Martha confronting a neighbour, Helen Cox, who had pinned Nellie Maher to the wall outside the school gates.

'You lay a hand on Nellie, and I'll tell your mother that you walked down the road holding John O'Keeffe's hand last week.'

'That was only once!' Helen was startled.

'Doesn't matter. Get your hands off Nellie.' She did.

Martha was no more than eleven. How did we lose her so easily? For the first time in almost fifteen years, I felt myself overcome with grief. In the silence of my room, I cried out to her:

'Martha, Martha, give me some of your courage now. I have lost it all, along with the laughter we shared. Where is it all gone these days? Did either of us know it would be like this?' I knelt beside my bed, the rain beating off the rattling windowpanes and I wept.

For six months since Monica had left, shortly after Christmas, there had been tension in the staffroom. Social conversation had almost ceased entirely. The few lay staff left immediately after their duties. There was a resettling. Sienna had withdrawn into herself. Try as they might during our evening community gathering, Sisters Anthony and Frances could get few words from Sister Sienna who answered in monosyllables.

All in all, the atmosphere was dismal. I understood the humiliation it would cause Monica to leave in the middle of the academic year. It was out of my hands post the inspector's report which was also sent to Mother General Ignatius. She was quite annoyed that this negative attention had been drawn to the school in this way and by extension, to the order. She acted swiftly, her only concession being to allow Sister Monica to finish out her first term and leave under the anonymity of the school holidays. Under strict instruction I was not to inform the staff until after her departure presumably so the matter would not be discussed between the clink of the sherry glasses and the Christmas pudding! No doubt it still was!

However, the extraordinary staff meeting held upon return was met with a stony silence and glances of empathy in Sienna's direction. I did have support, like Nicodemus in the night, I got the occasional knock on the door when no one else was around. In general, the comment was *Not sure about the way this was handled but it can't be easy.* Such comments, while well intentioned, did little to reassure me. It was painful and difficult for all concerned. We all knew that this was going to take time.

A year later, before the beginning of Summer, Sister Sienna requested leave of absence from the community in Carrigeen and her duties as a teacher. Both were granted. She took up a two-year course in pastoral studies at the Milltown Institute. She never went back to teaching, instead choosing to work with vulnerable groups in the centre of Dublin. I met her many years later. We both understood we would never be close friends, yet she was generous enough to share what liberation her decision and courage to leave Carrigeen had brought. The day after Sienna left, I too ventured into unknown territory and took my first driving lesson. After many bumps on the coastal country road under the keen eyes and even voice of Vinny Mc Mahon, taxi driver turned instructor, I passed the driving test. This was my liberation.

Two summers later, in 1974, before dipping my head into planning for the following school year, I turned towards home for the first time in nineteen years. I drove the three-hour journey in the community's own Toyota Starlet, one of two we now owned, no longer dependent on taxis. The other car was driven by our two new additions, Sisters Maryann and Theresa. Maryann was in her thirties and Theresa in her late twenties. They had joined as vocations were beginning to slide. They were great friends having professed their final vows together despite their six-year age difference.

Maryann, the younger, was a catechist, one of the first from the Mater Dei Institute, with a passion for music. Theresa was an artist to the core. Spiritually sensitive she was also great fun and had no time for labels of any kind. Once a month she insisted on cooking dinner on a Saturday to give Anthony and Frances a break. What seemed impossible in the past was not just changing but welcomed. On those same afternoons she, Maryann, Frances and Anthony sat into the car and excitedly waited for Maryann's planned excursion to unfold. They usually kept the journeys to within an hour, but they could head in any direction. It was as exciting as it was simple, a picnic on the Flaggy Shore, a visit to Galway Cathedral, a walk around the grounds of Kylemore Abbey. One full day in August they drove to Knock. Usually for the closing day of the novena. On that day, all who were able or wanted, travelled and I drove the second car. Their liveliness and free spirit brought a whole new life to Carrigeen. It was as if the wild winds had blown in the front doors and were blowing all the old cobwebs of prejudice and inhibition away. The old often stifling order of things was giving way to more freedom of expression.

This also applied to family contact. I wrote a brief note every few weeks just to keep in touch. Though, when very busy or living through some crises, I lapsed. I did not always receive a reply, nor did I expect it. I wrote a long letter every Christmas and Easter, sent a card for each birthday even to the niece and nephew I had never met, Martha and Dan. I wrote of the nature of the community in which I lived and worked, the challenging and beautiful landscape and the friends I had made. I never wrote of tensions of any kind. I did not wish to trouble my family. I also regarded it as my duty not to. A regard for the community I had committed to. I realise now it was embedded as an important value in my formation.

I trundled along nicely excited at the prospect of meeting my family, wondering how it might all feel. I swept left to turn into the drive to the homeplace. New walls and piers had been built with large wrought iron gates. I hadn't anticipated that and very nearly scratched the passenger door but upon recovery reflected that they gave the entrance a regal look. The front of the house had not changed at all apart from the colour of the door which had gone from a forest green to a post box red. Fresh flower boxes of geranium and lobelia adorned the sills. Two sheep dogs came running to smell out the visitor. They were lively but once I grabbed them affectionately behind the ears and rubbed them, they settled. I was one of their own.

I walked in the open door observing the sunlight play in and out of shadows across the stairs I had climbed to see Martha for the last time and the same terracotta tiles leading to the kitchen at the back. I could hear the chorus of voices and smiled as I turned the same brass handle. Everyone turned, some jumped up.

'Mary, Mary, is it you? Ay Jaysus, I came especially to meet you and then miss the moment! How are you at all?' My big square baby brother, Tom, swept me up into his arms. 'My God you are only skin and bone. Are they starving you down in that place or what?' I felt the tears flow. Tears of joy, no explanations necessary. Mammy sat at the end of the table. She was as thin as I remembered her, but her expression was lighter. She stood very gently, 'come here my girl, my daughter'. She reached up and put her arms across my shoulders.

'You are not going to call me Sister Cecilia Mam, are you?'

'No. No. I have thought a lot about that. Mary it is, as I named you when you were born.' The contrast between this and our last meeting could not have been starker. I resolved to do what I could not do in the past and see my family more often.

'Well, I don't know what to call you! I only ever met you as Sister Cecilia but Mary it is then,' Angela, curly haired and plump with a radiant smile greeted me. James came fast on her heels with a warm handshake, 'Ah Mary, where have you been? It has been so long! We were thinking of sending out the search party.'

'Yes, it has been too long.'

'The kettles on and the lamb in the oven for later. We will have a good chat over dinner,' Mammy said.

'I am looking forward to it Mam. I have a few things in the car. Sisters Anthony and Frances sent up fruit and queen and lemon cakes and homemade lemonade.'

'Lads, give Aunt Mary a hand,' James gestured to two young men standing near French doors where the old back door used to be.

'Peter or John?' I asked, my hand outstretched.

'Peter is in Dublin, training in an architectural office but you know this!'

'I do but I am a bit confused with the two tall men before me,' I smiled.

'This is John and Dan, our baby,' James explained.

'John, you don't remember me, but I remember you, the two-year-old with the blonde curls like your mammy. O my, you make a fine, handsome young man.' He blushed and shook my hand.

'I'm Dan, you couldn't remember me. I have never seen you before.' Everyone laughed.

'No, indeed I haven't. Pleased to meet you Dan. Who are you like at all?'

'His grandfather, Jack,' Mammy replied. No one questioned it.

'And here is Martha,' Angela gently pushed forward a thin tall girl. She had her mother's smile, but I found myself looking at my sister's eyes. 'O Martha,' I stammered, 'you are beautiful.' I hugged her briefly as emotion overtook me once again. There was silence and surprise in the air as my silent tears flowed. Martha seemed confused. Angela put her arm around her daughter, 'go out to Aunt Mary's car and bring in that lemon cake, we could do with some.'

'Okay Mammy,' Martha replied

'I don't mean to be disrespectful Sister but Mammy, do you mean that tiny scrap of shiny metal outside?' Dan intervened, 'guaranteed to meet my Maker if I have an accident in that. Daddy wouldn't let Peter drive to Dublin in one of those.'

I blushed, everybody baulked. Then I giggled and everybody laughed.

***

I made my way upstairs. The original landing was still the same, the room Martha and I shared to the right across from the room in which she was laid out on the left, behind James and Tom's room directly opposite. Mammy and Daddy's room behind mine and a shared bathroom to the back as it used to be. That large bathroom was now gone and in its place was a small hall with a single bedroom for mammy to the left with her own facilities and opposite a shower and bathroom with a separate toilet. The two-storey extension to the back of the house was plain to see and explained the larger kitchen with French doors and conservatory downstairs. Granny's patterned carpet was gone, replaced by a deep midnight blue. It was subtle and warm. Yet I thought of granny, of her life here, of all the years she had given, now gone.

I was staying in my old childhood room. Apart from the structure and layout, the old mahogany wardrobe and dressing table, it was wholly changed. A typical girl's room of the seventies. This was now young Martha's room with a white bed. Posters of David Bowie were plastered all over the wall opposite the bed. A guitar stood in the corner beside the old wardrobe, but it was the walls painted magnolia with the old white sash windows which gave the room its light airy feel. Gone was the big flowery wallpaper with its large pink and purple roses rising out of a dark backdrop. Ours was a dramatic room. This seemed more restful. I loved the changes, but they made me keenly aware that the life inside my head was mine alone. I had memories I could scarcely share with young Martha. Even if I told her stories, the colours she imagined would be different.

In the early hours I found myself unable to sleep. I smelt the jasmine beside me. A single stem in clear glass beside a framed photograph of the entire family sitting on the cut grass of the lower meadow drinking the milky tea Mammy brought down from the house, a break while saving the hay. I don't know who took the photograph because we were all there. Mammy and the toddler Tom, Daddy, standing beside James, their arms folded leaning on their pitchforks, Martha and I giggling and stretching out. Everybody was smiling. I switched on the small lamp and gazed at it for a long time. Contentment was blowing over that meadow. I felt it in my young self. I felt the natural love that shared family adventure brought. I thought of the new generation. They had it now. I slipped out of the bed and stood at the window which once looked over the yard and the red barn. The perpendicular wall to the left was softened by Virginia creeper and straight ahead I could see half the length of the new lawn and the hills beyond, the green roof of the new barn tucked nicely into the horizon. The silvery light of a three-quarter moon fell on the world below as if nothing had changed.

18

These Past Few Days

'In these past few days when I see myself, I seem like someone else…'

That visit home was a revelation. While conscious of the radical nature of the changes happening in my own religious community nothing brought change home as viscerally to me as the presence of Martha and Dan. My niece and nephew, whom I knew of but never met until that moment. Their life force, their laughter, their reminder to me of my own childhood within these same walls, the lives that once existed here whom they had never known but somehow reflected.

After such a long absence, their presence was a source of sheer joy, and pain too. I was something of an enigma to them. I was forever Sister Cecilia in their eyes. Though they tried, I could never be Mary. I was reconciled to it. I did not revert to the past or pretend to be someone from the past. I had grown to love the tender spiritualities and grit of Cecilia in absolute certainty that she was born and rooted in Mary.

And so, I felt as I walked through the lower meadow as I used to do with Dad, his rough sunburnt hand across my shoulder or gently catching my fingers as we walked, the straw itching my skin within the wellington boots beneath my summer dress. I smelt the must rising from the damp earth. I stood beneath the old chestnut tree, its generous leafy branches and scented flowers hiding me from view as I leaned on its broad bark and looked back up the curving rising landscape where the top half of the house came into view. We know it. We have all heard it said: *if the stones could speak*. I vowed never to leave it as long again.

My mother of course was reason enough. Yes, her spirit was lighter which was a great source of consolation. After I started in earnest in religious life, I was not sure I would see her again so great was the trauma she had endured, the exact details of which I never fully understood. I approached the subject with Tom. He shrugged his shoulders and said, 'Today is good, is it not Mary?' I nodded my head.

'Yes but…'

'No buts. The past has already been decided. What is the point of going there?'

Inevitably, I sighed.

'Are you happy Mary?'

'Yes, yes I am.'

'Truly?'

'Yes Tom, truly.'

'Well then isn't that all we can ask for?'

There was wisdom in the man but avoidance too. 'Are you happy Tom?'

'Aye! Is it not obvious Mary? Do I seem unhappy to you?'

'No, not at all.'

'Well, there you are.'

'But you never married.'

'Ah Jaysus Mary, give a man a break! I had my chances, but I am not sure I am ready for the sacrifices required. Time enough.'

'Ah but Tom, you would make a great companion to any woman lucky enough to have you!'

'I know,' he laughed, 'I am not a bad catch at all! Handsome too…' he punched my shoulder and laughed and then whispered, 'but Martha sacrificed enough for us all.'

And there it was. Something in Martha's loss had stumped him. At twelve his trust in the world had been tarnished and it hadn't left him.

'What will it take to convince you? Really Mary, I wish you would leave Sister Cecilia behind! How often do we see each other? Can we not just be here, in this moment.'

'Oh, but we are Tom, we are. I am sorry.'

And so, I learned not to approach the subject again. James was simply a no-go area. His hard edge had softened, and I did not want to lose it. He was content and happy, and Tom was right, today is enough for today. Yet I knew the past was only a hair's breadth away lying in the heart's crevasse. The time was not yet right. It might never be, and I had to learn to accept it. Though I always remained hopeful, that acceptance took years. It was one of those sufferings which I prayed for the grace to endure. I knew that grace and mystery were twin sisters in that movement between God's spirit and mine.

And so, I leaned into that gap which I could not bridge on my own, resting in trust that healing would come. I did not need any divine signs. Martha was full of love and laughter. Tom is full of love. So am I. God is love. We are all one. We will be one again. There will be healing. There is nothing more to say.

Mammy and I sat in the back of the house in the quiet of the small conservatory where the dappled sunlight played on the terracotta floor. Mammy sat on her own chair, affectionately referred to as *granny's chair*, with its Foxford rug and its well-worn cushions: *Grandma's rules apply here*, and *Old Friends are the Best Friends*. The glass door leading out into the back garden was slightly ajar, leaving in some welcome, if damp, air after the heavy showers which had fallen for the past hour. The overhanging branches drooped, drenched in droplets falling on to the glistening sodden grass. The air was lifting. There we were sitting amongst the red geraniums and spider plants, sharing a pot of tea before I left.

Mammy was very serene. Clearly, in the intervening years, her body had changed. Her sallow skin bore the wrinkles of her seventy years. Her hands were mottled. She had two arthritic fingers in either hand including her wedding finger where the ring could no longer come off. It had been an issue during her last visit to hospital over a year ago when she had suffered a minor stroke. Startled at this discovery, I asked James why he hadn't told me.

'And what would you have done? What could you have done? Nothing. You have other responsibilities now. That's the life you chose.'

It stung. 'I would just like to know.'

'Okay'.

'Promise me that if anything like this should happen again you will let me know.'

'I will. But you must understand, you are at a distance. You cannot understand the demands...' he seemed to struggle for words... 'the immediate intensity of these kinds of situations.'

'Maybe I understand more than you give me credit for James.'

'I doubt it!'

'What do you mean?'

'Nothing, nothing at all.'

'Oh, but you do James. You do. Please help me understand.'

'I am sorry. Just let it go. What do I know of your life? Different worlds, that's all.'

'Not so different. Same human longings, same challenges to face each day. You sell the cattle or the horses or whatever. You run the farm. I run a school. We still have to get up each day with some conviction. But mostly, same mother, James. We both grew up in this house together. At least grant me that.'

'I am sorry Mary. I know. What you say is true. We have missed you; you know. Especially all those years ago.'

'I don't think I understood just how much.'

'No. But you are here now, and life is pretty good under this roof. I promise you if anything at all happens to mammy, I will let you know.'

'Thanks James,' we hugged before he left to visit the outside farm where he reared dry cattle.

I couldn't shake off a deep sense of being chastened.

***

'When did the veil go Mary?'

I automatically fingered the hairline at the back of my neck. Teresa, our local hairdresser, had trimmed it for me before I came home.

'That's gone a while now Mammy. I have not worn it since 1970, though I was the first to let it go. Some of the sisters still wear it. They feel it's going as the thin edge of the wedge, a failure to witness so to speak.'

'Maybe they are right.'

'Really Mammy?'

'Ah, what do I know? It is good to see your curls again even if they are grey and makes you less forbidding for Dan and Martha. Just so many changes.' She sighed.

'Yes, so many changes,' I surprised myself by sighing also.

Abruptly and in an almost forced tone as if to imply we are not going down that rabbit hole, Mammy giggled:

'Peter and John were terrified of you, you know, when they met you at that convent…St Brigid's… at your final vows.' She giggled again.

'They talked for a long time in the car on the way home before falling asleep: "Really granny. What colour is her hair? Does she wear it when she goes to sleep?" Of course, James frightened the life out of them asking Peter if he remembered the injured bat they had found together in the barn with its wings spread. He told him that your veil was made out of bat wings. Poor Peter was terrified, we all laughed and then he was confused. It didn't stop him from falling into a deep sleep, his head on my lap. Yes, gone is the veil!' She winked at me and laughed remembering. 'That was a strange day!'

She stared into the middle distance as if opening a door.

'Strange Mammy?'

'I am only rambling Mary. Take no notice. We were all exhausted, that's all!'

'From the effort it took?' I almost whispered.

'Yes,' she said without pretence.

'I am sorry Mammy.'

'You have nothing to be sorry for. It would have been all the same had it been your wedding day, which in a way it was. Any family occasion was going to be difficult to get through that time.'

'Under the circumstances?'

'Under the circumstances.'

'Daddy died so suddenly! Grandad lived into his eighties. Was it the strain of Martha's sudden death?' I found myself asking my mother the very questions I had vowed not to ask given the pain she must have endured.

'Oh indeed, it was a lot of things Mary. I have spent years wearing myself down asking. The questions only bring torment. I left it in God's hands a long time ago. Otherwise, I would go mad.'

'Torment?' I thought but refrained from asking. Questions which bring torment? We have no control over sudden death. No agency. 'Do I bring it all back to you?'

'It's just… I have seen so little of you since that time, you know? I had two lovely and lively daughters full of life…' her voice trailed… 'and then…in a whisper…', she raised up her hand and let it fall gently into her lap

'Oh Mammy,' I knelt beside her chair and caught her hands in mine.

'Don't trouble yourself anymore, Mary. You are my lovely daughter, and you are here now. That is all that matters.'

'Yes, and like the veil, it is all changing. I can visit more often and even stay over like these past two days.' I was taken by surprise by the empowerment I felt when uttering these words. Another liberation.

It felt completely right.

'As long as I am alive, there will always be a bed in this house for you, you know that don't you?'

'I do mammy, I do.'

'Now tell me, that woman who spoke to me about the advantages of having a nun in the family… couldn't stand her!'

'Really?' I laughed

'Ah you know, there are some people who have it all sorted, all planned out. The kind of cuteness that passes them by coming back. I cannot stand it. The kind that says marrying the teacher is like having the outside farm! Makes my skin crawl!'

'Oh, mammy you're gas!'

'Well?'

'Well, what?' I was still giggling.

'Did the daughter stay in or not? …with all these changes you know. What's this her name was?'

'I am surprised you remember the conversation at all,' I laughed, 'Eileen, Sister Immaculata, now Eileen. Oh, she did stay. Actually Mammy, she is the real deal. A genuine woman with a generous heart. The last I heard of her; she was running after-school homework classes for kids on the verge of dropping out.'

'You know, that does my heart good to hear because strangely and despite the exhaustion we experienced at that time, that woman's self-serving comments struck me as completely out of place in what was otherwise a gentle reception. You see that's the thing, I find it hard to put my finger on, I hated losing you, but I can't deny that for an hour or so during the service, a strange and beautiful peace came over me. James, of course, thought he could not get out fast enough.'

'That's James for you!' I laughed and hesitated, 'thanks Mam for telling me that.'

'You know I have only heard myself saying it for the first time. The peace didn't last but it was there. A kind of reprieve. Anyway, I am rambling.'

'Do you remember Sister Xavier Mammy?'

'Let me see now. She's not the one who watched you like a hawk and kept her eye on the clock when you were here for poor Martha's funeral?'

'The very one! Well, she left, was gone at the first whisper of change.'
'Go away!'
'She was my novice mistress, incredibly strict! We were all shocked.'
'How long ago was that?'
'About five years ago. She lives in the States now I think.'
'She must have been one of the first to go.'
'She was.'
'Very brave really.'
'You're right. She was.'
'Have you ever thought about leaving?'
'Need you ask Mam?'
'Probably not. You always had something in you that was beyond me.'
'I don't know about that Mammy, but I do know I am where I am meant to be on this earth. Not every day, but most days.'
'Well, that's good enough. If every person getting out of their bed in the morning had that sense of purpose, we would have a very peaceful world.'

I looked out at the lush stretching lawn beyond the gravel. The early hydrangeas were in bloom a deep blue at the far end of the lawn where the barn used to be. 'What a peaceful view.'

'It is, isn't it? My favourite spot. I just watch the robins in the morning. One has his spot there, right there near the door and another further down the lawn, near the chestnut tree. Since Angela added the birdbath and feeding station, the finches and the wagtails have been a joy to watch. James says all we are doing is encouraging vermin with the birdseed but that falls on deaf ears.'

'When did he move the old red barn?'

Shortly after he took over the farm. After Jack died. He knocked it all together and replaced it as you can see. It was a good decision.'

'It was. I would never have imagined the view or its impact. Though I was fond of the old red barn. Many a chat I had in there with Daddy. In fact, the last chat I had with him was there.'

'Is that so?'

'Yea, he showed me some newborn kittens.'

'Life moves on Mary.'

'Indeed, it does. Angela is great, isn't she?'

'The best thing that ever happened to James! The children are great crack. They give me heart. A touch of Tom's humour in all of them.'

'Tom?'

'What about him? He is very much his own man Mary. Always was. I tell you; he did not leave my side for about five years after your father's death. But I was not afraid for him. He was self-assured since the day he was born. When James and Angela finally moved in, he gently made his exit. The boys are very close. It is a great blessing. You know, when there is land involved it isn't easy, but he went off and did his own thing.'

'He seems to work all hours.'

'I agree.'

'What's this he is in again?'

'Pension funds apparently.'

'I wouldn't have a clue.'

'Me either. He is just here, there and everywhere. He flew out to London this morning.'

***

And so, as I swung my Toyota Starlet right onto the road that would eventually take me back to Carrigeen. I still had the warmth of Mammy's embrace, a comfort blanket around me, a reassurance that we had connected. I absorbed all the images, the changes, the light, the laughter and let the challenges of the past few days settle within me on the three-hour journey home. Yes, home, the windswept granite barracks of a building battered from Atlantic storms without, the struggle and resilience of the characters within, and the smell of fish on a Friday. I had come to love this place that I had barely endured in the early years. It was raw. It was weather beaten. It was honest, like the wrinkled face of the seafarer or the calloused hands of a lifetime of work.

19

What the Old Men Say

I came back to a flurry of gossip. Fr. Leo, who wore the collar but dressed casually, had set up the folk group, sat in the kitchen of almost every household in the parish, visited every person living alone, and even managed to make crusty, old Tadhg smile, was gone. Yes, gone! Not to a new parish but to a new life. And he wasn't alone. Teresa Mc Gregor and her children went with him.

I thought of the many encounters we had pre and post Sister Monica, of her passion and anger, of her grief and love, of her protective grasp of her then fragile daughter and I could see it all. Two dynamic people who had glimpsed what was possible beyond the horizon of their own heart-scape. I was sad that we lost such a compassionate priest, but I was not sad for him. I still cannot imagine the courage it took to leave it all behind.

Fr Leo was pastorally present to his congregation. He had a deep spirituality. It would surely hurt him to no longer be able to celebrate the sacraments. He would miss the camaraderie of his colleagues. Those who cared for him would make efforts to stay in contact. Yet 'ways lead on to ways' and there will be inevitable partings. He was loved by those he served.

He would be missed by the lonely. Yes, there is the very real loneliness of the last left in the family sitting at the kitchen table listening to the wind coming in over the sea and the existential loneliness of the spirit that glimpses the unexpressed suffering of another soul. Leo would never leave behind the conviction of divine love. It lived in him. He lived within its beautiful light filled source.

He was quickly replaced by a younger man in his mid-thirties. Fr Gerard Tuohy arrived in his cassock, and everything went from there. Another very reverend. The resilient people of this westerly peninsula just got on with it. The light-hearted natures of Maryann and Theresa were burdened at times and their tolerance sorely tested. His expectation of tea served upon each visit to the convent was too much for them, they refused on principle. Sister Anthony always picked up the slack and served it anyway.

When given the opportunity, they joined him with their own mug of tea, sat deliberately casual and attempted to engage him sometimes in issues of the day, the well-worn Humanae Vitae and the priest as servant or authority. He sighed, threw out the occasional comment but would not be drawn. They read *The Journey of the Magi* to him. 'I don't do poetry' was his response.

'But you must!' Maryann protested, 'the scriptures are full of poetry!'

'Ah yes but the scriptures are divinely inspired.'

'And that is why you must see the layers Fr Gerard.'

'There is no duplicity in God,' he replied

'No, no, there is mystery but that requires imagination!' Theresa couldn't help herself.

I smiled to myself as I listened to them recounting their experience. I recognised much of my younger often unexpressed self. My formation was less informed than theirs. The vow of obedience was understood as the suppression of self as distinct from a free and more meaningful giving of oneself. I am old enough now to recognise the battles worth taking on. Fr Gerard and his assumptions was not one of them.

***

It was around this time when I first began to consider the possibility of new horizons. Doors were opening, counselling, facilitation, retreat direction, pastoral work. I had no idea what. I came across many mothers with little social contact burdened with a lot of hard work. The one woman who had immediate connection with the girls who came through the doors of Scoil Mhuire was Peggy. She had a keen eye for the less obviously isolated or oppressed. She put things in place. Drew my attention when I failed to notice, but once she left work, her heart expressed itself in her brushstrokes. Every few months she travelled to The Dandelion Market in Dublin selling her paintings. A whole new world awaited her. She enjoyed the colours, the smells and the people she met there.

'Echoes of London, Camden Market,' she said, 'it still has the sixties vibe. The smell of incense and Tibetan bells around every corner.' She always came back invigorated.

We worked well together and pulled each other through many difficult moments. Sometimes we walked together sharing only the odd word taking in the air after a difficult day. We understood each other. But I also understood that Peggy had boundaries over which no one crossed. She was never offensive, but she rarely came to our Christmas or Summer gatherings. We never spoke so intimately again as that day in Kinoulty. Peggy had learned to keep her deepest self under lock and key. To remain her friend was to never ask.

***

Life inevitably rolled on. There were days in Winter when a melancholy came knocking on the door dressed in her slanted relentless rain. Days when the sea wasn't grey, it was angry. Sometimes at night you could almost hear the stillness beneath the whistling wind stripping the furze bushes bare. Yet, there were days too when the setting sun of a frosty dusk fanned out like a flame across the still surface of the sea and poured its gold into my heart.

It was on such an evening as I sat beneath my stained-glass Sower and before the altar of the Sacred Heart filled with such images, that I noticed Sister Paul was not sitting in her usual place before the tabernacle on the main altar, third row on the right, more or less parallel to me. We always shared this hour in quiet contemplation before retiring for the night. We might just smile at each other but usually we shared a few words before or after the hour. Others sometimes joined us but eight to nine pm was ours. Creatures of habit and otherwise busy. At peace with the world I fell into the deep prayer of gratitude, and longing for the healing of broken hearts. Only the distant gong marking bedtime stirred me.

Sister Paul had not come. As I passed enroute to my own room, I saw the light on within hers as it seeped out around the edges of her ill-fitting door. I knocked. The only sound I heard was the settling of the community around me. From Paul's room, nothing. An instinctive dread kicked in and I gently turned the handle on her unlocked door. There she was in an undignified, crumpled position on the floor, her right leg caught beneath her. Her left arm was outstretched. Her face lay to one side with her mouth open. I knew instantly that she was dead.

Her spirit was utterly gone. She had left us. Nonetheless, I tried for a pulse. Her hand though lukewarm was already turning blue. I raced down the stairs, grabbed the phone in the hall and rang Dr Larkin.

'I will be there in twenty minutes. I will notify the guards. Your breathing is erratic. You have had a shock, Cecilia. I suggest you have a cup of tea with sugar.'

My hands shook. Paul was our Reverend Mother. Who was now in charge? I made my way to the landing and struck the gong. One head peeped around a door in the distance. Sister Claire returning from the bathroom. I gave two or three good blasts until all ten of us, now nine stood anxiously in the half moon landing.

'Our beloved Sister Paul is gone…' I tremored.

'Gone? Gone? Where exactly?' Sister Francis uttered, already knowing the answer.

'She's dead. I found her a few moments ago in her room.'

There was a collective intake of breath followed by sobbing.

'What do you want us to do Cecilia?' Anthony asked.

I went into autopilot.

'Dr Larkin is going to be here very shortly probably along with Sergeant O'Dea. Get dressed as quickly as possible. Anthony, please sit with Paul and pray for her. Maryann, go down to the kitchen and put on the kettle. It is probably going to be a long night. Theresa, go now and prepare yourself to meet Dr Larkin and Sergeant O'Dea when they arrive. Show them up.'

'I cannot believe this is happening.' Sister Francis' voice cracked. 'I know that Anthony and I would like to prepare her for burial.'

'Yes, yes we would,' Anthony was staring into the middle distance.

I put my hand forward and held Francis' hand. 'I'm afraid that is not possible tonight. Our dear Sister Paul will be removed to the hospital mortuary in Kinoulty. A post-mortem will have to be carried out to establish the cause of death. That is why Sergeant O'Dea is coming. It is required by law.'

'Surely not,' Sister Elizabeth sounded upset and indignant, 'they are taking her away?'. And she sobbed.

'It is standard practice in this situation. We are going to need each other now. Paul's family will have to be informed. There is a lot to do.' I was about to suggest that all nine of us would kneel with her for a few moments in prayer when I realised that some of the community would find the sight that greeted me too difficult. I also wanted to leave Sister Paul her dignity. Before any further thoughts were formed, Elizabeth had already dropped to her knees. We all followed suit reciting the prayer for the dead. It was brief and it was moving.

'Okay, let's go.'

***

Sister Paul had died of a catastrophic brain haemorrhage. Had she survived she would have been left incapacitated. It would take us some time to accept that her death was a happy release. We offered mass for her in the convent chapel the following morning as dawn broke. Exhausted we faced the day and as the news broke among the community it was clear that Sister Paul's requiem mass would be celebrated in the parish church. She had been principal of the school for over thirty years. On retirement, she visited the homes of those who lived alone or in trying circumstances, often negotiating with services on behalf of those who were not able.

There were two old and weathered bachelors, Paddy Moses and Mickey Joe, shy men, who rarely stepped outside the confines of their small holding and never outside their parish. Bent with the damp, their neighbours left bread, milk and sometimes a cooked dinner on their doorstep, at Christmas a few bottles of stout and a small ham. Two or three were given the privilege of a chair amongst the detritus of their lives in their darkened kitchens. Sister Paul was one of them. On the day of her burial, they stood at the back under an arch edging the main entrance to the church. Both were formally dressed in suits that had not seen the light of day probably since they buried their mother or father, their white shirts yellowed at the collar and wrists. Their single tie black. That sight moved me beyond tears. All the wordy tributes washed over me. Paddy Moses and Mickey Joe possessed me that day.

Later that evening we sat together in our community room. First in silence fully entering the pause in this time of grief and change. Then in a tender solidarity we took care of Francis and Anthony who had taken their professional vows with Sister Paul nearly 56 years before. They were bereft. Sister Elizabeth had been appointed reverend mother. Elizabeth was the quiet woman amongst us, yet each of us could point to a moment when she had shown strength. Nonetheless, she seemed overwhelmed. She still taught art in the school but was nearing retirement. She would finish out the year. Now I knew that if I could at all, I would also change direction.

20

The Poisoned Tree

It took some time to recover from the exhaustion sudden death brings. We were considerate and kind, utterly tolerant of each other for our irritations had not changed. We looked in faith for the signs of Spring and new life in the lengthening of days with the low light over the sea. A certain weight began to shift. It was late March deep in the recesses of Lenten fasting and prayer, deep in the lull of my own sleep that an insistent knock on my bedroom door woke me. It was Elizabeth.

'What is it Elizabeth? What time is it?'

'It is three o'clock.'

'The hour of the dead,' I whispered out of my unconscious mind. I have never regarded myself as superstitious.

'The hour of the dead,' Elizabeth repeated in a dreamlike trance. Then more formally, 'your brother James is on the phone. I said you would ring him back, but he insists it won't wait and neither would he disclose his purpose.'

'James, is it?' I grabbed my dressing gown and ran but stopped on the turn of the stairs to take a second, my heart racing with the sense of dread. 'Lord whatever it is, whatever lies before me now, be with me,' and on I went. Elizabeth followed on shortly behind. Gesticulating to me she indicated that I should lift the new extension in the parlour. Pushing open the heavy oak door, I stepped on to the mahogany floor and lifted the phone handle. I heard the click of Elizabeth's disconnection from the hall as I gushed 'James is that you?'

'It is.'

'Is it Mammy?'

'It is.'

I left out a cry.

'She is gone Mary. She is gone. I am sorry. I am sorry.'
'Oh James,' I cried, 'tell me it's not true.'
'It is Mary, I'm afraid. But don't worry. We are all here with her now. Angela and Martha would do you proud. They have whispered the Act of Contrition in her ear and are gently saying the rosary beside her.'
'Did she die at home James?'
'Yes. Why would you think otherwise? I promised you I would let you know if Mammy was sick or in hospital.'
'Yes, you did.'
'Tom is on his way from London.'
I felt a sibling jealousy rise at being the last to be informed. Ashamed, I dismissed it.
'What happened, James?'
'The truth is we don't know. She went to bed early. She said she was tired. She looked pale but nothing too out of the ordinary. Martha got up to go to the bathroom and noticed Mammy's slipper near her bedroom door. She just checked. The lamp was still on and her magazine open on the bed, but Mammy was stretched across the pillows as if she fell sideways while sitting upright. That's when we were called.'
'What do you think happened?'
'It's hard to know.'
'I wish I was there.'
'But you're not and you can't be.'
'I am on my way.'
'Really Mary, there is no point. Dr Murphy is with Mammy now. The ambulance is waiting to take her, and the guards are just arriving.'
I knew the drill all too well. 'Okay James, I know this scene. We had a similar situation with Sister Paul just over six weeks ago.'
'You did? I am sorry to hear this, Mary.'
'It doesn't matter James. I am just saying I understand. But I want to come home,' I felt myself behaving irrationally, like the child in me was breaking out and stamping her feet. I gushed on 'I was barely there for Martha's death. I wasn't there for Daddy's. Things have changed. I want to be there for Mammy's.'
'I won't go down this route with you Mary but fine! If that's what you want, fine! You have always made your own choices.'
'Oh James, I'm sorry. I just want to be with my family.'

'Okay Mary, I hear you but there is no point in you coming until Mammy is returned to us.'

'I want to be with you and Tom. There are only the three of us now.'

'Mary, there are only two. You chose another family a long time ago.'

It stung like a hornet's venom. 'James, what are you saying?'

'You could have been there for Martha.'

'Martha? Martha died suddenly. No one could have known!'

'That's right Mary. She did. I am sorry. I am just upset. That's all. Martha was found in her bed and now, Mammy. It is bringing up a lot, that's all. If you want to come home, come home Mary. We will find a bed for you.'

'I am sorry too James. You have more than enough to deal with right now. I won't come home immediately. You all need some space. But I will come home before the funeral. I want to be there to receive Mammy home.'

'Okay Mary. We have not even thought about arrangements.'

'I will ring you later on when we all have had time to think. Please give Mammy a kiss on the forehead for me before she goes in the ambulance.'

'Can't touch her Mary. You can give her a kiss when she comes home.'

'That's right. I am not thinking straight. Thank you, James.'

'None of us are Mary. Take it easy.'

Thank you, James. For everything. Give your Martha a hug for me.'

'I will. I will surely.'

***

Elizabeth was waiting in the hall.

'I have the kettle on. Let's slip down to the kitchen.'

We sat on stools on either side of the well-scrubbed table where all the baking was done.

A cup of steaming, sugary tea sat before me but I neither saw nor drank it, so fast were the tears that flowed. I sobbed so that I could hardly catch my breath.

'Your mother,' Elizabeth spoke as a matter of fact rather than question.

Between the sobs, 'my mother,' I cried.

'Yes, nothing like the loss of your mother.' She gently tapped my hand and sat silently until the tsunami had subsided. 'Drink the tea. It will help. Ordinary things do when all else is out of control.'

'I won't drive now.'

'Good decision.'

'But I will go some time tomorrow.'

'Oh, you can discuss all that with your family. I take it, it was sudden?'

'Yes.'

'Like Paul's.'

'Yes.'

'That's hard.'

'Hmm... it is,' I gritted.

'Okay, here's the hot water bottle. Do not get up for morning mass. We will do the praying for you and for your family. Forget about everything for the next few hours. You will need stamina to face all this.'

'Thank you,' was all I was capable of uttering. The small child was still with me and Elizabeth had her firmly by the hand.

'Let the head rest. Our thoughts are no good when they are scattered.'

I fell beneath the blankets. My head hurt. James' words flowed in every direction, but I could not make any sense of them. I eventually fell into a fitful sleep. When I awoke, the light behind the curtains announced it was morning. The silence of the house suggested it was later than I realised. All were gone about their duties. My head no longer hurt. My heart was paining me.

Half an hour later I found myself sitting in my usual space before the side altar of the Sacred Heart. I had slipped down like a ghost avoiding all contact. I felt weary. I felt I was disappearing. I did not lie prostrate before the altar as I had done in response to Martha's death. I had no need of the dramatic gesture, and I was too exhausted. I could not pray. Scattered words and phrases wandered in and out of my focus:

Mammy

My God, my God, why have you forsaken me?

You are my lovely daughter, and you are here now...

Mammy I am sorry. I am sorry I was not there.

Deep in Thy wounds Lord,

Hide and shelter me...

You can give her a kiss when she comes home...

It was the images that dominated. Our last encounter: the rain drenched grass outside the open door as we spoke, her curious eyes when searching for the robin that had just disappeared behind the potted begonias, how she raised her lovely long hands sweeping them in half circles to express herself, the laughing exchanges which her barbed comments provoked, her gentle revelation of an experience of peace at my final profession. It was like a gift now and I leaned back resting in the lap of God.

Then within moments the tense exchange with James resonated. I found it hard to name what it was that lay between us. I knew we were good. We trusted each other. Yet, the carefree affectionate relationship we had when throwing conkers at each other or helping each other stacking hay was well and truly gone. It is inevitable that childhood days end. This felt different.

Some poison lay between us that I failed to understand. It seemed apparent to me now that he never wanted me to become a nun and had never accepted my decision. That is how I interpreted *'you have always made your own choices.'* I both regretted and accepted it was a price I had to pay. With some spiritual pomposity, even now in my wiser years, I regarded it as the necessary sacrifice of one who gives herself to God. I was soon to discover it was an empty assumption.

V

21

The Crushed Reed Revisited

I relished the sight of the turbulent sea and the crashing waves against the cliffs beyond as I drove the two kilometres along the coast road before turning right for Kinoulty. A three-hour drive lay ahead of me, and I was glad of the silence. Anger alone might have driven me. A full thirty hours had passed. I had burnt a few bridges.

I was embraced by the easy affection of Theresa and Maryann, spontaneous in their expressions of sorrow on my behalf. They, along with (now) Mother Elizabeth, had come back to the convent during school lunch hour. I had eaten early under the attentive eyes of Anthony, a bowl of soup, toast and tea. I could not manage the haddock served. I had hoped to escape quickly and quietly to pack, leave and avoid questions for which I had no answers, some of which I knew I needed.

Establishing funeral arrangements, a simple bed to sleep in, I had looked up the yellow pages for accommodation near our farm and identified one I thought suitable. I needed to talk with James. Simple stuff really but nothing is simple when a family is overwrought.

'Any idea of the funeral arrangements?' Theresa asked brightly.

'No,' I almost whispered

'Well how could you know 'til the hospital releases your mother,' she continued answering her own question.

'I just want you to know we are here for you,' Maryann offered helpfully but then continued 'when are you going home? This afternoon, I suppose. Would you like company? Consider it done if you would.'

The very queries I was trying to avoid were out in the ether awaiting a response. Elizabeth responded: 'Cecilia and I will discuss all this after lunch and let you know.'

A heavy silence fell around us.

I made my excuses and left them to their main course after Elizabeth announced that she would be available to meet me in the parlour in half an hour. It was a directive. I sat at my desk in my room and wondered where the warm woman of the night before had gone. Paul had never been so dictatorial and had rarely met any of us in the parlour. Perhaps Elizabeth was just establishing her authority before the younger sisters. I didn't know. I didn't care. I had other concerns.

I packed my bag including my formal navy suit and left it at the foot of my bed before making my way downstairs to meet Elizabeth.

'How are you, Cecilia?' she greeted me with concern, yet her tone was formal. I felt compelled to provide some answer, though I barely grasped how I felt.

'I'm okay.'

'Good. Your duties are being attended to by Mrs Hannon. She is a very capable lady.'

'Yes, she is,' I demurred.

'Always good to have capable people at times like this, don't you agree Cecilia?'

Though baffled by the conversation I replied, 'I do.'

'Now, to your own situation.'

'Situation?'

'Yes. Do you have any idea of your plans yet?'

'I will ring James after this conversation, but I have my bag packed and I intend to leave in the next hour.'

'I don't think that will be possible.'

'Why not?'

'I am not available until late tomorrow afternoon. It is my intention to travel with you as befits the occasion.'

'I would like to be with my family today! I also want to receive my mother's body home. That is likely to be tomorrow morning.'

'But you don't know that for certain, do you?'

'No, but under the circumstances I would like to have time alone with my family.'

'It is a long journey, and a companion is good in times like these.'

I could feel the panic rise. 'Yes, but...'

'No buts, I insist! I have been given the responsibility to oversee my community. I insist I travel with you and pay respects to your family.'

'I insist you don't!' I could feel my voice separating from my body.

'My word Cecilia! You insist I do not come!'

'No, no absolutely. Please come and pay your respects as you would have it. I very much appreciate that. Truly! But I want to leave this evening by the latest. Please Elizabeth.'

'I will have to think about this. It is a matter of profound regret to me that you question my judgement.'

'I am not questioning your judgement at all! I just want some personal time with my family.'

'There is the practical matter of two cars. If you take one, we are left with only one should issues arise. I have a responsibility to the entire community, not just to you.'

'Yes, yes, I understand. I can take the bus to Kinuolty and get the train to Dublin. I can organise for my nephew to wait and pick me up there. Today's bus is already gone. That would mean not getting home until tomorrow evening.'

'Exactly! So, whether you wait for me or get the bus and train and make your own arrangements, it will be the same thing!'

'No, no it won't. I will miss the possibility of receiving my mother's body home.' I could feel the tears stinging my eyes but the anger I felt at the fences being placed before me, prevented me from showing them.

'Maybe a phone call to your brother would sort all of this out. Why don't you make that call?'

'That is my intention.'

'I will be finished with some paperwork here in half an hour. You can call him then. James, isn't it? The boy at home?

'Yes.'

'It will all work out in the end. You know that don't you Cecilia?'

'I hope so,' was all I could muster.

And thus, the afternoon slid from me as easily as melted butter from a hot spoon.

***

'Hello Sister Mary'

'Angela, is it?'

'Yes, yes. We have a bed here for you. When will you come?'

'I would be there by now if I could. Right now, I am not sure of my times.'

'Oh?'

'If I can at all I will leave this evening, otherwise it will be the morning.'
'I see.'
'It's complicated'
'Yes, I'm sure,' but Angela did not sound convinced.
'If you need the bed for anyone else, please feel free. I have found a B&B a mile away…'
'That would be Joan's but there is no question of it whatsoever.'
'That is very kind of you,' I could hear the tremor in my voice
'Sister Mary…'
'Mary, please!'
'Mary, this is your mother. You are coming home to the house where you grew up.'
'Thank you,' I whispered.
'Not at all. The only thing is you will sleep in your mother's bedroom. It is the only one we have. Martha is very upset, and we couldn't ask her to move.'
'Of course, I understand, but is Mammy not being laid out at home?'
'No. The removal will be from Costelloe's Funeral Home.'
'Costelloe's?'
'Yeah. Joe Costelloe. He set up the funeral home ten years ago. Yes, you would not be aware of that.'
'Joe Costelloe the publican?'
'Yes, the very one.'
'And why not at home?'
'It's just… it's just too difficult.'
'Difficult?'
'She will be coming home but to family only. The notice goes into the paper tomorrow. The house will be strictly private.'
'Strictly private?'
She sighed. 'Yeah, yeah, none of this is easy.'
'I suppose not,' I sighed almost in resignation, feeling myself disappear again. 'When are they releasing Mammy?'
'Tomorrow. Hopefully the morning but it could be the afternoon.'
'I would like to be there when she comes.'
'I am sure James and Tom would like you to be here too.'
'Is Tom home?'
'He should be arriving in the next hour. He flew from London into

Dublin and landed an hour ago.'

'Oh, okay,' I longed to be there.

'James is with the undertaker now. Would you like him to call you? I know he is anxious to speak with you and Tom. It is hard for him to make decisions around funeral arrangements on his own.'

'Yes, I am sure it is. I have to say I am surprised that the wake will not be at home.'

'I think that was something Tom and he agreed a long time ago.'

'Really?'

'Look, I could be wrong. Memory makes fools of us all.'

'Yes.' We both knew Angela was back-tracking.

'You think you will be here to receive your mother's body home?'

'Most definitely.'

'I have to go. The neighbours have been calling all day.'

'Give Tom and James my love.'

'I will.' And she was gone with a click.

Elizabeth had disappeared. she was probably back at the school. I could not move until I had her consent and some sense of her intentions. I grabbed my coat and headed out down the back road to Lough Dubh. The bracing wind was bitter and in spite of my tightly tied hood, it seemed to find its way around my body. Yet the silence beneath its gales, the old stone walls, the rusted gates, the abandoned sheds I had just passed, all seemed to console and make real my own passing humanity. 'Mammy,' I cried openly on the empty road.

'Mary,' she seemed to cry back to me in the sudden gust of clustered gales. I must have walked five miles before landing back in time for tea.

'Oh Cecilia, I thought you would be gone by now,' Theresa looked at me curiously. Elizabeth glanced at me. But boldly I replied,

'So did I!'

'Arrangements at short notice are never straightforward,' Elizabeth was in like a shot.

'Nobody chooses the hour of their death,' I replied, 'death will always be an inconvenience.'

'We all understand that death is so much more than this Cecilia,' Elizabeth replied in an even tone. I felt silly. The air was stifled.

Anthony emerged from the kitchen, 'I have made your favourite! Bread and Butter pudding with custard.'

A tear fell for her compassion. Silence. Anthony put her hand on my shoulder. 'Take heart Cecilia. The Lord will not crush the bruised reed.' The depth of her words touched my soul, and I knew immediately that this is the landscape, the only landscape, where I could negotiate the rage and loneliness within me.

'Please excuse me.'

I left and made my way to sit beneath my favourite stained glass of the farmer sowing his seed in the furrows as the sun rose. The browns, the greens, the amber. The earnest simplicity of the roughhewn man, his thick shoes, his kemp trousers, his well-worn hat, his broad hands spreading the seed from the sack strapped across his shoulders. It was a grey March day and the setting sun outside did nothing to illuminate the colours. The image was already burned within me. I had no need of any sun to let it shine more brilliantly than it did in the late afternoon when its rays filter the glass on cloudless days. All those I knew and loved came to meet me: Daddy, Mammy, Martha, James, Tom. I fell into a fitful sob and covered my eyes:

Lord, my heart is torn. I have no words. I understand nothing. After all these years. After all this dedication. Nothing! James! What do I have to do to understand you? To help you understand me. What is it that ails you? Is it me?

I suddenly realised that I had mixed feelings about going back to the homestead. I longed for it and dreaded it too. What would it be without Mammy? I knew that hole on its own could swallow me. Why in these latter years did I always feel the edge of a sharp word whenever I encountered James?

I am tired. I am not able.

I put my head back and sighed into the darkness. I remained there for a long time. Not a sound. Not a word. All cried out, I raised my head and opened my eyes to meet the flame of the sanctuary lamp.

At that moment I realised, I don't have to be… I don't have to be anything. I don't have to be able. Nothing is the right word. Nothing at all depends on me. Love or fear will carry me. That is all. I sat in the darkness for a long time just imagining all the fear leaving my body. I wanted love, only love. The stone began to shift. 'Thank you, Anthony,' I whispered into the dark, 'for bringing me back to myself.'

I resolved to accept whatever Elizabeth had planned and in so doing accept that she was some place on her journey that I could not, nor did I need to, understand. I would manage. Love alone would help me manage. I knew this love. I had experienced it. It was liberating. In the end, Elizabeth decided that it was unnecessary for me to wait another twenty-four hours, and the community would manage without a car.

'In the event of something unforeseen, Paddy has agreed to provide a backup service. You do understand that this is not something I could presume upon because we no longer use his services.'

I nodded. She asked me to book bed & breakfast with our neighbour Joan O'Dea. I happily acceded to this request. The sisters would arrive the following day for the wake and stay for the funeral.

James, and maybe even Tom, were of deeper concern. I knew I would have to meet the moment. As the sea disappeared in my rearview mirror I headed for home, the images of the past two days washing over me. My chaotic feelings were beginning to settle. I felt ready, insofar as one could be. I had a brief call with James that morning. We both cried. Mammy's body was arriving home in the early afternoon. There was anger still in me, but it was no longer about Elizabeth. It was about loss. I put my foot on the accelerator.

22

The Long Goodbye

The sun came out from behind the windswept clouds as I glimpsed the house at the end of the lane. 'The Boys' as I would come to call them, James' sons, hung around the front door. Dan, at least an inch taller than when we had last met less than a year ago, approached as I swung around and asked me to park to the side of the house. The hearse was due. Action all round, he opened the door of my car and whipped out my small luggage bag -

'Are these to come in too?'

'What?'

'The boxes?'

'Yes, just two cooked chickens and two fruit cakes Anthony and Francis sent up.'

'Great. This watching duty has us all on edge and all starved.'

I couldn't help smiling. He was so like Tom in his spontaneity.

'I'll take care of this.' Then more gently, 'granny is due any minute, it won't be long.'

His urgency prepared me as I stepped out. Peter came towards me, another tall, broad shouldered, thin man with a tuft of thick blonde hair falling across his high forehead. Stretching out his hand,

'Peter,' he said. 'We missed each other on your last visit.'

'That is right. The architect in Dublin,' I already detested the reference as I heard myself speaking.

'Not quite there yet.'

'But you will be. You will be.' Our spurious talk was cut short as the hearse turned into the gateway. I had no time to think. I was taken aback by the inner lights that illuminated the coffin. A lump formed in my throat. My heart began to race. James, Tom, Angela and Martha poured out. Angela stood with her children on one side of the main door.

'Quickly Mary', Tom pointed to the gap he and James had created between them.

We stood as sister and brothers, a guard of honour on the opposite side. We held hands. Mine were cold, James' were calloused yet had the sweat of a man under pressure, Tom's were big and swallowed my palms. I squeezed each on either side. The squeeze was reciprocated. James turned to me and smiled. Silence descended. The wind blew about us, but the sun held out. No one stirred.

After a few moments, Joe Costelloe Jnr stepped out and with the aid of his son Martin unscrewed the coffin from the floor of the hearse, easily sliding it onto the waiting trolley. It was clearly a light load. They pushed it a few feet over the gravel when the boys stepped forward. We will take it from here. Just as they shouldered her coffin, Tom coughed as if to clear his throat. He let go of my hand, threw his head back, shut his eyes and began to sing our mother's favourite *Let the Rest of the World Go By*.

He squeezed his eyes tightly, as if, had he opened them, his voice would fail. Though he struggled, his notes were strong and clear and immediately brought back so many memories of one of our Christmas traditions when we had a sing song after dinner. Mammy always started it off, a small sherry in her hand, she began very softly:

Is the struggle and strife
We find in this life
Really worthwhile, after all?
I've been wishing today
I could just run away,
Out where the west winds call.

My heart splintered into a thousand pieces. James whipped his hand from mine and began to sob uncontrollably. Angela looked alarmed and Martha pained to watch her dad so upset. It was clear she had rarely if ever seen her dad cry. By the final verse we all joined Tom in his delivery:

We'll build a sweet little nest somewhere in the west
And let the rest of the world go by.

She was placed to the right of the front door into what used to be the parlour, now a snug for James and Angela with its upholstered couch, Queen Anne chair and small television in the corner. On this occasion, apart from simple fresh greenery on the windowsills, the room was stripped bare. We were asked to wait outside as the undertakers prepared Mammy for 'viewing'. That awful term. That awful word. We just wanted to hold her hand and kiss her goodbye. As the door opened Martha stepped forward.

'Martha,' Angela called gently, 'leave it to Daddy, uncle Tom and auntie Mary.'

'Just leave me do this Mammy. I promise it will only take a few seconds.'

And that is all it did, as she stepped in and placed a small posy of fresh narcissus and crocuses at Mammy's feet. She did not even attempt to look up. She, Angela and the boys made their way to the kitchen. The three of us stood in that room stunned by the scene before us. There was Mammy, thin and beautiful and very dead. The life force, gone. A present absence. We were tense in our grief. James placed his hand across her cold forehead. Tom took her hand. I stood at her feet. Simple pearl beads interlaced her fingers. I recognised them as the beads Martha, and I had received for our communion a lifetime ago.

'That's a nice touch,' I whispered.

'What? Yes, Martha's beads.'

'Are they Martha's? Did they not go with her?'

'No,' James gulped, 'curiously, Mammy insisted she wanted something of yours to go with Martha. Her two girls,' she used to say, 'her two girls.' He shook from the sobs that followed. Tom quickly put his arm around his brother's shoulders and led him to the window where they both stood looking out toward the birdbath in the side garden where the finches and the wagtails chattered. That intimacy between them was beautiful and painful.

They wanted me included. We loved each other but I was outside their significant experience of shared grief. I felt my stomach fill with a deep-seated anxiety, but I resolved to remain strong, held my mother Maeve's hand and bent to give her that kiss on the forehead I had so longed for. Just as I finished there was a tap on the door.

'Aunt Kathleen is on her way. Sheila will be here in an hour.'

'So much for "house strictly private",' James sounded irritated.

'They are family James. In fact, your uncle Jim is coming from Athlone this evening. I think the last time we saw him was at our wedding! You are going to have to grin and bear it. They have their memories too.'

'What would I do without you Angela?'

'I don't know,' she smiled. 'She looks lovely, if you can say that about … about her now. Then she always was.'

'Was what?' asked Tom distractedly.

'Beautiful really,' Angela trailed off.

'You're right Ange, you're right,' Tom stood with his hands in his pockets. 'Do you remember Seamus Moloney?'

'Who?' Angela replied

'The photographer?' I proffered.

'Yeah him. He had a fierce crush on Mammy, always wanted to take her picture. Any local event she ended up in the paper. Do you remember? Point to Points or summer festivals or the dog show, God forbid, even when she didn't have a dog!' We all giggled.

'That's right!' I had forgotten.

'Dad didn't fancy him much,' James threw in with his back to us.

'Could you blame him?' Angela smirked.

'Era, Seamus Moloney never stood a chance!' James swooped around and winked at Angela. The mood lightened.

***

The evening passed around the kitchen table regaling stories of mammy. Her favourite colour, yellow. Her first and only visit to a cinema in her later years to see Richard Harris in *Camelot*. Her love of music: John Mc Cormac, Louis Armstrong, Duke Ellington, Sean O'Riada: '*Mise Eire*' all said spontaneously when his name was thrown up. I did not know this. I was the outsider now. Their natural spontaneity made me feel it even more. I felt stripped bare, but I suppressed the knot of grief I felt rising in my chest. The flow went on. And of course, her party piece.

'You had us all in tears there Tom!' James threw out.

'Couldn't let the moment pass,' he replied

'You were right Tom. It was fitting. Heartbreaking but fitting,' I smiled.

We discussed how no one ever underestimated her when playing cards. Her passion for Michael Collins. Her refusal to ever discuss the civil war. We acknowledged that there were areas of our parents' lives about which we knew little. That was a painful realisation.

Uncle Jim asked for a few moments on his own with Maeve. He came into the kitchen leaning on his cane, looking a little more bent, tears in his eyes declaring, 'Maeve was the best of sister-in-laws. Jack was very lucky to meet her. Don't get me wrong. Jack was, if I may say so, a handsome man and a great provider. Just look around you! But sometimes he was stubborn. It was his way or the highway. But Maeve brought out the best in him. He died so young. Too much! Poor Maeve. May God be good to her', he sighed. Changing the mood he asked, is there 'Is there a drop of whiskey going? Who is this tall chap?'

'I'm John,' and so the evening grew into night.

Sheila had called earlier with her husband Rob. She left after an hour. Said she would come back early the following day before mammy left for the funeral home. She had aged substantially. I don't know what I expected. The pictures in my head were out of date. She approached me briefly and with her lifelong warmth.

'Ah Mary. It has been so long,' she said as she looked at me with her outstretched hands on my shoulders before she drew me to her for a hug. 'Martha's funeral, wasn't it?'

'Yes,' I said

'Such an awful business.'

'Yes,' I almost whispered, 'tragic.'

'And then your father! He had so many regrets.'

'Regrets?'

'Around Martha.' I must have looked puzzled, 'you know … that she did not complete the studies she loved so much.'

'But how could she? She died.'

She looked at me hard. 'That's right,' she said firmly and then 'and he died of a broken heart.'

'Yes, he did,' I said, 'no other explanation.'

'I don't know how your mother survived it at all. After your father's death, she rarely left the house.'

'Really?'

'Yes. Apart from your final profession. That took serious effort.'
'Did it?'
'Yes, but she would not have missed it for the world. "I want to acknowledge my daughter"; she would say because she had refused weddings and funerals. "Mary, my lovely Mary."'

I could feel the tears welling. 'Oh, don't mind me *raimeising*. I will see you tomorrow.' And with that she was gone. Tom passed her as she left.

'Sheila made a hasty exit,' confirming what I thought I was imagining.

***

As was customary, we made a rota as to who would sit with Mammy overnight. It was agreed that Angela and Martha were off duty as they were preparing breakfast the following morning. Three chairs were placed to accommodate the boys who insisted on sitting out the rota together from ten to midnight. We volunteered for two-hour slots. Mine began at midnight and ended at two, followed by Tom and James and the boys again from six a.m. Tom produced a bottle of twelve-year-old Redbreast. Eight glasses were produced and handed out to each of us as we stood around Mammy's remains. Though there was some to-ing and fro-ing as the whiskey was being poured, a kind of spontaneous consensus was reached that, as James suggested, each of us would give one recollection of Mammy.

We started with the grandchildren. Martha mentioned her first doll. John, her hat with the pheasant feather to the side, Peter, the look she gave you that said you were dead. We all laughed. Dan, her smell. He had her jumper wrapped around his neck. Angela, the day her mother-in-law approached her and gently handed her, her string of pearls to wear on her wedding day. Tom, preparing the vegetables with her on Christmas morning as a teenager. James, the morning she found a distressed cat at the back door and helped her deliver her kitten. I, the last conversation we had together, the contentment I found within her.

'To Mammy,' Tom raised his glass

'To Mammy,' we repeated, and all drank down our undiluted shot of whiskey.

***

I was glad to rest for two hours in the bed my mother slept and died in. She loved me and I her. I did not allow myself to consider anything else. I slipped down at midnight and sent the boys to bed. Peter kindly offered to stay but I insisted he go and took out my breviary to pray.

Ant 1: The Lord will guard you from every evil, He will guard your soul.
Ant 2: If you, O Lord, should mark our guilt, Lord who would survive?

And so, I prayed for over an hour with images of my mother's life dancing around my words. Then I sat, my hand resting on the edge of her coffin beside hers. I could feel myself nodding off when Tom walked in and sat on the chair opposite. 'Go on off to bed Mary. You are going to need your energy for tomorrow.' I agreed. As I turned to go, he said, 'Glad you are here. It makes a difference.'

'So am I Tom. So am I,' I replied. As I climbed the stairs, I reflected on what my absence had cost. My mind was working on adrenalin. I fell in and out of sleep and eventually decided to rise. I descended the stairs at five thirty a.m. with the intention of joining James. Maybe I knew what I was doing, maybe not.

23

What is Truth?

*'My heart is moved by all I cannot save,
So much has been destroyed…'*
—(Adrienne Rich)

'Tom, you're still up!'
'Yes I am.'
I glanced at a freshly opened bottle of Jameson and jug of water sitting on a small table below the sash window beyond the head of the coffin. Tom must have brought it in along with the kitchen chairs, two on either side of Mammy's remains. 'Well Mary, you will have a small Jameson.'

'I don't know. My head hurts. Maybe I will sort a cup of tea.'

'Go away with your tea Mary. 'Tis your heart that's hurting,' James threw me a glance.

'Come on Mary,' Tom softly intoned, 'how often do you get the chance to spend time with your brothers with no one else around?'

'Send that Sister Cecilia out the door Mary,' James scowled.

'Alright. I will have that whiskey, a small one but with white lemonade. I am not a whiskey drinker. I can't manage it with water.'

'Done,' said Tom as he left for the kitchen.

'Sit down Mary, sit down.'

'You know James, Cecilia is as deeply me as Mary. We are one and the same.'

'Aye sure I know. It's just the formality I associate with the name and with all that goes with that.'

'Like what?'

'Convent life and stuff.'

'Nuns?'

'Those too,' and we both laughed.

'It isn't like that at all.'

'Did I miss something?' Tom entered with a bottle of TK lemonade under his arm and some fruit cake on a plate. He handed me a glass. I sipped. It tasted mighty good at that moment in time.

'Well?' he queried.

'Oh, we were just talking about nuns,' James quipped.

'Oh, not that James. Leave it. Mary is Mary.'

'Not so Tom. She has just told me she is Cecilia too.'

'Of course she is. She didn't give her life up for nothing! Mary and Cecilia are one and the same person.'

'Thanks Tom but I didn't give my life up either. I am living a very particular life that's all. No either or, just different.'

'Well, I am glad to hear you did not give your life up, Mary. Not the way Martha did,' James spoke to the middle distance, his voice trailing off.

'For God's sake James don't go down that route,' Tom looked directly at James, but James turned his head.

'And why not?' His tone was sharp. He drained his glass and stood up staring out the window with his back to Tom and me.

'That was a very dark period in all of our lives. Leave it with the dead,' Tom pleaded.

'What is it they say about truth Tom?'

'What is the point? You are only causing more damage.'

'*The truth will set you free.*' James swung around and stared directly at me, 'Isn't that right Mary?'

'Yes, yes of course James,' I said weakly with the dread that had taken root now spreading across my chest.

'Well, our relationship has no future without you having the truth.'

'For God's sake James! She is here to bury her mother and if Mammy didn't say it, why should we?'

'Tell me James. Tell me it all.' I was resolved in my request. I could feel his resentment in every cell. I could not explain his obvious anger and implied judgement. I was beginning to feel angry myself

'Pour one more for me Tom. I am going to need this,' James held up his glass.

Tom's eyes caught mine. Pools of sadness surrounded him. 'Prepare yourself Mary. This is not easy.'

'Martha had a baby. Did you know that?' James was direct.

'Oh my God, no! Of course I did not know that.'

'Daniel was his name! But you didn't know that either did you?'

I drew my hand across my mouth. His words blew the roof right off me, but his anger pulled me into the torrent.

'Do you have to start there, James? Do you? Less of the cruelty. There has been enough of that!' Tom continued in more hushed tones 'It was September. I will never forget it. I had just returned to school. Martha was due to go back to UCC. David Carroll had spent the Summer in London earning money to pay for the costs of his final year. He was making good money working as a clerk in a post office, or something like that through some contact he had. He decided to stay on until the third week in September. Had he come home earlier it might have all been different.'

'I doubt it. Daddy was not for moving,' James was very matter of fact, almost confident like someone who had thought about this moment for a long time.

'Apparently Martha was worried, afraid she might be pregnant. But she said nothing. I do remember her being very quiet that summer,' Tom continued.

'Was that the Summer she went to Knock with Granny?' I heard myself ask.

'Yes. The only reason I remember is that she went without a word of objection which I thought was strange because granny was a bit of a dose at that stage.'

'She wrote to me. Asked me to pray for her. I thought that strange too…but I never imagined…'

'What exactly? That she needed help?' James intervened. 'Well, she did!' I felt myself disappearing.

He continued, 'Daddy lost it completely. Just lost it. I arrived back from the mart, and I heard shouting. Shouting! I had never heard a voice raised in this house. I ran into the kitchen and there was Martha in a corner crying uncontrollably. "Please Mammy, please!" she cried. Mammy stood at the threshold of the door as Daddy stormed up and down the hall. "He is no man of honour. He would not put his hand on my daughter in that way if he was." Martha went to stand up, "It wasn't like that! Please Daddy!"

"Wasn't it?" He was white with anger. Respect, respect, respect, it was about respect!

'Hah!' James threw his eyes up to heaven. 'I can still hear him. "No respect for you! Do you hear me, Martha? No respect for you or for your family." I had never seen him like that. To be honest I was stunned, Mary. I could feel my legs shaking so I can't imagine how Martha felt.

She pleaded again, "It wasn't like that Daddy, please."

"O but it was," he roared, "or you would not be in the fallen state you are in. Can you deny it?"

I remember that very clearly. It was like his words were preparing the trap she had to fall into.

"No," that's all she whispered. Not another word. She sounded defeated.

"David Carrol will never enter this house again. Do you hear me?" And that was that.'

James' account was so literal and so graphic it astonished me. The scene was clearly seared into his memory. He must have played it over and over. He barely took a breath:

'I was rooted to the spot. I understood very quickly what was going on. I was shocked at Martha's situation but even more shocked at Daddy's response.'

'What was Mammy doing?' I heard myself ask, but my voice felt dislocated from my body.

'Mammy appealed to Daddy. She begged him to calm down so they could get some time to think straight. He cried out that she was *ruined*. He threw his head back and sighed: "She is ruined. My beautiful daughter is ruined."

'What an awful term. But in fairness to Mammy, she fought back,'

"*Our* daughter Jack, our daughter. She is not ruined. We can manage this, please Jack, please!"

'Daddy did not seem to be able to see anyway forward. A tense silence descended. None of us moved. It was as if an invisible force held us to the spot. I don't know. I think we all felt scared. Yes, we were scared. That is the only word I can use to explain it all. We could have been in that state for ten or twenty minutes. It wasn't any less. It might have been more, but it seemed like an eternity.

"How? Tell me how?" Daddy collapsed at the bottom of the stairs and cried.

No one said a word. Total silence. Then Mammy gently suggested that there were places that helped families cope with these kinds of situations. But I could hear the panic in her voice. She kept repeating, "We just need time, Jack." But Daddy insisted that that was the one thing they did not have. The rage had left him as suddenly as it had arrived. I took the fire stool and sat beside Martha. She took my hand. We whispered together. Don't worry Martha, I told her.'

James bent his head forward brushing his hand through his hair. '"O my God, my life is over," was all she could say. She wailed into the tea towel on her lap. The thing is she was right. It was.'

***

Tom took up the story. 'I arrived all bright and breezy from school. I was after being picked for the school's Gaelic football team. Delighted with myself. I knew the minute I walked in the back door that the atmosphere was off. It was as if there had been a death in the house. There was no one I could talk with. Daddy was in this very room speaking in formal, even tones to Martha. I stood outside listening. I realised he was dictating. I barely heard Martha's voice. "Where?"

"Whittington Hospital London."

Whittington Hospital London? I thought to myself. *What is going on?* I knew better than to interrupt. I waited for over an hour. Mammy and James arrived home. They had been to see Dr Walsh where Mammy received a letter of recommendation to a nursing home for expectant mothers. James, to be fair, took me out the back to the barn where he explained all that was going on. I didn't even see Martha that day. She refused to come to tea and went straight to bed.'

'O my God! O my God!' I put my head in my hands. Please, please no more, just give me a few moments.

We all stared into oblivion. I stood with my back to my brothers and my dead mother looking out that beautiful window and listening to the dawn birds who chirped happily and so freely in the garden beyond. After some time and now on autopilot I reflected aloud, 'Poor Martha. She must have felt so alone.'

'And she was,' James stated matter of factly.

'What was Daddy dictating?' I asked.

'A letter to David. He did not want him anywhere near Martha in case it would complicate things,' James replied.

Tom continued, 'it was all nice and neat. Martha was going to the Navan Road in Dublin to see out her pregnancy and have her baby. The baby would be given up for adoption. Martha would eventually get her life back, but the important thing was not to let anyone know, not even in the extended family, so that her....'

'And of course the family's...' James interrupted

'...reputation was kept intact,' Tom threw his hands in the air and sighed.

'What was Mammy's position on all this?' My thoughts were racing. I was finding it difficult to concentrate.

'She said that there was no point in ruining two futures. David was a talented musician, hadn't we heard him ourselves playing his own composition and that she knew he loved Martha but burdening him with a child meant he would not finish his degree and probably leave him as a clerk and a frustrated, unhappy man for the rest of his days. She wasn't angry with him the way Daddy was. That is why she maintained her relationship with Martha and Daddy didn't.'

'That is true,' said Tom. 'Martha never spoke to Daddy again after he dictated that letter. Not a word.'

'Really! Not a word,' I was aghast.

'No, not a word,' James looked all in.

'Next evening I came home and called into Martha's room. She was lying on the bed, quiet and pale as a ghost. I lay across the end of the bed. "I don't know what to say to you Martha," I said. "I know," she said, "I have no words myself." But she was glad I was there. I promised to take care of her when I grew up.' Then his voice reduced to a whisper, Tom recollected, "Do you promise?" she smiled. I promise, I smiled back but I never got the chance...' Tom's head bowed as silent tears fell to his knees.

I swept over to him, leaned over his chair and put my arms across his chest. He caught my arms. We both cried. If only I could have done this for Martha, I thought to myself. The atmosphere in the room was raw.

***

'You may as well hear it all now,' James gulped.

'There is more! Please don't tell me there is more!'

'Well button up because there is,' James let out a sigh.

'I don't know that I am able for this James, not to mind Mary,' Tom put his hand up just as Mammy used to do.

'But you know the story Tom,' I looked at him.

'Exactly!' Tom replied.

James, ignoring us, continued: 'As I told you Martha gave birth to a baby boy, but he was not a candidate for adoption. He had a very slight hair lip. Martha told me later that it was in David's family. She had met his uncle Con, a tall man with a fine moustache to cover his lip. She loved that child. '"He was my own" she'd say, "he was my own flesh and blood, and I was forced to leave him." And that's when Mammy and Daddy parted ways.

'Parted ways? What do you mean?' I asked

'She came home at the end of March, six weeks after Daniel was born. She was as thin as ever. She begged every day to bring him home. "Who is looking after him now?" she pleaded. But Daddy would not agree. He said that all this effort had been made to save her reputation, that she should think of her sister too who would be equally destroyed if word got out. There had to be another way.'

I felt my stomach collapse.

'Mammy fought hard. She asked him what way he could think of to save their grandson. It was the first time I heard her use this word. I was delighted with her. Daddy was softer in his tone. He always addressed her as Maeve when he was soft and serious. I used to regard it as a kind of romance. Now I realise just how much he depended upon her. He was lost without her agreement. He said it was *unfortunate*. For God's sake!' James threw his hands up in despair.

'Unfortunate?' I asked

'The plan had been that by then Daniel would be with… How is this he put it?... *with some fine family being reared as their own*. He appealed that that was his intention all along' James crossed his legs and leaned back. 'It was hard to tell if he was trying to convince himself or Mammy. She was having none of it!

"But he isn't Jack. He is on his own in a home above in Dublin." She put her head in her hands and cried at the kitchen table. I can see it all like it was yesterday. He stretched his hands across and caught hers. She looked directly at him. That's when Daddy agreed that they could do better than a home in Dublin. The plot was hatched. Mammy put the wheels in motion. She was not for turning. I guess she had her regrets too. Daddy was embarrassed and uncomfortable, but he agreed that they would go to see Sheila and Rob in Ballinrobe. Martha was not allowed to travel. They left early in the morning and came home late that evening. They both looked stressed. They spoke only once: "Sheila has agreed to take your baby. Rob needs a few days to discuss it with her. Understandable." Martha was hanging on every word. She no longer cared what anyone thought of her. She just wanted Daniel to be given a chance. Rob and Sheila arrived a week later and said that they would do it. That is when Sheila took complete control. She was so loving to Martha and to be fair so was Rob.'

'Yes,' Tom added, 'I was coming downstairs when I overheard Rob saying to Martha "I promise, when he comes to my house, he will be my own son." Rob is very decent but not exactly the huggable type and Martha threw both her arms around him. He seemed genuinely moved.'

'So, what happened? Where is Daniel?' Tom and James exchanged glances.

'The women agreed to get him. Sheila drove in their old Ford with Mammy beside her with a parcel of fresh clothes for the baby. Mammy told me years after that they were apprehensive. She went into town the day before and rang from Dr Walsh's phone. For confidentiality you see. She did not trust the public phones. I imagine she needed his support. She spoke with a Sister Bernadine who seemed on edge. She implied that the baby has been unwell. She mentioned fever and weight loss. She was defensive. She suggested that they come the following week. Mammy would not agree. She put down the phone and ran to Daddy and Martha waiting outside in the trap. "Now! We have to leave now, right now, straight to Ballinrobe." '

James continued: 'They went home to get the car parked in the barn. Daddy had only bought it a few months before and was unsure of himself. They insisted Martha stay behind. She had a haunted look in her eyes but said nothing. I suppose she was afraid to upset the plan, but it all seemed cruel. They arrived three hours later in Ballinrobe.

Mammy and Sheila left for Dublin at the crack of dawn the following morning. It was already too late. The baby had died during the night but as Mammy surmised later, he may have already been dead when she called. In any event it was all too late.'

The four of us shared that room. I looked at my mother's dead body. I drank in her peaceful face. I was overwhelmed reflecting on all that once lay hidden in this loving woman's heart. Why did she never tell me? I knew I had no answer to that.

***

Tom almost whispered, 'It destroyed Martha completely. Mammy found it difficult to get her out of her room. She refused to get out of bed. Then she took to getting up before dawn and wandering around the kitchen, later leaving to walk for hours across the hills. Things started to improve. We all thought so, didn't we James?'

'We did.' He didn't lift his head.

'She helped Mammy make the tea in the evening though she ate very little and spoke even less. She went directly to her room after tea. I called into her a lot on those evenings. Sometimes, she said nothing at all, but I stayed and did my homework. It worked. She helped me with maths on the odd occasion or would quote something from poetry if I was writing an essay. She was very sad, you know. She said she had only slept once with David after a party in May. She said it was all a fumbling and innocence. I said I didn't need to know. I was only thirteen. I said as much to Martha, told her I didn't have a clue. "I don't care. You will have a clue sometime and I want you to know" was what she said. "I want the world to know that what we had was pure as a mountain stream. Beautiful." Then more fragile: "Why did he never contact me, Tom? Why? Do you think he wrote, and Daddy burned the letters?" I shrugged my shoulders. I did not know what to say.'

'You see the thing is, David did come.' James' edge had resurfaced, 'He did call to the house a week after the term began at the end of September. Martha hadn't shown up. He had received a letter from her which didn't make any sense, he said. Daddy told him that Martha had moved to London, was training in nursing at Whittington Hospital. David refused to believe him and told him so. Daddy was outraged that this upstart of a young man who had caused all this trouble would not take his word. He told him he wasn't welcome. David shouted out

Martha's name over and over. Daddy pushed him and when David did not get any response to his pleas, he left kicking every stone as he went. All the while Mammy sat in the kitchen crying. I was out the back, heard it all. It was never spoken of. Never. Daddy changed. Went into himself. I rarely heard him laughing after that. And then when Martha did not turn up at all one morning, Mammy sent me to get her. It was almost midday.

"I am exhausted, James. I am exhausted from it all," she pleaded. "See if you can talk sense into her because I can't."

But there was no talking sense to anyone. Martha had been dead several hours.'

James crumpled up in his wooden chair and the dam burst. He placed his hand over his mouth to prevent his sobs from disturbing the sleepers upstairs. He refused any consolation. Tom and I glanced at each other feeling helpless and hapless, all three of us caught in this cataclysmic sorrow. We waited for James' sobs to ease. We sat in silence for some time. My legs were dead weight beneath me. I still had questions for which I needed answers. I understood that we would probably never visit this again. It had already cost too much.

'Thank you, James. Thank you for telling me.' He lifted his head and nodded. 'I am sorry for asking, but we may as well finish it now. How did Martha die? Was it her heart?' I knew I could take nothing for granted.

'Yes and No. She did die of heart failure but because of digitalis poisoning. All those early morning walks gathering foxglove to make her brew.'

'She took her own life!' I cried.

'She obviously could see no way out.'

'O my God, my God. I clinched the side of the coffin with both hands. Poor Martha. How she suffered.'

'And then we were obliged to keep *that* a secret!'

'What?' I asked in a miasma

'Her suicide! Lest she be buried in unconsecrated grounds.'

The anger was again spewing out of James. 'I'd have buried her under the shelter of the Oak tree in the meadow. No one's business but our own!'

'You know James, it is not everything I see eye to eye with you but on that we are one!' Tom raised his glass.

'I am glad to hear that, Tom. I am! Really! You see Mary; Mammy and Daddy were protecting you. They knew you would have to come to bury your sister. They did not want your family's life sullied opposite your community. It might be detrimental to you. They did not take that risk. So yes, heart failure is on her death certificate, but we knew the whole story.'

'Stop it! Stop it right now James. The fact that I agree with you on Martha's burial does not give you licence to destroy Mary.'

'Isn't that just the point Tom! They had one daughter's life destroyed. All covered up because there was no point in destroying a second one! '

'They were protecting themselves and maybe even you and me!'

'Protected, is it? Protected?'

'Yes, James, yes! Protected! From the prying eyes of a very judgemental world.'

'How does having to deny the existence of your nephew, the circumstances of your sister and your fathers' deaths protect you? It has nearly driven me insane!'

'I know James, believe you me I know.'

'Honestly, Angela was my saviour. I told her everything. Everything Tom and she didn't judge. She was very happy to come into this family.'

'And we are very lucky to have her. Angela is a gem. But tell me this James in the interest of the honesty you proclaim, did she ever tell her parents?'

'You have stumped me there. You have stumped me there.'

'So, you agree the world is judgemental.'

'Small communities are.'

'If small communities are, it is only because the big communities are too. You have more of a chance of hiding in a bigger city, that's all.'

'Is that why you never came home once you left Tom?'

'Ach, I don't know. That would be to say too much. The past doesn't dominate my life.'

'No, nor mine but it colours it all the same.'

'For sure.'

***

'You okay Mary?' Tom suddenly emerged from the dramatic exchange I had witnessed which left me rooted to the spot. The neat yet challenging narrative which I had lived with my eldest and baby brother, our collective loss of Martha, was no longer so simple. I had stepped into the nightmare which they had lived through. The landscape had changed. I was now in that nightmare, but they were already ahead of me.

'I think I need to put the kettle on,' was all I could say. I went to stand up, but my legs gave way.

'Let me do it. I'll make some strong tea Mary. Besides, the boys will be down in twenty minutes or so.' James turned as he headed out the door, 'I am sorry if I was a bit harsh Mary, but I am glad that you know. You and Martha were once so close, you had a right to know.'

I nodded. I was simply unable to speak. Tom pulled his chair around in front of me.

'I want you to hear something now Mary and to hear it clearly.' He leaned forward looking directly at me. 'All that you have heard, you have heard under the very particular circumstances of this room. Grief, I suppose is what you call it. James and I do not live with this burden every day. Yes, it is a deep wound, but it is not our present reality. We lived through all of this years ago. You can see all the happiness around us here. You saw how contented Mammy was when you last visited. You need to hold on to that.'

'I hear you Tom,' I heard the resignation in my own voice. There was nothing I could change now but I was haunted by Martha's suffering and the doubts about my parents whom I had never before questioned.

'I hope so Mary because you need to hear that. That happiness does not come out of nowhere. We had good parents, you know. They did their best.'

'Did they Tom? Really?'

'Yes, I think they tried very hard. In the end it cost them even their own relationship. They were caught in a crisis and made some bad decisions.'

'Seriously bad decisions.'

'They knew that more than anyone else. They lived with the consequences and those consequences were devastating. Isn't that punishment enough?'

'Yes,' I could barely get the word to my throat, feeling the tears flow from Tom's compassion. 'Daddy? James mentioned Daddy's death.'

'He did and it isn't pretty. Daddy died in January. He never recovered from Martha's death the previous summer. Mammy moved into Martha's room. She helped Daddy in any way she could, but she seemed to be going through a darkness of her own. We all were. We carried on our own tasks but there was seldom a word at the table for a good three months or so. James went out every other weekend. Sometimes he stayed out all night. He never speaks about it. I kept my head in the books. A letter arrived in October from some friend of Martha's. Some exotic name.'

'Cosette?'

'Yeah, that was it. How did you know?

'Because Martha wrote to me about her. It is not a name you forget.'

'Well, it was a good letter. Very genuine. She said she didn't know of Martha's death, that she would have come, that Martha was a beautiful spirit and that David and herself were great together. How broken-hearted he seemed. Daddy collapsed completely. He cried almost every day. Mammy asked Dr Walsh to come out. He did. They spent hours in this room. The three of them. He prescribed tranquillisers for him. In the end, Daddy just could not live with the decisions he had made. At least that's my take on it. He swallowed the pills along with a whole bottle of poitín. James found him in the barn. Mammy signed everything over to him.'

'So, it wasn't when he married Angela?'

'No, the week after Daddy was buried, she went into Kennedy solicitors in town and signed it all over. We were all a bit shocked at how quickly she did it but maybe she wanted to let go of it all and give James reason to go on. The first action James took was to knock that barn out of existence. Mammy told him she was relieved to see it gone. She could no longer bear the sight of it.' Tom sighed lightly. 'You have it all now Mary. There is no more.'

And I recognised the guests that had come to visit me. All the demons that filled my house.

'Here Mary, here is a good strong cup of tea,' I took the hot cup gladly and felt its comfort, not so much in substance, but in the love with which it was given, even if the giver was now the less angry James.

It was sweet tea. I tasted the sugar and was glad of it. It gave me the strength to climb the stairs as I leaned heavily on the banister and stubbed my toe once even though I was wearing slippers. I barely made it to my mother's bedroom before I heard the boys stepping softly down the stairs.

24

Giving to the Mystery

I heard the click of the lock and leaned my back against the door where Mammy's dressing gown was still hanging. I looked at her bed. I saw her there: spending many hours reliving what might have been; longing for her dead daughter; recollecting the love she and Daddy once shared. I saw too that it was a new room for her, a new beginning and James had built it. I could see it all more clearly now. A bed like a nest where she slept uninterrupted, loved tenderly to her dying day. I smelt her soft fleece around me and slid to the floor. Glad to be of some distance from the landing, I sobbed until I had no more tears to give. Crawling on all fours, I climbed into her nest and slept.

The remaining two days, even though my mother's wake and funeral, passed me by. I felt as if I was in a surreal landscape where all the players were actors. I played my part. I stood between my brothers accepting condolences from people I did not know. I felt my brothers' presence shoulder to shoulder with me. Now that the whole truth was out, what could have driven us apart, united us. The three of us knew now that our bond was unbreakable. We knew and understood the characters in our own story. Despite the outcomes, we loved them. We questioned them too. It was painful. It was raw.

As the queue of sympathisers moved, I shared affectionate recollections from those I remembered. Donal Lenihan, our neighbour, his firm hand upon my shoulder, so genuine; 'It has been years Mary, years.'

'A lifetime,' I managed to utter.

'Your poor mother,' he sighed.

'My poor mother,' I repeated.

'How did she survive at all when Martha died, and you disappeared on us all?'

I barely held it together. I wanted to tell him that it was Martha who disappeared. I said nothing.

'Still, Maeve was feisty. She needed to be. I remember the occasional spat between herself and mum.'

'Leonora?' I asked

'The very one!' he laughed,' she was not an easy woman, our Leonora. Two great women, nonetheless.'

'How long is she gone?'

'Six years.' The queue was loading from behind.

'Mind yourself Mary.' He left as quickly as he came.

I greeted the sisters when they came with such love. I could not show my soul. When Theresa and Maryann hugged me very tightly, I felt as if my body was in automatic pilot. I was polite but not warm in response. I watched as James made sure all their needs were met, thanking them for coming. I did not sense it was hypocrisy but a man who had settled the contradictions within himself. A kind of maturity hard won but which I did not fully understand. He was kinder to me over those days. He wept a lot at Mammy's grave. I stood still as stone. I was unable to pray. I barely understood myself.

The following morning, I was unable to get out of my mother's bed. A weight sat upon my chest. Whether I turned right or left my bones ached. I was expected back to the convent later that afternoon. I knew I would not make it. I rang from the landline later that day postponing my return for twenty-four hours. I was not seeking permission. I was being respectful and explained the facts of the situation. Elizabeth was graciously accommodating. Yet this interruption of routine, this letting go of demands and expectations was a new and ultimately, welcome experience.

In the quiet of the late afternoon amid the resettling that falls upon a house after a funeral, I borrowed a pair of wellington boots I found inside the backdoor and made my way to the lower meadow. It was the second week of April and there was still a chill in the air. Nonetheless, the buds everywhere were on the cusp of unfurling. The leaves of the Hazel and Birch trees, though their branches were bare almost black against a threatening sky, were ready to burst at their tips. The grass beneath my feet was damp and very green, the ground uneven. There was an earthy smell. I was immediately reminded of all the life burrowing its way through the dark soil. I felt my own smallness. I knew all this would be here after I was gone. I found that consoling. Again, it came back to me, nothing, no thing. Like the worm, life is given to us. We don't earn it. I don't have to be able. I don't have to do. I can lean into the graciousness of a world freely given.

This was the meadow where we had saved the hay, chased butterflies, listened to stories of the past and sometimes let our thoughts wonder to possibilities of the future. I glanced back at the house, its upper stone walls rising above the mound beyond. Though its structure was sturdy, resilient against the darkening sky, every cell within me was overwhelmed by the voices heard and the voices silenced beneath that roof. I knew I had to deal with this, all this other window on my family. My childhood recollections had not changed but the colour of the lens through which I reviewed the memories was darker.

As a nun, I had committed to my family's absence from my everyday life. There was a cost. Christmas and Easter I always felt the tug. Weddings, graduations, and of course, Daddy's funeral. I still do not have words for the pain of that time. So convinced was I of the worthiness and necessity of my sacrifice that I scarcely considered my absence from them through critical experiences. I thought I had suffered but I knew nothing of theirs. I could not forgive myself for that. I resolved to spend some time later that evening with Tom and James, before I left.

No one was in the mood to cook. After a dinner of leftover lamb, sandwiches, tea and current cake, James, Tom and I retreated to the front room. The boys had put back the furniture and lit a fire in the grate while I was walking the meadow. It seems all three of us had the same idea. Just as I was about to approach Tom to suggest it, he leaned across the kitchen table and whispered,

'Mary, we can't let you go like this,'.

Though I knew immediately what he meant, I still asked 'Like what?'

'Raw! Bloody awful raw. Come on. James is waiting for us to join him.'

As I walked in, I caught James by his two elbows and drew him into me. He leaned in, 'I am sorry Mary. I needed to tell you.'

'You did James,' I was firm. 'I had a right to know.'

'Timing wasn't good,' Tom suggested.

'But maybe inevitable,' I sighed.

'You have buried your mother and are now tormented by the grief we experienced all those years ago.'

'I need to say something.'

'You do!' they replied spontaneously.

'Yes, I do. Let's sit down. It is true. I am raw. I am shocked. I just have no words.' Tom went to step forward. I stopped him.

'No Tom. I need to say this. I am truly sorry, truly, truly sorry for anything you have had to bear on my account: silence, suppression. My very absence from the devastation you were left to deal with.'

'But what could you have done? None of this was your fault.'

'No, it wasn't my fault, but I never stopped to really question Daddy's death in particular. I seemed to accept what I was told so readily. But more than that. I regarded myself as suffering even more than you because I could not share the loss with you. May God forgive me! *You* were the ones who were deeply seared by it all. You had to face the very real consequences to which I was oblivious.'

'Ah Mary, there is not one of us who could have imagined what was before us. Don't be so hard on yourself.'

'Besides, we knew you were praying for us!' James threw his eyes up to heaven and laughed. 'Seriously, we needed those prayers. Mam survived what I thought she might not. Not only did she survive, but she also came into her own. We had some great times.'

James continued, 'Tom and I have been talking. We would like it if the three of us could meet up once a year, family events apart.'

'On our own,' Tom threw in, 'just to remember them. We don't have to talk about anything if we don't want to. We just do something good together in their honour.'

'I would love that,' I felt their love. It was tangible.

And so started the plan to walk a self-styled pilgrimage just one day over the summer months in their memory. Our first was to Mount Melleray where Mammy's parents were married in a private ceremony. We attended early morning mass and later walked through the woods of the Knockmealdown mountains. But that, while consoling, was much later.

***

Upon returning to Carrigeen, I was very glad that a full week of Easter holidays still beckoned. My community was kind. A hot water bottle in my bed. A fresh sandwich plated and in the fridge when I missed lunch, no questions asked. Fresh spring flowers on the desk in my room. A book, left by Theresa, *On Death & Dying* by Elizabeth Kubler Ross, the title of which sent me into such tears I dared not open the pages. For three days I sat for hours beneath my Sower. I could not formulate my thoughts. I had a deep splinter within me fast becoming infected.

My sleep was restless. I woke up with images of an angry young man under an arch at my sister's funeral. Had he tried to reach out but would not have known how to contact me? Had I even thought of him? Spectres of my sister's tormented corpse haunted me.

My mother's words from our last conversation…. 'You are my lovely daughter, and you are here now'… 'a strange and beautiful peace came over me' referring to my final profession, consoled me. Twenty years later she leaned into it. She remembered. Teasing it out for myself, I felt that despite her troubles, my mother had glimpsed the thrust of her daughter's spirit and my reason for choosing the life I did. Right from the beginning, she had asked me to be true to myself. That mattered to me then. It matters to me now.

I had recurring dreams of walking across the meadow with my father. The grass was long, ready for cutting. The sun was always shining. But in one dream the sky grew dark. It started to snow. We turned a corner heading for home. A dark presence appeared, looming above us, glaring. We stood petrified. My father looked up. He melted. He just disappeared. There was a grey patch left on the snow beside me. I woke up with beads of sweat across my back and my heart thumping: 'Oh Daddy,' I cried, 'Daddy, I will never see you again.'

On that third day, while sitting before the sanctuary lamp it came to me. Now that Paul was dead, there was only one person with whom I could share my burden. She had written to me. Left a lovely postcard: a watercolour of the sun rising over the sea. Early on a Thursday morning I found myself knocking on Peggy's door.

'Peggy,' I said apologetically. She looked startled but recovered quickly.

'Cecilia!' Are you alright?'

'I am evidently not.' I stepped inside her door and cried, unable to lift my head.

'Oh Cecilia, come in, come in. It can't be as bad as all that, is it?'
I just nodded.
'Okay.' She led me to her bright kitchen where the sea stretched out before us.
I sat down. 'Do you remember that day in Kinoulty.'
'That day? The one we swore we would never mention?'
'That one.'
'Please Cecilia. I cannot go back there. You can leave now if that is your intention.'
'No, it is not my intention.'
'Then why mention it?'
'Because today is my Kinoulty day.'
'Oh!' She looked at me hard. I nodded my head. She sat down.
I knew instantly that I was in the right place with the right person. She caught my hand, and I poured out my story. Many times, I observed her placing her hands to her face as I spluttered out the words. 'Oh my God! I can see her! I can see her with her face in the towel watching her life fall apart, any modicum of power she had…taken away,' she whispered.
'Modicum of power?' my mouth full of warm spittle and my nose running from the relentless tears, I barely repeated the words. 'The thing is, she had none. No power at all.'
'Yes. I was lucky,' she whispered through her cupped hands, 'I found Uncle Jimmy or he found me.'
'It is compassion that found you. Why could it not have found Martha?' I bent my head and sobbed. This woman who had suffered so much and who, like Martha, had parted with her child, was saddened. We both understood it was a different kind of parting.

***

Three hours later we found ourselves down on the strand, the light April rain filtering our turmoil. I felt the cool air easing my hot cheeks. After a long silence having walked to the far end of the strand, Peggy turned to me.

'Find a stone,' she said, 'not just any stone. One that is smooth from the relentless washing of the sea or one that appeals to you for itself. Whatever it is, it must speak to you.'

We both went in search of our stones for some time.

Almost immediately I found a smooth white stone. *Your names are written in Heaven* came to me, but it just didn't fit. I found some beautiful shells with the plaintive sound of the sea when I held them to my ear. I found a mixture of coloured glass and stone. I found jagged stones that spoke to me but weren't the whole story. And then, I found another smooth white stone with a deep purple vein through its centre. This was my stone. I sat on a rock nearby looking out to the horizon, my mind floating on the distant sea, resting and exhausted. Peggy took her time. I understood she had a plan. I did not try to second guess it. I was beyond all that.

Finally, she came towards me with a smooth blue-green stone. Quite beautiful and dark.

'The truth is,' she seemed to struggle, 'I never think of my daughter. Never. I can't.'

I was rooted to the spot.

She continued, 'There was a little boy, Daniel, who did not live. I thought of her for the first time in many years when you named him. My daughter lived. I never named her. I don't ever expect to meet her, and I don't intend to look for her.' She stared out to the sea as she spoke. 'But today, I will name her. The name I give her is Martha.'

I was stunned. Martha was *my* sister yet at that moment it seemed right that her name would go with a child who would otherwise have been nameless in her mother's memory. Two babies time and worlds apart who would never meet. One dead, one living. Both acknowledged. I felt Martha would approve. Peggy waited for me. I nodded.

'Now,' she said, 'look at your stone. Let it speak to you. It will tell you why you chose it from amongst so many other offerings. It *will* tell you. You know already if your soul is listening. And when you are finished, place a kiss upon it and cast it into the sea. It is not your story to keep. It has a life of its own and you are part of that. You cannot keep it. It is alive in you today, but it does not tell the story of the whole of your life. That in time will be your stone.'

I think for the first time I truly understood the same line that had come to me earlier, except now I could complete it:

'To the person who overcomes, I will give some of the hidden manna, I will also give that person a white stone with a new name written on it, known only to the one who receives it.'

'Oh Daniel,' I thought, 'Your life had significance. It is significant today. You are my sister's son. You have spoken to me today.' And that is grace.

I climbed on to a small headland nearby, gently kissed the stone, and cast it into the sea to the plaintive cry of a gull in the distance. We walked back in silence.

***

Later we cooked omelettes and spoke of mundane issues: returning to school, the summer ahead, remedies for sleep. As I lifted the latch to go, I turned to Peggy, I hesitated, 'I cost you today. For that I am truly sorry.'

She refused to meet my eye. 'You survived and I survived. We know what it takes to survive. We both have a gift to give the world now.'

I went out into the night and reflected on my way home. Though still exhausted, I felt a burden lifted. I understood why it was that Peggy seemed to identify with those students or their mothers who had gaps in their lives. I knew her final words gave me the possibility not just of a future but a future with a purpose.

'We have a gift to give to the world now,' I repeated over and over. We had survived and not just survived; we had insight. I would not leave my role as principal but rededicate myself to every young girl that walked through that school door.

I also knew that evening as I closed the door of the convent behind me that I needed to make amends for the way I had freely spent the past few days without reference to my community.

Epilogue

*'I cast my lot with those who
age after age, perversely, with no extraordinary power,
reconstitute the world.'*
—(Adrienne Rich)

Peggy and I worked hard to bridge gaps where we saw them. The bus from Carrigeen carried the odd woman with more than five pounds in her pocket. It was not systematic. We had no policy. Circumstances presented themselves. There was no plan, but our core value was responsibility. The bus was a last resort but a critical exit strategy. For each one we enabled, I was forever conscious of those I had failed. That was over forty years ago. Had I been younger or less experienced when all this unfolded, I would, like my father, have been destroyed. Daddy was barely forty-nine when he died. He had his farm and his family. This was his life. I do not choose to put words in his mouth. I have no idea what ultimately drove him to such despair but surely loss, guilt and indeed, the tenderness of the love he once knew were factors.

I was just shy of forty. My days changed for sure. My world darkened. Each bitter experience of suffering so readily communicated now; displaced people, abandoned children, people caught in the futility of conflict, cracks appearing on the floor of our world, like they did in mine, all speak to me of a young woman with blonde curly hair and brown eyes who longed to be a philosopher. She is every man, woman, child, every gentle sigh of surrender, every haunted despair, every desire to live that is thwarted. Though it took time and a lot of shedding. I was lucky. I had Peggy, my brothers, my community, an enduring faith and my journal. I wrote it all out in an attempt to make sense of what I could not.

I glimpse an empty station as I pass on a train and am reminded of how fleeting it all is; a child stands still, looking through a window caught in his thoughts as all around him rush about. I hold the hand of Sister Nancy as she struggles to let go, to place her foot in trust on the threshold where a thousand angels meet and pass from this life to the next. I surrender each moment to live deliberately because Martha did not.

Each evening, I sit before Christ upon the cross. Sometimes I just sit. Always I search for the meaning of a suffering God. They say Christ's deepest suffering was to witness, in his dying moments, all that was to befall humanity. The haunting sight of history's cruelties, which only a heart of love can see, cracked open His core.

What happened to Martha crushed me for a very long time. Fr Ignatius, Sister Paul, my mother, Peggy, the love of Tom and James, life itself, taught me that truth brings understanding, and survival, responsibility. Now, I watch for every opportunity to live. I put one foot in front of the other, each step a possibility, a footprint already disappearing on dewy grass.

***

Though eighty-seven and with murmurings of the possibility of a retirement home, I still visit my handful of friends in the small coastal town of Carrigbawn, north of the peninsula, fifteen kilometres from Carrigeen. I live with two others in Ard na Greine, a semi-detached house, one of a semicircle of twenty houses overlooking the sea. I boil a soft egg for Sister Helen because she likes it that way. Helen is younger than me at seventy-eight, but she has lost her energy. The world has changed too much for her. She is overwhelmed. I respect many of the changes. They are necessary. I like having my own autonomy. After the betrayal of years of toxic revelations, I don't argue the toss with anyone. Though I know the story in my own heart.

Sometimes I find change overwhelming too. The school I once taught in is now a community school serving hundreds of girls and boys. The convent in Carrigeen closed fifteen years ago. The old building is still there, battered by the Atlantic. It had a brief life as a retreat centre run by Theresa and Maryann but there was no one to replace them when they retired. It was sold on to a local builder who hoped to convert it to a hotel. Last I heard there was a possibility of it being converted to a refugee centre to accommodate Ukrainians.

In the early afternoon, I call to see Joe, a neighbour three doors down. He has read the paper by then and we discuss the latest topic. I bring him his favourite rich tea biscuits for dipping in his blue mug, the one Kate bought him in a craft shop in Dingle fifteen years before. He recalls that holiday, his *happiness* holiday, many times. Then he recalls his late wife, Kate. *The Dutchman* was their song, but it was he who took care of her. We smile together as I go. We know what it is to sink face down to a bottomless ocean only to turn a little to the right, a little to the left, disoriented but conscious of a faint, distant light, falling in and out of consciousness, caught in the riptide of grief, we wake, floating under a gentle sun, the quiet lapping all around us. We know we must live. We choose to live.

***

I know the day will come, maybe soon, when I too will have to leave this throbbing life behind and walk the solitary path. I know I will find myself upon the solid ground of the lower meadow with a young woman holding her baby son. We feel the fresh strands of soft hay sway about our thighs amidst the rising pollen as we walk. Red admirals will land on wild sorrel. We will glimpse the top half of a stone house overlooking us from a short distance and hear the sound of a young retriever barking from the yard. We have no words. We walk forward together with only the pure light of love to guide us.

Principal Characters

Ballymac:
Mary O'Brien/ Sister Cecilia
Martha, older sister
Jack, father
Maeve, mother
James, older brother
Tom, younger brother
Angela, wife of James
Peter, John, Dan, nephews
Martha, niece
David Caroll, Martha's boyfriend
Cosette, Martha's college friend
Sheila & Rob, aunt & uncle

Leonora & Donal Lenihan, neighbours
Fr Healy, parish priest
Sister Cletus, Junior School teacher

Boarding School, Rossnagh:
Sister Maria, dormitory mistress
Sister Brigid, missionary outreach
Sister Aloysius, retired member of the community
Sister de Lourdes, visiting speaker

The Novitiate:
Mother Columba, mother superior
Sister Xavier, novice mistress
Sister Anthony, choir mistress
Sister Mary Ann, peer
Sister Immaculata (Eileen), peer

Ballygraigue:
Sister Celestine, deputy principal
Sister Eucharia, principal
Mother Agnes, reverend mother
Fr Ignatius, spiritual advisor
Marian Smith, student
Nuala Minogue, student

Sheila Nolan, local choir mistress
Monsignor, parish priest
Siofra O'Grady, student
Paddy, bachelor

Sisters Josie, Bernadette, Augustine, Aidan, retired
Sisters Peter, Ligouri, Borgia, carers
Sister Agnes, peer
Sister Rita, peer
Nancy Doolan, Legion of Mary

Carrigeen
Sister Paul, retiring school principal
Peggy Muldoon, school secretary
Sister Monica, teacher
Sister Sienna, teacher
Sister Elizabeth, teacher,
Sister Anthony, lay sister
Sister Francis, lay sister
Sister Teresa, teacher
Sister Maryann, teacher
Fr Ryan, parish priest
Mick, Jody, distant cousins of Peggy
Tommy, school caretaker
Dr Larkin, local doctor
Helen Larkin, wife of Dr Larkin
Jim Muldoon, father of Peggy

Patsy, granduncle of Peggy
Mary O', Patsy's friend in London
Mary McGregor, student
Teresa Mc Gregor, mother to Mary
Fr Leo Spillane, acting parish priest
Fr Gerard Tuohy, parish priest.

John Delaney, driver
Sister Claire, teacher
Mrs Howard, teacher
Mary Kelly, student
Brid, student
John O'Sullivan, brother of Helen Larkin
Vinny McMahon, driving instructor
Paddy Moses, elderly bachelor
Mickey Joe, elderly bachelor

Acknowledgements

Thank you for the companionship and support of Killaloe Hedge-School Writers who offered a critical filter during the first readings of this book.

I am grateful to David Rice, writer, former journalist, former head of the Rathmines School of Journalism and founder of this group. Thank you for your support, energy and generosity in bringing this work to a close.

Thank you to Helena Guerin, editor and 'world building' enthusiast who despite your busy life as a young mother and lecturer, proved an important critical ally.

Gratitude to: Jessica Brown, poet and writer, for your real and sensitive support. Siobhán Ní Riain and Maggie Bresson for your constancy and sincerity, simply unparalleled. Una Flynn and Marie MacNamara who read first drafts, and later Aisling Walsh, all of whom provided valuable commentary.

Thank you to Dominic Taylor who offered to publish this work. Dominic's advocacy for The Limerick Writers' Centre is important, admirable and critical to the cultural life of Limerick and its hinterlands.

Finally, thank you to my husband, Liam, my friend, who understood and facilitated the time and space needed to put words on this story.

About the Author

Veronica Molloy born in Cork, she lives in Ballina, County Tipperary. She holds a primary degree in Religious Education and English Literature and a research master's degree in theology. She has worked as a secondary school teacher and more recently as a school chaplain. In the past, she has been the keynote speaker addressing both chapter and provincial gatherings for religious communities of women. She published poetry in the Clare arts funded *The Creel* and more recently in separate publications *River People* and *Writers Unmasked*, edited by Ron Carey through the Limerick Writers' Centre. Originally a member of the Killaloe poetry group, she is a member of Killaloe Hedge-School Writers. *All I Cannot Save* is her debut novel

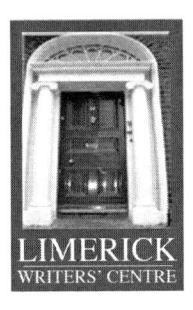

The Limerick Writers' Centre, based at The Umbrella Project, 78 O'Connell Street in Limerick City, is a non-profit organisation established in 2008 and is one of the most active literary organisations in the country. Our goal is to build a community focused on storytelling, personal growth, exploring literature, and the powerful impact of publishing. Our mission is to enhance your journey as an author, helping you connect with more readers and leave a lasting impression.

At the Centre we share a belief that writing and publishing should be made both available and accessible to all; we encourage everyone to engage actively with the city's literary community. We actively encourage all writers and aspiring writers, including those who write for pleasure, for poetic expression, for healing, for personal growth, for insight or just to inform.

Over the years, we have published a broad range of writing, including poetry, history, memoir and general prose. Through our readings, workshops and writer groups, our aim is to spread a consciousness of literature. Through public performances we bring together groups of people who value literature, and we provide them with a space for expression.

We are dedicated to publishing short run, high quality produced titles that are enjoyed by all. Since 2008 we have published over 160 titles. At our public readings we provide an opportunity for those writers to read their work and get valuable feedback.

The Director of the Centre is Dominic Taylor ably assisted by a board of directors and volunteers.

The centre can be contacted through its website:
www.limerickwriterscentre.com